PERILS OF TH

Patricia Hall

Constable · London

First published in Great Britain 1997
by Constable & Company Ltd
3 The Lanchesters, 162 Fulham Palace Road
London W6 9ER
Copyright © 1997 by Maureen O'Connor
The right of Maureen O'Connor to be
identified as the author of this work
has been asserted by her in accordance
with the Copyright, Designs and Patents Act 1988
ISBN 0 09 477580 X
Set in Palatino 10pt by
SetSystems Ltd, Saffron Walden, Essex
Printed and bound in Great Britain
by Hartnolls Ltd, Bodmin

A CIP catalogue record for this book
is available from the British Library

Prologue

She woke at the same time every night, struggling against the suffocating coils of sleep to escape the panic of the dream. She felt as exhausted as if she had really hurried, mile after breathless mile, down the canyons of city streets, with the child always in sight ahead of her but out of reach, the fair hair swinging – had she not heard someone say that you did not dream in colour, though this child's hair was the gold of cornfields caught in fitful summer sunlight – but the face always turned away, as the little girl, barely hurrying but always tantalisingly out of reach, trotted this way and that between faceless passers-by. She knew that she appealed to those passing strangers for help, though she was not sure why, or what she was telling them so desperately, but the answer was always a blank stare, a faint shrug, an imperceptible turning away from her by innumerable strangers. And so the child went on, never hesitating, never faltering, never ever looking back, a small compact figure, better schooled than Orpheus not to tempt the Fates. And she inexorably followed, her fear and despair increasing until they overwhelmed her and at last she woke, sweating and breathless and, she guessed, often crying out loud in anguish and frustration as the child's image slowly faded in the faint grey light of dawn.

1

'How much, flower?' The voice was flat, unemotional. It might have been demanding the price of potatoes. But the question made Laura Ackroyd catch her breath sharply in a moment of panic.

The dark car had pulled almost silently into the kerb beside her without her being aware of it, and the voice of the man leaning across to speak to her through his open window had caught her unprepared. He edged open the passenger door invitingly.

'Come on, sweetheart, how much?' he asked. The question was harsher this time, more insistent, and the eyes, flickering from breasts to thighs, left no doubt about the merchandise which had attracted the driver's attention.

Laura leaned forward into the car trying to get a good look at the kerb-crawler while hunching her shoulders to limit the view down her skimpy T-shirt to bra-less breasts. But the flickering light cast by the streetlights, half hidden amongst trees, was too dim for her to make out more than an indistinct image of a middle-aged square-jawed man with short hair of indeterminate colour and those greedy eyes.

It served her right, she thought angrily. The tight black mini-skirt she was wearing was so short that it revealed her stocking tops, the cut-off T-shirt under the black leather jacket left little else to the imagination. She would think twice about Lycra in future, she thought grimly.

She had dressed for the part, though without much enthusiasm, so as not to stand out from the crowd and had got what she should have expected. She felt stripped naked by this inevitable encounter, which exposed all too many gaps in her ensemble and her deception as she tried to conceal her embarrassment. She had no one to blame but herself, she knew, for giving in too easily to her boss's more dangerously imaginative notions.

She mumbled something in reply to the customer, who was still scowling at her from the interior of the car as he waited for an answer to the proposition she had sought and most definitely did not want.

'Have you got a place we can go?' he asked. 'I'm not looking for a quickie in the car.'

'Sorry,' she said, surprised at how dry her mouth had become, how breathless she felt.

'Eff off, then, slag!' he said, slamming the door in her face and swinging the car away from the kerb and accelerating so viciously that Laura had to step sharply backwards to avoid it. She shook her head in disbelief and wished her editor a long and painful encounter with the torments of hell. She was shivering and clasped her arms around herself to persuade herself that she was cold, though she knew she was not. Her cheeks were burning.

There was a peal of raucous laughter from behind her and Laura turned back towards the woman she had been talking to before they had been interrupted. Gradually the laughter subsided into a fit of coughing. The two women were now almost concealed in a patch of deep shadow half-way down a street of Victorian terraced houses, each with its own small walled garden and narrow uneven pathway leading from the deeply recessed front door to the pavement outside.

Ornamental trees had grown tall and shaggy over the years creating caverns of darkness between the pools of orange light cast by the handful of lamps which still functioned. In almost every shaded spot beneath the trees a woman or two stood poised, ready to move forward quickly when a customer approached, eager to attend to the drivers' needs. As the cars cruised past the women stalked jerkily, like ungainly flamingos, long legs in high boots below skimpy skirts or skin-tight shorts and bomber jackets. They were silhouetted against the fitful light as they leaned in at car windows before opening doors and sliding into the passenger seats with practised ease. The cars accelerated away urgently, the deal done in seconds, the consummation to be achieved elsewhere in little longer.

At the far end of the street a dog began to bark menacingly and Laura thought she could hear angry voices. Her heart was still racing after her exchange with the man in the car and she began to have even more serious doubts about the wisdom of her assignment.

'You'd never meck a living if that's the best you can do, love,' Sherry Maguire said, a husky voice tinged with contempt as well as laughter as Laura moved back to join her again in the shadow of the trees. Make the time-honoured excuse and leave, Ted Grant had instructed cheerfully when she had shown some reluctance to accept his brief to explore Bradfield's notorious red light district. She knew now that was easier said than done.

'You'd best stick to reporting,' Sherry said, and Laura could only nod in agreement, humiliated by her experience and hoping it did not show. Her companion was a tall buxom woman, breasts bouncing round and bra-less beneath a tight T-shirt, glinting bottle blonde hair piled on top of her head, boots up to her thighs, skirt wrapped skin-tight around her bottom.

'I wasn't actually looking for customers,' Laura said huffily.

'Just as well, an' all,' Sherry said. 'But you see? It's like I were telling you. It's dead easy if you do really want to score.'

'So how many women are there working down here?' Laura asked. 'Just in Whitley Street?'

'Oh, a dozen that I know of,' Sherry said. 'Actually on t' street, that is. Doing it the hard way.'

'There's an easier way?'

Sherry grinned, an eerie sight in the flickering orange light which filtered through the bare branches above them. Her eyes remained expressionless in a chalky, old-young face, a cigarette glued to her glossy red lower lip.

'There's three or four classes o' working girls,' Sherry said, as if explaining something to a five-year-old. 'Same as any other job. There's the kids, straight out o' school at four o'clock, if they've bothered to go at all. A quick trick before tea-time, like. And there's quite a few students an' all, these days. Undercutting the going rate, them. Amateurs, in it for t' pocket money. Then there's the bloody junkies, desperate for a fix. Do anything, they would, they're that shot to bits. And then there's us, on t' street as a career, you might say, like you've seen tonight. And then there's a cut above, i'n't there? Little advertisements in t' newsagents' windows, or in phone boxes, an appointment book like a bloody dentist or summat, and charging t' bloody earth an' all.'

'That sounds better than this,' Laura said, shivering slightly as a cold breeze rustled through the rubbish in the front garden of the terraced house behind them and rattled the tree branches above their heads.

'Aye, if you can afford a decent place to work,' Sherry said, matter-of-fact now, as if discussing the pros and cons of any business. 'If you've got kids at home you daresn't risk it. The social'd have 'em in care soon as look at you if you had clients on t' premises regular.'

'You've got children?'

'Two,' Sherry said shortly. However informative she was prepared to be about her work, it was obvious to Laura that her family was strictly off limits.

Another car cruised past slowly, not stopping, but as it began to pick up speed at the end of the street there was a sudden shout and again the sound of a dog barking angrily.

'Here comes trouble,' Sherry said. 'We could do without these beggars. It's all getting bloody out of hand.'

They could see a group of people assembling at the far end of the street. One ran into the road shaking a fist at the rapidly disappearing tail-lights of the cruising car before running to join the rest of the group of men and dogs who had set off at a determined march towards where Laura and half a dozen other women were standing.

'The vigilantes?' Laura asked.

'Aye, that's what they call themselves,' Sherry said contemptuously. 'Interfering busybodies, more like.'

The approaching group were mainly Asians, distinguishable even in the half-light by their traditional baggy white trousers and long tunic tails flapping beneath dark jackets, although a few of the younger men were in jeans and bomber jackets, the uniform of Bradfield's youth of any race.

Their leader, a youngish man in traditional dress with a heavy black beard and close-fitting white cap, swept the handful of working women along the street in front of him forcefully, without actually touching them, though Laura thought he would have few qualms about handling them as roughly as it took to chivvy them out of the street completely. Just behind him strode a white man in a clerical collar incongruously worn with denim jacket and jeans, chubby-faced and bright-eyed when the street lights caught his expression of zealous enthusiasm.

The young Asian quivered with pent-up aggression as with an

imperious gesture he stopped his followers and the dogs a few feet from where Sherry and Laura were standing.

'We are fed up with this,' he said loudly to Sherry Maguire as he drew level. 'We have told you many many times that we don't want you here with your immoral habits. This is a respectable area. We are trying to bring up children decently here. Please go.'

He was supported by a voluble chorus in English and what Laura took to be Punjabi. One of the dogs strained on its leash and began to bark again. The cleric said nothing but nodded vigorously at every point the group's spokesman was making.

'And we've told you, Mr Ahmed,' Sherry said grimly, 'we've as much bloody right here as you. It's a public street. You can't shift us. You've no right.'

'No, it is you who has not right,' the young man came back angrily, misunderstanding, perhaps deliberately. 'What you do is not right. It is wrong.'

'There is a better way, you know,' the cleric said earnestly to Laura, obviously not recognising her although she knew him well enough as the regular contributor of a religious column to the *Gazette*. 'Believe me, Jesus can make a difference to your lives.'

Laura opened her mouth to object and then thought better of it, but her companion had no such inhibitions. 'Oh, belt up, Holy Joe,' Sherry said contemptuously, but she kept a far more wary eye on the young Muslim men who were edging themselves into a threatening circle than she spared for the churchman.

How the confrontation would have ended Laura never knew. As the simmering fury on both sides threatened to spill over into violence the street was suddenly filled with the sound of screaming tyres and the flashing blue lights of half a dozen police cars and vans.

'Oh, shit,' Sherry said, glancing around for somewhere to run and then shrugging resignedly as she realised that the cars had come from both ends of the narrow street and the uniformed and plain-clothes police spilling out of them had an unusually determined air about them.

Laura had no more than a few seconds to watch in astonishment as, to cries of encouragement from the protesting residents, the police began to take hold of the women and bundle them

11

into vans. She had no sense of personal danger, having slipped mentally into her normal observer's role, before someone took a firm grip on her own arm.

'Right, flower, you're nicked,' said a voice she recognised, although she could not at first place the stocky plain-clothes officer who had taken hold of her. She opened her mouth to complain and identify herself and then, without seriously considering the consequences, held back again and said nothing, letting him push her roughly into the back seat of one of the cars and climb in beside her. It would be an interesting angle on her story, she thought, to find out just how the women were treated on what she knew were their regular trips to the police station and the magistrates' courts.

'You're new round here, aren't you?' the man beside her said. She realised with some surprise that this was the same man who had drawn up in the dark unmarked car and propositioned her those few minutes earlier. While she digested that disconcerting information, the police car pulled sharply away from the kerb and followed the vans on to Aysgarth Lane, the main road into Bradfield town centre. The arrests had taken no more than five minutes from start to finish.

'It's for real, then, is it, that red rug?' the police officer went on conversationally, running a hand roughly through the curls which Laura had teased out into a copper cloud for her evening investigating street life. She gritted her teeth rather than let him see her wince.

'Bloody 'ell, it is an' all. I thought it were a wig,' he said to the driver who half turned to look, before turning back to the wheel with a snigger.

Furious, Laura pulled away as far as she could and leaned a burning cheek against the chilly car window, her fists clenched in her coat pockets. She wondered how far he would go and knew that she was angry enough to want to find out. What had begun as research for a feature on the growing antagonism between Bradfield's prostitutes and the mainly Asian residents of the streets they worked in was already expanding in her mind's eye into a polemic on abusive policemen, with the added spice of some first-hand, eyewitness reporting. And she did mean hand, she thought, as she pushed her importunate companion's off her thigh. It was a story she knew Ted Grant would

12

not pass up, in spite of his generally mindless support for what he called 'the forces of law an' order'. Ted was not a man to let a principle get in the way of a good story.

It was a short drive to the central police station opposite Bradfield's Victorian town hall but long enough for Laura. She got out of the car in a towering rage, face flushed and eyes flashing, and marched into the station ahead of her tormentor to stand in line with the other women waiting in the custody area to be processed.

'You take it all very lightly,' she said through clenched teeth to Sherry who was waiting just ahead of her in the queue of arrested women, some of them sullen and silent, others apparently unconcerned. Sherry dropped her cigarette end to the floor, ground it out with her boot heel and lit another, in defiance of the no-smoking notices on the walls.

'Occupational hazard,' she said with a cheerful shrug. 'Nowt to be done about it. You reckon to get fined every now and again. Make allowance for it in t' price. There's no hard feeling wi' t' police. They're just doing their job. Within their rights.'

'Not that one, he wasn't,' Laura hissed, nodding towards the plain-clothes officer who was glancing in her direction again and laughing with other officers in the doorway, evidently at her expense.

'Gave you t' treatment in t' car, did he?' Sherry said with a grin notably lacking in sympathy. 'He's a randy beggar, that one. Always on t' look-out for summat for nowt, he is. A lot of coppers try it on. I tell them they can pay up like any other punter if they want owt. But some o' t' lasses let 'em have a favour now an' again.' Sherry turned her attention to the waiting custody sergeant and eventually it was Laura's turn. Her importunate companion from the car moved sharply alongside her, giving her a sidelong grin and a knowing wink as he did so.

'I'm Laura Ackroyd of the *Bradfield Gazette*, and I want to make a complaint,' she said fiercely to the sergeant, who barely glanced up at her from his record-keeping as she took her place in front of his desk.

'Oh, aye?' the sergeant said sceptically, at length, glancing at Laura's arresting officer, who merely shrugged dismissively. 'Aye, well, it makes a change from all the Liz Hurleys and Madonnas we get in here of a Saturday night.' He handed her a closely typed card. 'Those are your rights. You can make one phone call. And you can have a solicitor.'

He began to flick through the contents of her bag and soon came to the conclusion that perhaps she was who she claimed to be. He gave his colleague a puzzled glance and looked at Laura a shade more warily.

'The charge is soliciting, Miss Ackroyd, and you seem to have made the mistake of approaching one of our officers in his car. That, if I may say so, was not a very bright move at all.'

'I want to ring my editor,' Laura said.

'You mean she's for real?' the arresting officer said incredulously. 'I don't bloody believe it.'

'Leave it, John,' the sergeant warned. 'I'll sort it. You'll have to take your turn for the phone, Miss Ackroyd. In the meantime you can wait in a cell like the rest of them. It looks like being a busy night one way or another.'

Chief Inspector Michael Thackeray stood at his office window drumming his fingers on the sill and looking down at the straggly cherry trees which struggled for a breath of carbon monoxide-free air in Bradfield's main square. Behind him Laura Ackroyd slumped in a chair and watched his broad shoulders strain against the crumpled white shirt, wondering inconsequentially if she could persuade him to learn to iron his clothes.

'I'm sorry, Michael. I'm completely mortified by the whole thing,' she said. Her fury had seeped away during her brief spell in a cell, leaving her pale and drained.

He turned and stood looking at her silently for a moment, torn between genuine anger and an overwhelming desire to take her in his arms. During the hour she had spent in a basement cell, she had tied her unruly cloud of hair back in a pony-tail and, in the short skirt and dark stockings she had adopted for her foray down Whitley Street, she looked like some perverse schoolgirl waiting for the verdict of a particularly strict headmistress.

'Don't you understand what a dangerous game you were playing?' he asked quietly.

'I wouldn't have got into a car,' she said defensively. 'You know I'm not that daft.'

'It's not just that. The whole place is simmering anyway with

14

these Asian vigilantes they've got patrolling down there. There's going to be real violence soon if we're not careful.'

'Was that why the women were arrested tonight?' Laura asked, a touch of asperity in her voice now. 'Just to keep the locals happy?'

'It was the uniformed branch's party, but I expect that's what they were thinking. The residents have a point. Respectable women can't be seen on the streets round there at night without being propositioned – as you seem to have discovered for yourself.'

'I was asking for it, is that it?'

'Wait till I see Ted Grant,' Thackeray muttered angrily. 'He must be out of his mind sending you on a jaunt like that.'

'Leave him out of it,' Laura said quickly, knowing only too well how her boss would react to any comment the policeman might make on the suitable deployment of his staff. 'I could have said no. I didn't think it through properly. It was my own fault.'

Thackeray shrugged slightly and ran a hand through his unruly dark hair, his blue eyes still uncertain. Laura had not asked for his intervention in her case. Working late, he had learned on the station grapevine, which sizzled red-hot with the news, that she was in a cell and he had found her there, hunched in the corner of the bunk with her arms round her legs and her chin on her knees, a shamefaced grin lighting up her pale face as soon as she saw him. Vouched for by their own DCI and Laura's editor, they had let her go with a weary warning not to behave so recklessly in future.

'And you said you wanted to make a complaint? Was what happened in the car that serious? What are we talking about? Indecent assault or just harassment?' Thackeray asked.

Laura did not meet his eyes.

'He pestered me all the way back to town in the car,' she said.

'Pestered?'

'Touched. Stroked my hair, put his arm round me, put his hand on my thigh . . .'

'He thought you were a tart,' Thackeray said explosively. 'And you didn't disabuse him when you had the chance. Why the hell didn't you tell him who you were?'

'Michael!' Laura said, furious herself now. 'There's no reason why tarts should have to put up with that!'

'You're being naïve, Laura,' he said, coldly now. 'Not one of those girls – '

'Women!'

'Women, then. Not one of them would have complained if it had been them.'

'So what happens if I pursue it?'

'It'll be investigated. John Franks is a good officer, at the very least he'll be under a cloud for a while. If the driver doesn't back up your story he'll probably get away with it.'

'And the driver's hardly likely to do that, is he? He enjoyed every minute of it,' Laura said resignedly. 'Are you saying drop it, Michael?'

Thackeray looked at Laura's flushed cheeks, her obstinate chin and the green eyes which reflected her disappointment too clearly for comfort. He knew that the disappointment was with him as well as the police force which would in all likelihood close ranks and decline to give Constable John Franks what she thought he deserved. When he lay awake in the night struggling to see a future for this relationship, he could never decide whether it would be temperament or profession which would drive them apart. Tonight he would put money on his profession.

'If you want my advice, then, yes, drop it,' he said with a sigh.

'I'll think about it,' Laura said coolly. 'I'm sorry if I've embarrassed you with your colleagues.'

'It's not a question of embarrassment, it's a question of proving it, and what would be gained if you could.'

'He's not likely to get his paws on me again,' Laura said sharply. 'Though I'd have thought you might have minded more about that . . .'

'Laura . . .' Thackeray began, and the pain in his eyes made her catch her breath before they were interrupted by an urgent knock on his door. Sergeant Kevin Mower put his head round, grim-faced.

'Sorry to interrupt, guv,' he said. 'We've got a body, a young woman, looks like murder.'

Thackeray picked up his jacket and put it on without looking at Laura again.

'Where?' he asked.

'Whitley Street,' Mower said, raising an eyebrow the merest fraction at Laura as he spoke.

16

'Oh, damnation,' Laura said to herself as she watched the two men leave the room without another word or a backward glance.

2

Not for the first time Michael Thackeray felt a curious dislocation between what he knew and what he did not wish to know. That the human body pumped eight pints of rich red blood around, safely confined within its walls of muscle and tissue and bone, he could accept with equanimity. A bit of general knowledge lodged at the back of his brain with occasional relevance to his professional concerns.

Yet to his chagrin, even after twenty years of hardening his heart to such things, the sight of that same blood, puddled and splashed and congealed around the naked body of a young woman, who had evidently struggled frantically to turn the ebbing scarlet tide of her life, caught at his throat and wiped all expression from his eyes.

He stood for a moment at the girl's bedroom door, trying to steady his breathing and watching the pathologist Amos Atherton making his examination of the corpse. He was aware of the sharp eyes of his sergeant at his side, watching for signs of weakness. He took a deep breath, squared his shoulders and took the couple of steps across the stained carpet and into the investigation of a murder.

'Made sure of her,' Atherton said, wiping the sweat from his broad brow with the sleeve of his overall. 'At least six stab wounds, mebbe more. I'll get a better look when I've got her on the slab.' He hauled himself upright from the ungainly crouch from which he had been examining the body, which lay sprawled half on the bed and half on the floor. The pillows and quilt were sodden with rusty stains and smears of drying blood.

'Left nowt to chance,' he said. 'Severed the jugular. You can move her now when your lot have finished taking their snaps.'

'Do we know who she is, Kevin?' Thackeray asked Sergeant Mower.

'Louise Brownlow, guv. A student at the university. Shares

17

the house with a couple of other girls. Her parents are abroad apparently.'

Thackeray absorbed that slowly. After what had happened in Whitley Street that evening he had almost without thinking assumed that the dead woman would be a prostitute. He should know better than jump to conclusions, he thought, especially conclusions that Laura would treat with the contempt they deserved.

'And the weapon?' He addressed the question equally to Mower and Atherton, who had closed his instrument case and was stripping off his plastic gloves.

'Nothing found, guv,' Mower said.

'A broad blade,' Atherton said. 'Tell you more tomorrow at the PM.'

'Time?' he asked, automatically, knowing that Atherton would shrug non-commitally even before the broad shoulders heaved.

'Not long ago,' the pathologist conceded. 'This evening, any road, likely within a couple of hours or so.'

Thackeray looked around the room again. It was, he thought, a typical student bed-sit, cluttered and untidy, the shelves piled high with books, a desk littered with papers in the bay window which overlooked the street, a kettle carelessly knocked on its side next to cups and dirty plates on the floor beside the gas fire.

'Are the other girls here?' he asked Mower.

'Downstairs, guv. I haven't asked them to identify her formally yet.'

'Not yet,' Thackeray said sharply. 'Not until she's been tidied up and made decent. Who found her?'

Mower glanced at his notebook.

'Woman called Roz Jenkins. Actually owns the house, she says. Doing a post-graduate degree. Lets rooms to other students to make ends meet.'

Thackeray drew a deep breath.

'Right. Let's get the bloody show on the road,' he said without enthusiasm or conscious irony.

Louise Brownlow's flat-mates were sitting huddled together on a sofa like refugees from a cataclysm they had only barely begun

18

to comprehend. Both women, Roz Jenkins, mature in figure and face, ruddy and spikily dark-haired, and her friend Jane Watson, barely out of her teens, fair and frail, were tense and red-eyed. They stared at Chief Inspector Thackeray with something akin to horror, as if he were personally responsible for opening up the abyss into which they had plunged.

'I shall need to ask one of you to identify the body, as I understand her family are not in this country,' he said gently.

Roz swallowed hard and nodded. She was evidently the more nearly in control of the two.

'I'll do it,' she said in a strained whisper which was barely audible against the clatter of hefty official feet and shifting of furniture in the bedroom immediately above them.

'They'll let us know when they're ready to move her,' Thackeray said. He glanced round the bay-windowed front room in which they were sitting. It was furnished with a couple of comfortable old sofas draped in vibrant Indian throws, its tables and shelves cluttered with books and newspapers, framed photographs, video tapes and CDs.

'This is your house, I understand?' he said to Roz.

She nodded. She was a heavy young woman with dark eyes under the severe haircut, dressed in the near universal student uniform of black leggings and a loose top, in her case dark blue and decorated with several strands of oriental-looking beads.

'I let the spare rooms,' she said. 'Jane and Louise both have bed-sits upstairs, and they can use the kitchen . . .' She broke off as it evidently struck her that Louise would not ever be using the kitchen again. Jane gave a convulsive shudder and the older woman put her arm around her protectively.

'Which of you found her?' Thackeray asked.

The two students glanced at each other. Then Roz shrugged.

'We both did, really. I came in about ten and Jane was making cocoa and we shouted up to Louise to see if she wanted some. She didn't answer, which I thought was odd because I'd noticed that her light was on when I came in, and we could hear music, so we went up and knocked on her door.'

'There was a CD still playing when the first uniformed man arrived, guv,' Sergeant Mower said from the hard chair by Roz Jenkins' desk where he had positioned himself. 'Wagner.' If

19

Mower had views on Wagner, which Thackeray was sure he had, he did not indicate by the slightest inflection of his voice what those views might be.

'She was into the *Ring*,' Jane whispered, her eyes filling with tears again. She wrapped her towelling bathrobe around herself more tightly as if to ward off evil. She had evidently been on the point of going to bed when disaster struck. Thackeray nodded but refused to be deflected from what he wanted to hear.

'So when you got no reply, you opened her door?'

'Eventually, yes . . .' Roz too stopped then, unable to continue, and Thackeray could imagine only too clearly how the two of them, gasping for breath, no doubt, and overcome with the nausea which had seized him too, had been plunged from their everyday world of domestic concerns into the nightmare of the charnel house that their friend's bedroom had become.

'The door doesn't have a lock?' he continued matter-of-factly, knowing that it was only by concentrating on the mundane detail that he could keep them from hysteria.

'No, a little bolt on the inside, but no lock,' Roz said dully. 'We didn't think we needed locks, the three of us.'

'And there was no sign that the front door had been forced when you came in? You opened the door with your key quite normally?'

Roz looked at him blankly for a moment and then nodded, and Thackeray glanced at Mower for confirmation.

'There's no sign of a forcible entry, guv. Doors and windows all secure. Back door closed but not locked.'

'And had you been in the house all evening?' Thackeray persisted, turning to Jane, who huddled further into her robe.

The girl shook her head dumbly, evidently finding it almost impossible to speak.

'I'd been out earlier,' she whispered at last. 'I came in about nine and had a bath, then came down to make a drink.'

'And you heard nothing out of the ordinary?'

Jane shook her head. 'I wouldn't from the bathroom. The water heater makes a terrible noise and I took my radio in with me.'

A uniformed constable put his head around the door.

'They're ready to move the body, sir,' he said.

Thackeray glanced at Roz Jenkins.

'Sergeant Mower will take you down to the mortuary where

they'll make her decent,' he said. 'Then you can make a formal identification. Can you cope with that?' Roz nodded and got to her feet. She was quite composed now, her round full face determined and her eyes blank.

'I can leave a WPC with Jane until you come back,' Thackeray offered. 'Will you be all right here tonight? Is there anywhere else you could stay?'

Roz shook her head firmly. 'We'll be all right,' she said. 'Jane can sleep in my room. We'll be fine. I'll look after her.' Jane looked up at her friend, her pale eyes filled with tears, the thin hands twisted together in torment, and Roz leaned down and embraced her before she moved majestically to the door.

'Then I'll leave the rest of my questions until the morning,' the chief inspector said, watching the younger girl who had shrunk into a corner of the sofa and closed her eyes, though the almost transparent lids were flickering convulsively. She was in a state of near collapse, he thought, and he wondered if it were simply a more sensitive temperament which led her to react so much more profoundly to Louise Brownlow's death than her friend, or something more.

Early next morning, Michael Thackeray rolled away from Laura and lay face down on the edge of the rumpled double bed, his face buried in his arm, his shoulders hunched, tension visible in every muscle of his body.

'Sometimes you make love as if the Pope's looking over your shoulder,' Laura said waspishly. 'Or your mother.' Or your wife, she thought, but angry as she was she did not quite dare add that name to the litany of her discontent. Thackeray's Catholicism and his mother were dead. Of his erstwhile wife he resolutely refused to speak, though Laura knew that it was ten years since she had broken down and drowned their baby son, whether by accident or design she had never had the courage to discover. That Thackeray blamed himself for the tragedy was almost as much as she wished to know.

Thackeray turned on to his back and watched her moodily as she slipped out of bed and her silky pyjamas and stood naked surveying the clothes in her wardrobe with an expression of profound dissatisfaction. Irritably she flung a deep gold shirt back into the wardrobe and selected a black one instead. Her own live-in lover had come and gone without seriously disturbing her equanimity. Or so she told herself from this distance in time. But this morose giant of a policeman disturbed it every time she looked at him and threw her into a turmoil even when he came to her bed, as he had done late the previous evening, speechless and exhausted after the night's grim work, too tired to make love until they had found themselves sleepily in each other's arms as dawn broke.

'Come here,' Thackeray said, making space for her to sit on the edge of the bed beside him. She shrugged herself into a towelling robe and tied the belt firmly around her waist, shutting him off from the view of her small pointed breasts and slim hips. She sat down gingerly on the edge of the bed.

'I mustn't be late for work,' she said stonily.

'Nor I. The post-mortem is at eight thirty. So tell me.'

She sat for a moment looking at the tall, broad-shouldered figure leaning against her pillows, his square face with remote blue eyes under dishevelled dark hair which never looked tidy softening slightly as he met her gaze.

'I sometimes feel used,' she said. 'You turn up when the mood takes you. You know I won't turn you away . . .'

'You think I make a convenience of you?'

'No, not that exactly,' Laura said, her eyes full of misery.

'You think I should go to one of your friends out on Whitley Street instead? I don't think I'll ever forget seeing you dressed up for that bloody meat market last night. Do you really think that's all you mean to me?' Thackeray's jaw was clenched tight and his eyes, full of pain, demanded an answer.

'No, no,' Laura said desperately. 'I know it's not all, but you say so little, you're here so little, it's breaking me apart!'

He pulled her towards him and wrapped her in his arms.

'Laura, I love you,' he said, as if trying the phrase out for size.

'Do you?' she said doubtfully.

He buried his face in her hair and groaned, not knowing how to reply. The word 'love' was one he had not used to anyone for much longer than the ten years since his marriage had ended and the sound of it on his own lips and hers terrified him more than he would ever admit.

'I thought you knew that,' he said, the words wrenched from him as if by the Inquisition.

'I never know anything with you,' Laura said bitterly. 'You're the most uncommunicative person I've ever met.'

'What can I tell you?' he said, suddenly angry. 'Last night I came to you from the blood-soaked bed of a young woman who'd been stabbed to death. It's almost impossible to describe what that does to you. I couldn't even begin to tell you how it feels. And because it's impossible, you build up barriers against feeling anything at all. It's the only way to survive. I don't want to hurt you. But I'm terrified history might repeat itself and I can't even begin to think about that. Give me time, Laura, please.'

He bent his head over Laura's, his dark hair mingling with her wild red curls, and they clung to each other in an embrace that had more of desperation in it than affection. In the end it was Laura who gently untangled herself from his arms and kissed his cheek. It was the longest and most passionate declaration she had ever prized out of him and it moved her more than she, with all her verbal felicity, could put into words.

'Patience isn't my strong suit,' she said with an attempt at a smile. 'But I'll try.'

'I'll try, too,' he said. 'But now I must go to work.'

His eyes, she noticed, had already taken on the bleak impassivity which sometimes drove her to despair. Damn you, she thought, you're going to crucify me and there's nothing I can do to stop you.

She thought of Thackeray again as, back in her own office, her editor, Ted Grant, disposed his troops at the morning news conference. Grant was not a man to leave any titbit unused if it could be turned to his advantage and she was aware that she had caught his bleary eye with more interest than normal.

'It's always the bloody same,' he said. 'It's either nowt at all or t' bloody sky falls in. Not only do we get a reporter arrested, but there's a blasted murder the same night, in the same place, and we bloody miss it.'

Grant was a heavy man whose complexion, never less than

shocking pink, took on a ruddier hue as the inevitable tension of the day wound to a crescendo when the main edition went to press at lunchtime. For eight o'clock in the morning, his cheeks had already taken on an ominously flushed look, and the assembled minions around the editorial table knew better than to interrupt him in full flow.

'You can do your piece about Whitley Street as a backgrounder to the murder, Laura,' he said, swinging to face the only woman who had achieved even a middling senior position on the paper. 'Then liaise with Fred. He'll be going to the police press conference mid-morning. You reckon she's a student, do you, this lass? Not a tart? In Whitley Street?'

Laura gritted her teeth, knowing that if the victim had been any less respectable than she appeared to be from first reports the coverage would have been that much less extensive. Dead students were front-page material, and would be for days to come: dead prostitutes were much softer currency.

'My information is that she's a student,' she said. She did not need to spell out where her information had come from. She and Michael Thackeray tried without much success to keep their professional lives apart but if the *Gazette* thought that it could gain an edge by taking advantage of the relationship Ted Grant would have no qualms. In fact, Laura did not suppose he would recognise a qualm if it came up and hit him between the eyes.

'Right,' Grant went on in his decisive mode, which his staff reckoned was modelled on his acquaintance with more than one of the more flamboyant London tabloid editors. 'When you've done your "How I got myself arrested" bit, you can get up to our precious seat of learning and start work on an "Are our students safe in their beds" piece. The students' union is bound to have summat to say. They're always ripe for a good whinge. And I dare say you can lay hands on one of your sociologist friends who can give us a spiel on the changing mores of British youth or some such crap.'

Grant had served his stint on a London paper and had never, to many of his colleagues' minds, recovered from the experience. Graduates like Laura he never forgave for having achieved the education he had been denied.

'I thought they all had rape alarms these days,' offered the chief sub-editor, Fred Powers, looking up from the pad on which

24

he had been idly blocking out page layouts. He sounded as if he deeply regretted such an innovation. 'You don't get a yes or a no, these days, from these lasses, do you? You get a maybe or a bloody klaxon and a charge of sexual assault.'

'Well, at least in those circumstances you can't imagine she's saying no when she means yes, can you?' Laura asked sweetly, having spent months early in her career convincing Powers that her rejection of his advances was not mere prevarication. But Powers' gibe reminded her of the unwelcome attentions she had suffered herself the previous night and her heart was not really in her riposte.

'Well, get up there and see what you can dig up,' Grant said brusquely. 'For all we know, this might be curtain up on a new performance by a Yorkshire Ripper. That'd give the circulation a nice boost over the summer.'

'Heaven forbid,' Laura said softly enough for Grant not to hear.

3

Bradfield University had grown haphazardly, expanding over twenty years from the dour stone Victorian technical college which had given it birth into an architectural hotch-potch of modern and converted buildings which straggled up one of the town's seven hills. Its early strengths had lain in textiles and the technologies of mining and heavy engineering, but as those industries had declined so had the need for graduates to serve them and the institution had ventured into new fields to survive.

It had embraced sociology and politics, peace studies and women's studies. It took to its heart exotic languages, some of which a trading and manufacturing town had drawn to itself as native-born Yorkshiremen eschewed night shifts and handed their old skills to darker newcomers from Pakistan. A brand new domed Islamic Centre rose at one side of the campus, neatly balanced by an institute for the study of Japanese language and culture housed behind the solid stone walls of a former woollen mill. Waste had never been greatly admired in West Yorkshire and where spinning and weaving machines once deafened their minders, students now logged on to computer networks and came to terms with the intricacies of Japanese script in near monastic quiet.

Laura had bitter-sweet memories of the place as she walked slowly up the hill towards the students' union. She had taken her own degree there ten years previously and although she had been born and bred in Bradfield she had not planned still to be living and working there so long afterwards.

She had joined the *Gazette* expecting to train and move on, as so many of her colleagues had done. But life had turned out to be less predictable than she had supposed as a new graduate stepping bright-eyed and eager into the *Gazette*'s newsroom. Her father, who had made good in Bradfield, collapsed with a heart-attack in his fifties, recovered from the illness but not the fright and retired to a villa in Portugal, all in the space of twelve traumatic months.

Laura had accepted with little grace his gift of a flat as replacement for the home in which she had grown up, the least he could do, she thought, in recompense for removing himself and her mother so far. They had never even spoken about the real cause of the ensuing coolness between them, the indifference with which he had abdicated responsibility for her much-loved but ageing grandmother, his mother. While Joyce Ackroyd was alive, Laura had decided without too much heart-searching, she could not and would not leave the town of her birth.

It was with a slightly melancholy sense of *déjà vu* that Laura pushed open the swing doors of the students' union, crossed the concourse littered with used polystyrene coffee cups, and knocked on the door of the office from which she had once sallied forth to do battle as a student journalist.

The room was no tidier but significantly less crowded than she remembered it. As she entered, a tall, thin boy in jeans and sweater glanced up from the computer he was using and raised a blond eyebrow. The only other occupant of the office, a young woman slumped at a corner desk with a cup of coffee and a weary expression, ignored Laura's arrival completely, allowing her trailing veil of dark hair to fall even further over her face as if drawing down a curtain.

'Can I help?' the boy said without enthusiasm. Laura introduced herself, and the name of the *Gazette* seemed to light a faint spark of interest in his pale eyes.

'You want our press relations person,' he said, glancing at his watch. 'I think she's in a class just now. And I've got one to go to in three minutes. Is it about the union? Can you call back?'

Laura smiled faintly. She had heard that modern students had been galvanised into hard work by the harsh realities of graduate unemployment. Here was the living proof.

'It's not really about the union,' she said. 'It's about the murder.'

'Murder?' the boy said, evidently surprised, and even the semi-comatose girl in the corner was energised sufficiently to turn her head and glance in Laura's general direction.

'Didn't you know that a woman student was stabbed last night?' Laura asked, astonished. 'It was on the local radio – '

'Jesus!' the girl in the corner said suddenly and explosively. 'I knew we should have given them free rape alarms. I knew something like this would happen.'

'Chris is our women's officer,' the boy said, getting to his feet and picking up a ruck-sack full of books from the floor beside him. 'Who was killed?' he asked almost as an afterthought as he made for the door. He shook his head when Laura told him. 'Didn't know her,' he said and went out, slamming the door behind him.

'I knew her,' the girl said faintly, her eyes full of horror. 'She's – was – on my course. I usually listen to the morning news but I was at a party last night, I'm a bit fragile.'

'I'm sorry,' Laura said.

'Was she raped?' Chris said. 'Ever since I took on this job I've been terrified we'd get a rapist. Where was she found?'

Laura told her what little she had gleaned about Louise Brownlow's death and watched Chris's face pale, until it became almost rigid with shock.

'In bed?' she said faintly. 'So it could be anyone? A boyfriend, even?'

'Did she have a boyfriend?' Laura asked.

'I've no idea,' Chris said. 'She wasn't a close friend or anything. Just someone I knew in class, quite bright, always answering stuff in seminars, you know? Someone you would know if you were in her year.'

27

Their conversation was interrupted by the precipitous entry of two young women, both dressed almost entirely in black, heavy boots emphasising the stick-like thinness of their Lycra-encased lower limbs.

'So it's happened at last, has it?' said the first over the threshold angrily. 'We told you it would, didn't we?'

'This is Laura Ackroyd from the local rag,' Chris said with a note of warning in her voice.

The two newcomers glanced at Laura with a fierce and critical interest close to contempt.

'Stef Andrews, chair of the Uni Women's Group,' snapped their evident spokeswoman. 'And this is Bev Smith. I suppose you're here about the murder?'

Laura nodded.

'We've been fighting this issue all term. But the men come up with one shitty excuse after another. There's parts of this town where women aren't safe at night, right?'

'Louise lived in Whitley Street,' Bev Smith said unexpectedly.

'So there you are then,' Stef said with self-satisfaction. 'What did I tell you? Even walking up to the halls of residence you can get propositioned. Down there it's a bloody nightmare walking a couple of metres from the bus stop to your own front door. It'll be some sad kerb-crawler lost his cool when she told him to get lost, right?'

Laura gave a small grim smile. She could personally vouch for the credibility of Stef's instant analysis, she thought, although her experience in Whitley Street was not one she wanted to discuss with anyone, least of all with these angry and frightened young women.

'Do you get a lot of support on this sort of issue?' she asked.

'No, of course we bloody don't. Most of the women here are too busy working themselves into the ground for their exams to get involved. Well, this little lot'll give them a shock, won't it? If Louise had had an alarm she might have been OK, right?'

'In bed?' Laura asked sharply enough to bring Stef up with a jerk. She had had enough, she thought, of knee-jerk assumptions.

'In bed?' Stef repeated, looking just slightly taken aback.

'She was killed in her own bed, not on the street,' Laura said.

'Not raped, then?'

'I honestly don't know,' Laura said wearily. 'Does it make it better or worse, in your book, if she was?'

The three students looked at her in silence for a moment, before Stef offered a slightly shamefaced smile, running a hand through her short, almost crew-cut hair.

'You must think I'm an insensitive brat,' she said at length. 'It's not because I care about Louise too little. It's because I care too bloody much.'

'Not raped then, guv?' Sergeant Kevin Mower asked his boss who returned, stony-faced, from the post-mortem on Louise Brownlow.

'No sign of recent sexual activity, according to our Amos,' the chief inspector said, standing in the doorway to his office and not making any attempt to take off his dark trench-coat. 'She effectively bled to death as a result of stab wounds, the most serious being the one to the neck which nicked the jugular vein. The weapon was broad-bladed, pointed – something like a kitchen knife, or a carving kife.'

'So whoever did it must have been covered in blood?'

'Almost certainly,' Thackeray said. 'I suppose for the girl's sake you have to be pleased about the absence of rape, but it makes it less likely we'll find any DNA evidence, which is a pity.'

'Forensic might come up with something from the sheets,' Mower said brightly. 'I take it she wasn't a virgin.'

'No, she wasn't a virgin. What young woman of that age is these days?' Thackeray asked sourly. 'But she was pregnant. Very early stages, Amos says. She might not even have been sure herself, but there were two lives lost.' Once a Catholic always a Catholic, he thought wryly as he saw the questioning look flash into Mower's eyes.

Mower switched off his eager expression abruptly and composed himself. He had worked with Thackeray long enough to know that there were times when a facetious crack would be taken in good part, and times when it most definitely would not.

He had intended to ask, quite sincerely, how Laura Ackroyd

was after her brief encounter with the inside of a cell the previous night, but now thought better of it. News of Thackeray's embarrassment had flashed around police HQ like Puck's girdle round the earth but Mower did not envy any officer who had the temerity to broach the subject with him, or anyone of senior rank either, for that matter. Michael Thackeray, he thought, was on the whole an easygoing boss, but when the man who had once played rugby for a police team was provoked into a tackle he went in hard and the opposition usually came off worst.

'Right,' Thackeray said. 'Whitley Street? What have we set in motion so far?'

'House-to-house inquiries, guv. Did anyone see anything last night, did they hear anything? – surely to God she must have screamed.'

'There was loud music playing, remember?'

'Tristan and bloody Isolde, no less,' Mower said, a glint of amusement, quickly suppressed, in his dark eyes. 'And I thought students these days only listened to techno jazz.'

'And a search for the weapon?'

'Under way, guv. Nothing inside the house that there shouldn't be so we're on to the front gardens, the yards at the back, and the alleyway, the little park at the end of the road. And the graveyard at St Jude's. They'll get a fine harvest of condoms from there, by all accounts. It's where a lot of the tarts take their clients.'

'It's a pity uniformed removed the women from the street just when they did last night,' Thackeray said gravely, not meeting Mower's eye. 'That's a dozen potential witnesses out of circulation.'

'Could be we're looking for one of their disappointed punters,' Mower said, equally seriously.

'What a bloody mess,' Thackeray said, and Mower did not think he was referring solely to the case. 'Come on,' the chief inspector said, turning on his heel. 'It's time we got down there ourselves.'

The drive through the town centre and out along Aysgarth Lane, a bustling thoroughfare lined with curry houses and Asian small businesses, was a short one. Mower glanced out of the window at the bright multi-coloured dress of the mainly Asian shoppers.

'This isn't going to make them feel any better about the kerb-crawlers,' he said.

'I've asked Les Dobson to draft in all the Asian officers in the division, and anyone else who speaks Punjabi, to help keep the tension down,' Thackeray said as Mower stopped at traffic lights and indicated a right turn into one of the narrow streets of Victorian terraced houses which led off each side of the main road. 'What about Whitley Street itself? How does that break down?'

'Mainly Asian, guv. Half a dozen houses with students in them. Just a few white families. A corner shop at the end. And St Jude's, of course.'

'St Jude's? Why have I heard of that?' Thackeray asked.

'Holy Joe? The Reverend Miles Bateman, popularly known as Joe? I suppose Miles doesn't have much street cred. Anyway, a bit of an evangelist, by all accounts. Packs the place out three times on Sunday. Very popular with the youngsters, all happy clappy stuff and rock and roll for Jesus. And he writes the God slot in the *Gazette*. That's probably where you've seen the name.'

Thackeray nodded, recalling reading the work of a man he regarded as a fundamentalist ranter in the Ian Paisley mould.

'And an ally of the Muslims in trying to get the area cleaned up?'

'Right,' Mower said as he drew into the kerb a couple of houses down from the murder site, which was still cordoned off by blue and white police tape and hemmed in by half a dozen police cars and a control van. Uniformed officers were visible at various front doors up and down the street but there was no sign at all of the 'working girls', a few of whom would normally have been lounging in gateways and on the street corners even at this time in the morning.

'Most of the women are due in court sometime today, guv,' Mower said, unable to resist the merest hint of a grin. Thackeray ignored him and sat for a moment taking in the scene. Whitley Street had seen better days. The solid stone terraces with their bay windows and small front gardens had been built for the burgeoning lower middle class of a booming Victorian Bradfield, the families of the men who had accounted for the bales of wool which came half-way across the world to Yorkshire to be turned into high quality cloth.

31

Clerks and salesmen and supervisors had lived out their lives here, but now the trees they had planted in their front gardens had grown tall and top heavy with neglect, the stone was beginning to soften and decay and the roof slates to slip. Upwardly mobile Asian families, most of whom had arrived as impoverished immigrants from rural villages in the Punjab, were beginning to look for something smarter, though not too far from the comforting embrace of the mosque.

As the two men got out of the car a tall, bearded figure in a white tunic came striding towards them, stepping over the straggling tapes in his hurry and brushing aside the outstretched arm of a uniformed constable who tried to restrain him.

'You are the officer in charge?' he asked peremptorily.

'This is Mr Ahmed, guv,' Sergeant Mower said quickly. 'He's been organising the street patrols round here.'

Thackeray nodded impassively. The official police reaction to the Asians' self-help patrols had not been warm.

'Can I help you, Mr Ahmed?' he asked.

'This is the final straw, is it not? You cannot wish any more reason to move on these women who have been creating such a nuisance?' Ahmed spread his hands expressively to take in the massive police presence around them and raised his dark eyes to heaven. 'They are immoral, these women, and they bring immoral men to our streets. And now look how it ends. How can we bring up our children safely here and protect our women from insult?'

'There has been a murder, Mr Ahmed,' Thackeray said. 'But I'm not yet in any position to even guess who committed that murder or what his – or even her – motive might have been.'

'It is nothing to do with us,' Ahmed said flatly.

'You can be so sure?' Thackeray said sceptically. 'None of your young men carry knives?'

Ahmed looked down for a moment with just the slightest discomfort. 'We do not kill young women in their homes,' he came back again fiercely.

'No? Well, we will be talking to everyone who was on the street last night later on,' Thackeray said. 'Including you, Mr Ahmed.'

'I am a man of God, Inspector,' Ahmed said, outraged.

'We will need to talk to you later,' Thackeray insisted, dismissively. 'And on the other front I think you'll have to continue the discussions you've been having with our community liaison people.'

Ahmed looked stormy at that and his fists clenched at his sides. He muttered something in Punjabi and was turning away angrily when to his evident surprise Mower responded in the same language. Ahmed glanced at the sergeant for a second before responding more quietly with a shrug, and then marching away down the street towards a cluster of men with dogs who had been watching the exchange from a distance.

'What was all that about?' Thackeray asked.

'I can't translate exactly, guv,' Mower said circumspectly. 'But he was calling our esteemed community relations people something unspeakable. I suggested he restrain himself, that's all.'

'I don't think he'll take that advice for long, do you?' Thackeray asked, his eyes on the gesticulating group of men who were now moving into one of the houses further down the street.

'No, guv, I don't,' Mower said flatly.

Detective Constable Val Ridley had been with Louise Brownlow's two flat-mates since early that morning. She had urged them to eat breakfast, sat drinking tea with them, and encouraged them to dress by the time her two more senior colleagues arrived.

Thackeray strode into Roz Jenkins' sitting-room, which looked dusty and slightly neglected in the bright morning light, and nodded to the two women.

'I'd like to talk to you separately,' he said. 'I don't mind who goes first.'

Roz and Jane looked at each other uncertainly for a second and then, as Thackeray suspected would usually happen, Roz made the decision.

'I'll wait in the kitchen,' she said. She was wearing a full dark skirt this morning, with a long, loose, jewel-coloured patterned shirt, and she swept out of the room with the air of a slightly amateur prima donna, without a backward glance. Mower, never slow to appreciate an attractive female, even one who billowed as she walked, followed her with his eyes and a slightly sardonic grin on his good-looking face. He was not used to being ignored.

Jane, painfully thin in jeans and a pale blue sweatshirt, and still looking grey with fatigue and shock, sank down again into the corner of one of the battered old sofas and glanced nervously at Val Ridley, looking for support. She let her fine fair hair fall across her eyes, as if trying to hide from whatever life had to throw at her next.

'Val will stay with you,' Thackeray said reassuringly, and nodded to Mower, who also turned on his heel and left without a word. His brief was to take Louise Brownlow's room apart for clues now that the forensic teams had finished their collection of evidence.

With quiet deliberation Thackeray took off his trench-coat and sat down opposite the women in the second of the two sofas. As the springs protested and sagged under his bulk he took his time to weigh up the young woman who sat opposite him, almost visibly trembling.

'Was Louise a close friend, Miss Watson?' he asked quietly.

Jane shuddered slightly.

'I suppose,' she said. 'Since I came to live here, anyway.'

'Which was when?'

'In October, at the beginning of the academic year,' Jane said.

'So tell me about her,' Thackeray said, very aware of the fragility of the girl's composure. She sat twisting her hands together in a knot for a moment before she began to speak.

'She was a good friend,' she said slowly. 'A good listener. She was doing languages – German and French. Spent last year in Grenoble at the university there.' The facts came out in a jerky stream, as if the shock of what had happened had already begun to wash the reality of the dead girl out of Jane's mind.

'Was being a good listener important to you?' Val Ridley asked quietly and Thackeray flashed her a look of appreciation.

'Yes,' Jane said quickly. 'It was. I'd been having some problems this year and Louise was always there when you needed her ... Louise and Roz were great.'

'Boyfriend problems?' DC Ridley asked.

'No, no, more family problems really...' The girl evidently did not want to elaborate and Thackeray came in quickly, taking the cue to ask one of the crucial questions he wanted answered about Louise Brownlow.

'Did Louise have a boyfriend?'

'No, no, she didn't,' Jane said quickly. Too quickly, possibly, Thackeray thought.

'An ex-boyfriend? Someone she had finished with, perhaps?'

'No one I know about,' Jane said. 'No one who came here. She was coming up to exams and working hard. She went to church sometimes, that's all. St Jude's. A lot of students go there. I don't think she had time for anything else.'

Thackeray raised an eyebrow at that. Even on the pathologist's slab, Louise Brownlow had been an attractive young woman, blonde, blue-eyed and slim with no hint yet of her pregnancy. In these days of allegedly hard-working students, he would have found what Jane was saying difficult to believe even if he had not been sure that the dead girl must have had a recent relationship with the father of her child. But that piece of information was one he did not intend to broadcast at the moment.

'So tell me exactly what happened yesterday, Miss Watson,' he said. 'From the time you last saw Louise alive.'

Thackeray listened with a vague sense of dissatisfaction as Jane repeated her story of the night before. She had come home, had a bath, begun to make cocoa and been aware of nothing untoward in the house until she and Roz Jenkins had decided to offer their house-mate a drink.

'Nothing unusual? Think very hard, Miss Watson. The slightest thing might help,' Thackeray persisted.

'There was nothing unusual,' she said, a single tear running down her pale cheek.

'The back door was unlocked? That seems rash after dark in a neighbourhood like this.'

'Yes, I hadn't noticed that. Roz usually takes charge of that sort of thing, locks up at night and so on. I'd no idea that door was unlocked,' Jane said, looking even more anxious. 'Do you think someone came in that way?'

'We have to consider all the possibilities,' Thackeray said neutrally. He dismissed Jane and while he waited for Roz to arrive looked more carefully round the room. On a bureau in one corner were several framed snapshots and portraits, most of them of young women, two of whom, Jane Watson and the dead girl, he recognised. He picked up a full-face photograph of Louise Brownlow and was trying to decipher the enigmatic

35

expression in her blue eyes when Val Ridley brought Roz Jenkins into the room.

'May I take this picture?' he asked. For no more than a moment Roz looked as if she had been struck across the face, but she composed herself almost instantly.

'Of course, if you need it,' she said, shrugging slightly.

'She was very attractive,' Thackeray said. 'She must have had more boyfriends than most.'

Roz shook her head and again denied knowing anything useful about her tenant's private life. Thackeray's frustration grew. Roz Jenkins was older, more confident, more in control, than Jane but just as mystified, apparently, by Louise's horrific death, just as uninformative about her relationships.

'Miss Jenkins,' Thackeray said at last in exasperation. 'She was found stark naked. That either means that she was getting ready for bed alone and someone burst in on her and stabbed her. Or she was getting ready for bed with someone she knew. Now there is no evidence that a stranger came into the house last night. There's no sign of a break-in. You say no one else could have had a key that you know of. The back door was inadvertently left unlocked but there's no sign of an intruder with burglary in mind. Nothing is missing, as far as we know. So who did Louise know who might have been with her listening to *Tristan and Isolde* with no clothes on? Was it you? Or was it Jane? Or was it someone else?'

Thackeray had intended to shock the woman into giving a little more than had so far been forthcoming, but there was absolutely no sign, beyond a minutely raised dark eyebrow at his vehemence, that he had succeeded.

'Inspector, I've been letting rooms here to students for the five years I've been working towards my PhD,' Roz said with dignity. 'I don't ask them about their private lives. If they want to confide in me that's fine. If they don't, I don't intrude. If they choose to have visitors, that's fine too. This is the 1990s, not the 1950s. I'm as desperate as you probably are to find out who killed Louise. Men who do things like that should be locked up and the key thrown away. But I honestly can't point you in any particular direction. If she had men friends, I don't know who they are.'

'Would she have let someone in and out by the back door, do you think?' Thackeray persisted.

Roz shrugged eloquently again.

'She could have done, I suppose, given what was going on out on the street.'

And with that Thackeray had to be content.

'So what are they trying to hide?' Thackeray asked Val Ridley ten minutes later as, frustrated, they joined Sergeant Kevin Mower in the dead girl's bedroom upstairs.

DC Ridley shrugged. 'I thought Roz Jenkins was being incredibly protective of both her lodgers, sir,' she said slowly. 'I don't believe Louise could have had a boyfriend who made her pregnant without at least one of them knowing about it. But why keep quiet about him when he has to be the most likely suspect? It doesn't make sense. And the Watson girl looks right on the edge, to me. But why? Is it the murder or something leading up to the murder that they're not telling us about? Or did they stab her themselves?'

'Which will be difficult to prove without a weapon if they continue to back each other up,' Thackeray said.

Mower listened to all this with an enigmatic smile. He said nothing but turned in his seat at Louise's desk overlooking the street outside, where uniformed police were still pursuing the routine of house-to-house inquiries. He flicked over a few papers.

'Where do you want to start, guv?' he asked Thackeray. 'There's a diary, but it's full of entries which will take some working out. Lots of initials, possibly a code. But our Louise wasn't as squeaky clean as her friends seem to want to make out.' He waved a hand over the neat piles of documents he had collated. 'She's broke for a start. In fact, she's up to her eyes in debt as far as I can see.'

'That's not unusual for students these days,' DC Ridley said mildly.

'Yes, but most of them have some visible means of support, Val. All I can find in this kid's documents is long lists of outgoings and no income. No grant cheques going into the bank, no allowance from parents. One payment for what I would guess is the maximum student loan, though we'll have to check that.' He glanced around the room which was well enough provided

37

with books, a stereo and CD collection, and a wardrobe reasonably stuffed with clothes.

'She's not been dressing from jumble sales, anyway,' Val Ridley said, running practised fingers down a few skirts and shirts at random. She picked up a red kimono with a gold dragon rampant across the back and felt it lovingly. 'This is silk,' she said.

'There's a possible explanation, guv,' Mower said cautiously. 'Though you're not going to like it.'

'Try me,' Thackeray said shortly.

Almost reluctantly Mower crossed the room to the bed, stripped of its bedding now and covered in clear plastic through which the rusty bloodstains on the mattress were still clearly visible. He pulled open a brown cardboard box which he had evidently placed there ready for Thackeray's attention. It rattled as he gently emptied the contents out on to the bed.

Thackeray looked carefully at the tangle of black stockings, bras and suspender belts, an elaborate Basque, the lengths of rope and chain and the police issue handcuffs and sighed.

'I think . . .' Mower said, almost reluctantly, 'I think she was on the game.'

'Which explains precisely what they were trying to hide, those bloody stupid girls,' Thackeray said angrily. 'And why she might invite her visitors in the back way. It was her they were trying to protect.'

'And she may well have taken great care not to let them know who she was entertaining,' Val Ridley suggested.

'Either way it's a whole new perspective. Time, I think, to start all over again,' Thackeray said.

4

'Good God,' Detective Superintendent Jack Longley said, grimly astonished by the turn the murder investigation had taken when Thackeray reported to him later that day. 'You mean she was bringing them in off Whitley Street? Taking the kerb-crawlers to her room?'

'I don't know,' Thackeray said. 'I've got my people checking with all the women who work the street regularly to see what they know, or might have seen.'

'A bloody university student!' Longley said angrily. 'Surely they're not driven to that?'

'According to Mower, they are, sir,' Thackeray said. 'It's not unusual, apparently.'

'If she was my daughter . . .' Longley began.

'Yes, well, she was someone's daughter. The father's working in the Middle East for one of the oil companies, according to university records. Why the hell he wasn't supporting her through university I don't know, but there's no sign of it on her bank statements. No sign of a grant either. Which probably explains why she turned to a more unorthodox way of earning her keep.'

'Do you think her friends knew?'

'They say not. I've tackled them twice, and they still insist not, though I'm not sure I believe them,' Thackeray said. 'The Watson girl is scared to death about something. I'll have another go at her tomorrow. I'm bloody sure she knows more than she's telling.'

'Aye, well, it could be that the Jenkins girl realises that if she knowingly let Louise Brownlow ply her trade in her house she's open to a charge of running a brothel. They're so bloody sharp these days, these lasses, it's no wonder they cut themselves,' Longley said.

'Yes, well, there was no possibility of that,' Thackeray said harshly. 'Louise was cut all right, but not by her own hand.'

'Don't take it personally, lad,' Longley advised with unexpected understanding. 'You'll find him. And in the meantime, I need to know what the hell I'm going to tell the community liaison people? They're meeting the local Asian leaders this evening.'

'There'll be a police presence down there for days yet. I should think that'll keep the kerb-crawlers to a minimum for a while, which should please Mohammed Ahmed and his friends.'

'Aye, but that's just temporary,' Longley said. 'When it comes to the crunch, the residents want the women off their streets for good. The women don't want to shift, and they've got the backing of a few thugs if things turn nasty. Community liaison can talk till they're blue in the face but I reckon there'll be a nasty bust-up in the end.'

'Well, just for the moment I'd like things kept calm if possible, sir,' Thackeray said. 'I need to talk to the women on the street, and to as many of their clients as I can get my hands on, especially the ones into a bit of bondage as that seems to be what young Louise was willing to provide. I've got a couple of the lads out looking in the phone booths too, to see if she was advertising.'

'You say she was studying French?' Longley asked. 'Bloody 'ell. Strict French mistress, that sort of thing?'

'That sort of thing.'

Longley saw the distaste in Thackeray's eyes. 'It takes all sorts,' he said comfortably, shifting himself in his chair. It was common knowledge in the division that Jack Longley was now contemplating his not too distant retirement with something like enthusiasm. Most of the time, he had the air of a man who had seen it all, done what he could and was ready for a well-deserved rest.

'She was nineteen, sir,' Thackeray said flatly. He seldom shared his superior's complacency. 'Attractive, clever and only nineteen.'

'So what are we going to tell your friends in the bloody press?' Longley said, stung into a change of tack, a chilly look in his eyes as he pulled that day's *Gazette* from under the heap of papers on his desk. It was open on the second page where Laura Ackroyd's description of her Whitley Street arrest and detention was spread across several columns.

'We could have done without this nonsense,' Longley went on. 'John Franks is running round like a headless chicken in the canteen threatening to get the Police Federation to help him sue her for libel.'

'She doesn't identify him,' Thackeray said mildly, although he knew that that was not necessarily any bar to an action.

'No, well, I've got Les Dobson leaning on him to shut his big mouth and keep his hands to himself in future,' Longley said. 'He's dead keen to get into CID so I dare say he'll listen to sense. Is she going to make an official complaint, your friend?'

'I don't think so,' Thackeray said neutrally, intensely disliking the turn the discussion had taken but powerless in the circumstances to prevent Longley probing just as far as he liked. Laura had strayed inadvertently into his territory and he was surprised at how much he disliked the effect she was having.

'Aye, well, you can use a bit of influence there, can't you? Persuade her to put it down to experience, eh, Michael?'

Thackeray thought of the sheer unlikelihood of his being able to change Laura's mind on anything she felt strongly about and gave Longley a wry smile.

'Maybe,' he said.

Longley sat looking at him for a moment, a faintly puzzled look in his pale blue eyes. Thackeray had worked for him for more than a year but there were times when the superintendent felt that he was no nearer knowing or understanding the younger man now than when he had arrived from the other side of the county. He had come to Bradfield trailing a reputation as an effective copper, but an intensely private man. But in spite of the occasional malicious whisper which reached Longley's ears at Masonic meetings and Rotary dinners, the superintendent had found no cause to complain about Michael Thackeray's dedication to the job. He had just one worry about him, and it had been sharply intensified by Laura Ackroyd's dramatic and all too public incursion onto police ground the previous night.

'Serious, is it, this thing with the Ackroyd girl?' he ventured with, for him, an uncharacteristic delicacy.

Thackeray glanced away, his face impassive but his eyes angry, and did not answer.

'Aye, well, it's none of my business,' Longley admitted cheerfully. 'Just so long as it's not going to bugger up your career, that's all. You could still go far, Michael, in spite of this reorganisation nonsense. You're young enough and bright enough. You can come to terms with being a crime manager, and the rest of the jargon, even if I can't stomach it. But you don't need episodes like this Franks business. That's not done you much good around the station. And you know how quickly news travels up the line to County.'

'I don't want to tell the press what we suspect about the Brownlow girl's extra-curricular activities,' Thackeray said abruptly, changing the subject as definitively as he dared. 'I want

41

to keep the innocent student façade intact for a bit, while we check for boyfriends and do a bit of quiet probing of men known to have an interest in getting themselves handcuffed for kicks.'

'If the *Gazette* reckons she's a tart they'll soon lose interest, any road,' Longley said. 'You might get the *Globe* burning up the motorway to have a good sniff around, though, in case we've got another Ripper on the go. But if you want local publicity the student line's the one to go for. I'll get County to lay on a press conference tomorrow morning. Have you contacted the parents?'

'The Foreign Office is tracking down the father. The university has no record of anyone else.'

'Right, well, he's not going to be right chuffed to find his daughter dead. He'll be even less chuffed when you tell him what she was up to in her spare time. Rather you than me, lad. Rather you than me.'

Laura sat in the corner of the students' union coffee bar feeling elderly. All around her young people came and went in a swirl of laughter and gossip, heedless of the fact that one of their number lay in a cold mortuary just down the hill. Would I have been untouched by a death like that? she asked herself, sipping with distaste at her plastic cup of lukewarm brownish liquid, and thinking back to her own time here more than ten years previously. And she was forced to conclude that it would almost certainly have passed her by, as it seemed to have passed most of the students by, a momentary concern, if that, in the super-charged bustle of university life.

She was waiting for Stef Andrews of the women's group, who had promised to bring her some of Louise Brownlow's friends to talk to. It was nine o'clock on a blustery wet morning, the rain from the western hills putting a shine on the town's grey slate roofs but casting a terminal gloom around the ill-lit students' union building which was showing distinct signs of wear and tear. The persistent bass line from the juke box chimed well enough with Laura's mood, which was not a happy one.

She had got up early after a restless night alone. Thackeray had neither called her nor come round to the flat the previous evening which, she told herself, was no cause for complaint.

They lived separate and diversely busy lives, and had no permanent commitment to see each other. Even so she had eaten a sketchy supper, desultorily watched television and gone to bed to sleep only fitfully in a fever of frustration for what she evidently could not have and did not know how to give up.

She tried to shake herself out of her depression as she saw Stef shouldering her way through the crowds, face shiny, hair bristling, blue eyes bright with an enthusiasm which Laura, ten years or so her senior, envied this morning with an almost bitter regret.

'Morning,' the girl said, dumping a ruck-sack of books on the floor and taking the seat opposite Laura. 'This is Jackie. On the same course as Louise.' Jackie was a tall, painfully thin girl dressed in jeans and a loose black top, her brown hair a mass of unruly curls which almost concealed her pale, serious-looking face, devoid of make-up and showing distinct signs that she had been crying very recently.

'Jackie doesn't want her name in the paper,' Stef said belligerently.

'I'm only collecting background information,' Laura said soothingly. 'I don't need to attribute it to anyone. It's just for a little profile of Louise to go with the report on the police investigations. Had you known her long, Jackie?'

The girl took a deep breath and seemed to conclude that having come so far she might as well go the whole mile.

'We were in hall together for our first term,' she said. 'And we're both doing French. But Louise didn't stay in hall. She said she couldn't afford it.'

'Didn't she get a grant?' Laura asked.

'She never said much, but I think her father wouldn't fill in the forms. He was abroad somewhere. It all sounded very difficult. She had a job in McDonald's for a while that first term, and I know she was very worried about how she was going to pay her fare for our trip to France. Then she went to live with Roz Jenkins and she seemed a bit easier about money after that. I suppose Roz wasn't charging much rent, as she's a student herself.'

'I talked to people about Roz,' Stef said. 'She's a post-graduate so she's not really into the SU or anything, but she has a reputation for taking in people who need a bit of help.'

43

'Her own personal social service?' Laura asked sceptically. 'What does she get out of it?' She had been corrupted, she realised, by too many years of the Me society.

'What nasty cynical people you hacks are,' Stef said. 'Perhaps it makes her feel good. Who knows? Kindness isn't illegal, you know. And they've not managed to privatise it yet.'

'I don't think Louise was living there free,' Jackie said, in some irritation. 'She paid Roz rent.'

'Did Louise have a boyfriend?' Laura asked carefully, knowing that if she did he would be very likely to be Michael Thackeray's prime suspect for her killing.

Jackie shook her head. 'She never seemed to have time for much of a social life. She was working all the hours God sends, with a job and her course work. She came top in the first-year exams. She was very good. But it was as if she had something to prove, you know? Perhaps to her father, perhaps to herself. I'm not sure.'

'So no men?'

'It is possible to live without men, you know,' Stef said loftily.

'It isn't much fun, though, is it?' Laura came back sharply, although she was not certain her heart was in the argument.

'Louise never got much fun,' Jackie broke in impatiently. 'She worried me. She came into classes looking completely shattered sometimes, but really we were beginning to lose touch after she went to her new place. She didn't stay on for a coffee and a chat any more. I tried to keep in touch but she didn't seem to want it.'

Laura thought of her own carefree student days in this very building and was filled with a weary sadness for what seemed to have been crushed out of the place.

'Don't any of you have a good time here any more?' she asked in exasperation, the outline of her feature on the dead student and her way of life taking shape in her mind. 'Is it all a grind being a student?'

'No, of course it's not,' Jackie said dismissively. 'But there are some people having a hard time, right? No one's got enough money to get by on. Everyone's skint and borrowing hand over fist and I think that gets to some people more than others. And if we're not borrowing we're trying to find part-time jobs to make ends meet, like Louise.'

44

'There's one or two women gone on the game,' Stef said emphatically. 'It's that bad for some.'

'You have got to be kidding,' Laura said, more in hope than expectation.

'No kidding,' Stef said flatly. 'It's a known fact, right?'

'Can you find me someone who'd talk about that?' she asked, thinking about her series of features on prostitution that it had taken her weeks to persuade Ted Grant to commission. Here was an angle which would appeal to him, she thought. Stef looked dubious, the deep suspicion in her eyes telling Laura that she understood very well that if anything could guarantee a raid on the university by the London tabloids a tale of undergraduate hookers would be it.

'I can try,' she said cautiously. 'Call me at the SU office later in the week and I'll see what I can do.' She looked around the bar from which the crowds were now beginning to drift away, many of them munching as they went. 'And now I have to go to a lecture.'

'And me,' Jackie said. 'I don't know who killed Louise, but I hope he rots in hell.'

Sergeant Mower and Bob Kitchen, a young PC who had been drafted into plain clothes to help with the murder investigation, drove together to the low-rise block of council flats which Sherry Maguire had given as her address at the police station the previous night. She answered their knock dressed in a bright lemon bathrobe, fastened around her waist with only the most cursory attention to decency, her hair wrapped in a matching towel. She invited them in reluctantly.

'I've got to go out soon,' she said unwinding her towel and giving her hair a vigorous rubbing, which set various parts of her anatomy moving in a way which Kitchen evidently found fascinating and from which Mower deliberately averted his gaze, not wanting to give his younger colleague any encouragement. Two children sat in front of the television in the main living-room and Sherry gave the men a warning look.

'Go and watch that in t' bedroom, chicks, while I talk to these two nice men about some business, will you?' The children, a boy of about eight with flaxen hair and a much darker girl of

45

about five, glanced round silently and then did as they were told.

'Both yours?' Mower asked, while the younger man looked around him in some bemusement. Sherry Maguire's situation was evidently not what he expected.

'And why not?' Sherry came back a touch defensively. 'If their dads had stuck around I wouldn't be in t' business I'm in, would I?'

'And they don't know what you do?'

'No, they bloody don't, Sergeant Mower. And that's the way I want it to stay,' Sherry said fiercely.

'It'll get harder as they grow older,' Mower said.

'Aye, well, I'll have to cope with that when I get there,' Sherry said. 'Just now we manage, thanks very much. I work while they're at school. There's a good lunch-time trade. Or at least there were till t' bloody Pakis and vicars and such started patrolling t' streets. And then I get a baby-sitter a couple of nights a week. They're well took care of them two, so don't you go telling t' bloody social that they're not. They're better looked after than if I were trying to get by on bloody income support or in some grotty factory job, I can tell you. I do my best for my kids. No one can say I don't.'

Mower too glanced around the comfortably furnished sitting-room with its TV and video, toys and books, fitted carpets and three piece suite and the bottles of gin and whisky on the sideboard, and he recognised the justice of that. He had seen the inside of too many homes around the town to go along with the idea of virtuous poverty as a comfortable way of life, or necessarily less destructive than the path Sherry had chosen.

'You could afford to pay your fine?' he asked mildly.

'It's paid,' Sherry said flatly. 'That's not what you're here for, is it? Come on. I haven't got all day. My baby-sitter'll be here in a minute. I lost money last night thanks to you lot. I've got some catching up to do.'

The constable gave her an old-fashioned look at that, old moralities dying hard in spite of the temptations he was obviously susceptible to, Mower thought, lips twitching. He stared resolutely out of the window, not wanting to catch Sherry Maguire's eye.

46

'Last night,' Mower said, when he had regained his composure, 'sometime either just before the uniformed police raided Whitley Street, or possibly after, you might have seen someone going into Number 17. Can you remember?'

'You've changed your tune a bit, now, haven't you?' Sherry said, slightly resentfully. 'One minute we're nicked, a fifty quid fine and no time to pay, the next we're valuable witnesses. Make you sick, wouldn't it?'

'Come off it,' Mower said. 'You don't want a joker with a knife loose on the streets any more than we do. We know the dead girl was at the university until six, but after that we've no record of her movements. No one saw her come home, no one knows if she went out again, no one knows who she let into the house or if anyone let themselves in, for that matter. If you were in Whitley Street you might have seen something significant without even realising it.'

Sherry Maguire sat for a moment looking thoughtful. She was a handsome woman, the dyed blonde hair in a damp cloud around her face, pale-skinned and with a generous figure. But there were deep lines of tiredness around her mouth and eyes that were normally concealed by the careful application of make-up and the slightly forced vivacity with which she faced the world. Watching her now, half dressed and wholly unadorned, Mower wondered how long she could continue successfully juggling her chosen profession with the demands of two growing children. If in the end the social services intervened, he thought, and to judge by her defensiveness they might simply be waiting for their chance, she could slide away into desolation with the help of those half-empty bottles on the sideboard, or worse.

'Aye,' she said. 'I know them three lasses by sight. And I've seen men go in there a few times.'

'Students?' Mower asked. 'That sort of age?' But she shook her head at that.

'Not lads,' she said. 'Much older than that. More like their dads than their boyfriends.'

'Can you describe anyone? Could you identify anyone?'

'No chance,' she said dismissively. 'It was always dark when I saw owt and I wasn't taking that much notice. I've got other things on my mind when I'm on Whitley Street.'

'White, though? Not Asians?'

'Pakis?' Sherry said incredulously. 'We only see them beggars when they choose to come an' abuse us.'

"Have they ever threatened you with violence?" Mower persisted. 'Have you ever seen anyone with a knife, for instance?'

'One of the old beggars whirls a stick about now an' again,' she said dismissively. 'Nowt worse than that.'

'Last night? A car then?' Mower said, but again he got little response.

'No one parked outside, if that's what you mean. But a lot o' folk don't like parking in Whitley Street, any road, do they? They get right stroppy if they see the family car round there, do their wives,' she said.

'So did you see a man at Number 17 last night?' Mower pressed and was finally rewarded.

'Early on, before your lot turned up wi' t' cattle trucks, I did see someone going in there. Must have been about half eight. He came down t' street towards me and I thought I had him hooked, but he turned in the gate just before he got right up to me. A middle-aged bloke, typical punter I thought, coat collar turned up as if he didn't want to be recognised. Right shifty. But he couldn't have been a punter, could he? Not if he went in there?'

'Not a punter you knew, then? Not your minder? Not anyone else's minder?'

'I don't have a bloody minder,' Sherry said. 'I can manage without a man helping himself to t' profits, ta very much. But no. No one that I recognised. But as I say, it were dark, he had his collar up. Could have been anyone, really.'

'Can you describe him?' Mower said, trying to hide the excitement in his eyes at what seemed to be the first lead they had turned up since Louise Brownlow's body had been found. But the woman shrugged.

'It were too dark,' she said. 'That street light by number 17's been out for weeks. He was a medium sort of bloke, not particularly tall, not particularly fat or thin that you'd notice, had a dark jacket of some sort, longish, a car coat perhaps, or a duffel coat, wi' t' collar turned up. Just ordinary looking.'

'But not young?'

'Not in jeans or owt like that, no,' she said. 'He didn't look young. Didn't *move* young, you know what I mean? Like I say, I thought I were on till he turned in the gateway. He looked like a punter.'

'Good,' Mower said. 'We'll need a statement on that, Sherry.' He glanced at the constable, who had been busily taking notes, his eyes firmly fixed on his notebook, his face and neck slightly flushed.

'Just one other thing,' he said. 'Bondage? A bit of strict discipline? Where would I get that around here, do you know?' But the woman laughed at him, and then laughed again at his discomfiture.

'There's a few I'd like to give a good spanking to, pet,' Sherry said. 'But not for kicks. And not for money. Just for t' sheer bloody satisfaction. Them bloody magistrates this morning'd come top o' t' list, an' all.'

'Seriously,' Mower said and the laughter died out of her eyes and she suddenly looked old.

'There's a few about who'll oblige,' she said. 'There used to be a lass called Sal who had a place up on t' Heights. It's not summat you can do up a back alley very easily, is it? But last I heard she'd died. Overdosed on summat, silly cow. But someone did tell me there was a card in t' phone boxes in town, someone offering a bit o' discipline. But I couldn't tell you who it were.'

'Looks like you'd better do a quick scan of British Telecom's finest, Bob,' Mower said to the constable, who had been listening to his exchanges with Sherry with some bemusement. 'See if you can set yourself up for a caning.'

'Sarge.' The response was half protest, half resigned aquiescence. The two policemen got up to go and Sherry Maguire followed them to the door, giving Mower an almost coquettish smile and pulling her skimpy robe down to reveal even more cleavage between ample breasts.

'So what time do you get off duty, lover?' she asked as she opened the door to let them out.

'Long after your bedtime,' he said with an appreciative grin, and a regretfully elegant shrug of the shoulders, knowing only too well what Michael Thackeray's reaction to any extra-curricular activities of that sort would be. But before either of the men could step over the threshold they were pushed aside by a newcomer, a young girl in leggings and a leather jacket, fair hair cut brutally short above a thin face where the bruised look around the eyes paled into insignificance against a long purple and red weal across the side of her face.

Startled, Sherry stood aside to let the girl into the flat.

'My baby-sitter,' she said quickly, swinging the door to.

'Right,' Mower said faintly as the door slammed shut behind them. He glanced at his companion quizzically. 'What do you think?' he asked. 'Would you leave a baby with her?'

'Don't know, sarge,' the constable said, evidently puzzled by the question. 'Isn't she old enough?'

Mower considered the hunted look he had caught in the pale girl's eyes, the look of an animal frozen in the headlights of a juggernaut that it knew could not conceivably stop.

'Probably not, as far as age goes,' he said, more to himself than his companion. 'But in terms of experience, I'd guess she's too old, the best part of a lifetime too old. Have a look in the missing person files when we get back, will you, Bob? See if you can recognise her. She looks as if she's running hard from something, and that could well include us.'

5

Laura sat cross-legged on her sofa in a pair of cream silk pyjamas, carefully wiping the chipped varnish from her fingernails. She wrinkled her nose at the remover, a smell she had always hated, and pushed the cloud of newly washed and still damp hair away from her face as it fell across her eyes.

She had been feeling quite cheerful earlier in the evening as she had dumped her work clothes on the bedroom floor and slipped under the shower. Late in the afternoon she had achieved what she had not thought possible after her inconclusive interviews at the university – a call from Roz Jenkins agreeing to meet her to help with the feature she had heard she was writing about student life.

Intrigued, Laura had walked back up the hill to the students' union and found Roz, dressed entirely in flowing black, sitting in front of a cappuccino and a slice of chocolate cake in the corner of the coffee bar.

'So just what is it you're proposing to write?' Roz had asked with a composure that Laura found unnerving in the circumstances. She told her how her features on prostitution had taken on a new dimension with the news that students were going 'on the game' to help make ends meet.

'I don't know why you're so surprised,' Roz said. 'It's hardly news that kids are desperate, dropping out of their courses, taking two or three part-time jobs if they can get them. What's new?'

'My editor hasn't taken all that on board, so I suppose a lot of other people haven't either,' Laura said.

'It's a living,' Roz said dismissively. 'What's to get so worked up about? Women have something to sell and men seem to want to buy. That's what capitalism's all about, isn't it?'

'Oh, come on,' Laura said. 'How many mummies and daddies would go along with that? It's a bloody risky living, from what I've seen of it lately. Drugs, Aids, the police. And murder, possibly, if you're really unlucky. It's not exactly what parents had in mind when they sent their daughters off to university, is it?'

'Well, their daughters aren't little girls any more. They grow up and make their own choices, just like you did, I'd guess,' Roz said complacently.

Laura had to smile at the justice of that remark. She had not, from the age of eighteen when she finally left her detested boarding school, taken very much notice of what her father had advised, and had quite deliberately turned her face away from her mother's pleading eyes.

'Do you know how widespread it is?' she asked.

'What? Students earning a bit on the side? It's mostly rumour, but I'm sure there are some genuine cases. The women's group is getting very worked up about the whole issue. And they're talking about solidarity with the women on Whitley Street. They don't like the way the locals are persecuting them down there. Students and some of those women are in pretty much the same situation, after all. They can't live on social security and the students can't live on their grants, and there aren't any jobs worth talking about. Same difference, really.'

'So how come you're able to buy a house?' Laura asked, changing the subject briskly, conscious of the justice of some of

51

what Roz was saying but reluctant to admit it, even to herself. 'I didn't think post-graduates were much better off.'

'They're not, on the whole. I had a small legacy and used that to buy Number 17.'

'Which you rent out?' Laura asked with studied neutrality.

'If they can afford to pay,' Roz said, dismissively. 'I only share with friends. The house is paid for. The rents aren't really important to me.'

'So Louise and Jane were close friends of yours? You weren't just the landlady?'

'My trouble is I'm a great big softy,' Roz said, taking a mouthful of chocolate cake and masticating slowly and with relish. 'I collect up waifs and strays. Jane has all sorts of problems. Louise was broke and very bitter and twisted about her dad. But it all seemed to be working out quite well until this happened. I still can't believe it, really. I think you go slightly numb in a crisis, don't you? The brain detaches itself from what's going on.'

'So tell me about Louise,' Laura said, and for a moment she thought that Roz's massive self-composure was about to crack.

'She was very bright, very together, very caring,' Roz said. She glanced away, her dark eyes full of tears. 'I thought she shared things, but after this I'm not so sure.'

'You mean she had secrets?'

'She must have had, mustn't she? Someone she knew well enough to let into her room, the police say. But no one Jane and I knew about. Unless it turns out to be that bloody vicar who was supposed to be teaching her hymns on the guitar.'

'Hymns?' Laura asked, bemused.

'She played at the services at St Jude's, didn't she? If you want to know what Louise was up to you should talk to her happy clappy friends down there. I went a couple of times to keep her company but in the end it all sickened me. They don't like prostitution, either. They're running some sort of mission for fallen women down by the canal. Handing out condoms with one hand and texts with the other. I approve of the condoms, thought I'd help for a while, but the Bible thumping is too much, really.'

'The police are working on the theory it was a boyfriend rather than an intruder, are they?' Laura asked.

'I don't know what theory they're working on,' Roz said, scraping up the last crumbs of cake from her plate with such care that Laura thought she might actually pick it up and lick it so as not to miss the last smear of cream. Roz glanced longingly at the bar and then shrugged slightly and turned back to give Laura her full attention.

'We're all vulnerable from men, aren't we?' she said. 'Some of them smile and smile and play the villain.'

'*Hamlet*,' Laura said automatically. 'What are you doing research on?'

'The role of women in the Elizabethan revenge tragedies,' Roz said mechanically. 'Did you read English?'

'No, I did *Hamlet* for A level, that's all. So what is their role?'

'Oh, just victims, most of them. Except for the one or two who defy the conventions, do their own thing like the Duchess of Malfi, for instance. Though, of course, they all end up dead.' For a moment enthusiasm lit up her face and Laura could see the intelligence there, which tended to be concealed by the all too voluminous flesh in which it was encased.

But the spark faded as quickly as it had arrived and Roz had obviously had enough. Laura reluctantly let her go, watching her sail out of the coffee bar like a massive black whale with a surprisingly sharp brain. She went home, half appalled and half fascinated by the twists and turns that student life had taken since she had graduated, but sure now that she was on to a good story.

Finding herself alone for the second evening running, and not at all sure that she wanted to compare notes about Roz Jenkins with Michael Thackeray just yet, she had decided on a late night beauty treatment to boost her fragile morale. The prescription was not really working, though, she admitted to herself as she glanced at her watch for about the twentieth time in half an hour.

Her collection of nail varnishes stood in ranks on that evening's *Gazette*, which she had spread across the coffee table. She was not sentimental about her work and already a patch of remover had spread a pungent stain across her page two feature on the insecurities of women students after the Brownlow murder. The latest on the hunt for Louise's killer took up most of the front page, invisible now, although she knew that if pressed she would be able to repeat verbatim the police spokesman's description of the young woman's horrific injuries.

And she knew, without ever having asked Michael Thackeray in so many words, that the details which were released were heavily censored for public consumption, sometimes as a ploy to help catch a killer, sometimes simply to protect the sensibilities of more sensitive readers and listeners. She never pressed him to tell her more than he was willing to tell but she guessed from the wounded look she sometimes caught in his eyes that even after years of professional dispassion he could still be hurt by the cruelty he witnessed.

She sighed and went to wash her hands before resuming her seat and cast a dispirited eye over the nail varnish bottles, as unmoved by Cherry Brandy as by Blush Rose and Coral Whisper. The shrill peal of her door bell made her jump. She glanced one final time at her watch and saw that it was ten to midnight. She smiled wryly. Only Thackeray, she thought, would turn up now, and she felt that familiar shiver of excitement at his arrival. It really was time she grew up, she thought, as she picked up the entry-phone and told him to come up.

'You weren't waiting up?' he asked, as he took his coat off and cast an appreciative eye over her state of undress.

'Don't flatter yourself,' she said, deliberately turning her back on him to resume her yogic position on the sofa. 'Have you been working late?'

'As ever,' he said, dropping into an armchair facing her and stretching his arms wearily behind his head.

'Making progress?' she asked, surveying her nail varnish bottles again with feigned interest.

'Not much,' he said carefully, wanting to avoid the direct lie, but equally unwilling to put Laura in a position where her loyalties might be stretched by knowing what he did not want revealed. 'She seems to have been a model student, young Louise. Hard-working, no attachments – or none we've uncovered – but broke, of course, as most of them seem to be these days.'

'D'you know some of them are on the game?' Laura asked explosively, her eyes sparkling with anger. 'So the women's group says. It's the only way they can make ends meet. What the hell's going on, Michael? What are we doing to these kids?'

54

'Have you met any who are that desperate?' he asked carefully.

'Not yet,' she said. 'I've asked for some names.'

'Will you let me know what you uncover?'

She looked at him speculatively for a moment. 'Are you serious? D'you think Louise was that desperate?'

'I've no firm evidence for that,' he said untruthfully. 'But with very little evidence at all, I can't afford to leave any avenues unexplored – or stones unturned, for that matter.' He smiled faintly as he fell into the sort of jargon he needed for the next morning's press conference.

'But that avenue's not for quoting in the *Gazette*?' Laura said shrewdly.

'It's absolutely never even crossed my mind,' he said. 'At least that's what the press officer will tell you.'

'I'll see what I can do – if my contacts actually come up with anything,' she said.

He gave her one of the rare smiles which she knew he reserved for her alone.

'Am I forgiven? Can I stay?' he asked.

Laura laughed in relief as well as resignation.

'When did I ever say no?' she said.

'A shower, then,' he said, and took himself off to her tiny bathroom where she knew he would borrow her shower gel and towel, because he had so far refused point-blank to leave any of his possessions in her flat, any more than he had ever invited her to his own. When he stayed overnight he dressed himself stoically in the previous day's clothes and, she supposed, always drove home to change and shave before going in to work. It was a small way of signalling his determined lack of commitment and as such it infuriated her every time.

As he closed the bathroom door behind him she plumped with a smile for Scarlet Woman and slowly began to paint her nails. When she had finished, and the varnish had dried, she followed him into the bathroom and stood watching him as he turned slowly towards her under the stream of water, the dark hair of his body clinging seal-like to his skin, his blue eyes as inscrutable as ever but his naked body unable to conceal the effect she had on him.

'The door unlocked?' she said mockingly. 'You don't think I might turn out to be a female Norman Bates, then, inspector?'

'Women don't use knives,' he said complacently, reaching out for her with a dripping arm and unbuttoning her silky pyjama top which she let slip almost imperceptibly to the floor.

'Stereotypes, schmereotypes,' she said, pulling his glistening dark head towards hers with scarlet-tipped fingers and kissing him. 'I can't imagine where you get these old-fashioned ideas.'

She let her pyjama pants slide down to join the jacket on the floor as he pulled her into the shower beside him, realising that shower gel had advantages beyond the obvious.

'Is this what they teach you in those glossy women's magazines?' he asked, but she was much too preoccupied to reply.

6

'I don't care whose fault it was, I want her found.' Superintendent Jack Longley stood at Michael Thackeray's office doorway and made his displeasure felt in a voice which could be clearly heard throughout the CID offices and probably throughout the whole police station as well. Sergeant Kevin Mower, who had tactfully taken refuge in the murder incident room down the corridor, flinched and looked for sympathy into the cool blue eyes of DC Val Ridley. She was sitting pretending interest in her computer screen but listening just as hard as he was, but he found scant comfort there.

There were not many women in the station to whom Mower had not made at least mocking advances more than once during his time in Bradfield, but Val Ridley was one he had treated with great circumspection. She had never openly expressed dislike, but he was not encouraged by the chilly expression with which she assessed his trendily stylish clothes, his expensive haircut and his ready smile. He had asked her out once, been delayed by some demand of Thackeray's and found she had left the restaurant before he got there. He had apologised, almost grovelled he thought at the time, but since then she had made it pretty clear she was not impressed by much he either said or did.

'To let her go with a backpack was pretty bloody stupid,' she said now, addressing her flickering screen rather than Mower directly.

'You'd think John Franks would have more sense after the bother the other night,' Mower said.

'He was lucky to get away with that too,' Ridley said, a note of bitterness in her voice. 'I'd have thought Laura Ackroyd would have made a point of pinning the bastard to the floor when she had the chance.'

Mower caught the fury in Val Ridley's reflection and forbore to comment on that episode. It was obvious that nothing he could say would soothe her sense of grievance, based, he suspected, on the energetic part John Franks played in the macho games of the uniformed lads downstairs where she had served her apprenticeship as a WPC. Having worked her way into CID through a combination of persistence and intelligence, Val still had a chip on her shoulder in spite of the best efforts of Michael Thackeray and Kevin Mower to convince her that they did not regard a woman on their team as a liability.

Mower wondered wryly who else DC Ridley would like to see pinned painfully down. He rather suspected he might be included in her fury, although he was not sure why, beyond the fact that he was undeniably male and therefore, he suspected, in her eyes as culpable as any other of his sex.

Along the corridor, Longley had slammed the door of Thackeray's office shut and cut off from the avid audience outside the recriminations which continued unabated within. Thackeray contained his own anger behind a pale and tense countenance. He knew better than to answer Longley in kind. He had barely been able to believe the news that Jane Watson had packed a bag and left Roz Jenkins' house early that morning, under the nose of an inattentive PC Franks, telling no one where or why she was going or whether she intended to return. He had learned during the short time he had worked for Superintendent Longley that when his volcanic temper erupted it was best to let his anger take its course and save rational debate until later.

'I've told them to call Franks back in,' Longley said, taking Mower's seat, breathing heavily. His colour had risen and there were beads of sweat on the broad brow and the balding dome above. 'The beggar went straight off duty. I'll have his bloody guts for garters,' he said, coherence gradually returning. 'I've told Les Dobson what I think about sloppy uniformed constables. I don't want him in plain clothes again, any road, after the last little lot. Is that understood?'

'He's the last man I want in plain clothes,' Thackeray said reasonably, recalling Laura's hurt fury after her encounter with Franks.

'He must have been asleep on the bloody job. There's no other explanation,' Longley said.

'And no excuse,' Thackeray said flatly.

Longley was subsiding visibly and his colour returning to normal.

'Could this lass have done it, d'you reckon?' he asked. 'Opportunity? Motive? Capacity?'

Thackeray shrugged. 'She certainly had the opportunity. She seems to think she was in the house alone with Louise for some of the evening, at least, though she says she didn't see her or speak to her at all. She took a bath. Perhaps she was washing off the blood. As for the rest, I don't know. There's no motive that we're aware of. They were just friends, house-mates, not even very close if Jane is to be believed. And it seems an unlikely crime for her to commit. Atherton is talking about a frenzied attack on a naked woman, six blows with a knife we haven't even found yet, two of which could have killed her outright. Jane Watson is a little skinny girl, anorexic almost. She hardly looks strong enough to strike a child let alone a well-built girl like Louise. She's small, slight, nervous – '

'And she's done a runner,' Longley broke in, exasperated. 'If not because she killed her, then why?'

'I had the feeling she was very frightened by what had happened,' Thackeray said. 'But frightened rather than guilty.'

'So she knows summat she doesn't want to tell us, maybe?'

'Maybe,' Thackeray agreed. 'I'll talk to Roz Jenkins again. She might have some idea where she'd be likely to go.'

'Put out a call for her. I want her found sharpish,' Longley said. 'And search the place again. Anorexic or not, if she's got a carving knife hidden under her mattress, Amos Atherton'll have to revise his ideas, won't he? Never forget that the most likely murderer's always the closest to home, lad. Never forget that.'

Thackeray stood, his face rigid, as the superintendent swept out, slamming the door behind him. Behind his frozen expression he fought down the nausea which Longley's – he hoped innocent

58

– remark had triggered. For no more than a second he could see vividly a body slumped, unconscious and noisily snoring on an unmade bed, and another, tiny, pink and peaceful lying in bath water that was still warm and alive with bubbles which sparkled around the wide blue eyes of the child who would never see again.

He had wanted to kill his half-naked and oblivious wife then, had picked up a pillow to finish what she had herself begun, and then baulked, blinded by tears. He had run from the house howling like an animal with rage and guilt and grief until he bumped into some kindly stranger who calmed him down long enough to make sense of what had happened and called in Thackeray's own colleagues who did little to disguise their conviction that while Aileen Thackeray might have killed her child, her husband was equally, if not more, to blame.

That morning, when he had arrived at his own bleak modern flat early after leaving Laura Ackroyd protesting sleepily at his departure, he had pulled a suitcase from under his bed where it had been stowed for several months. Every couple of weeks, usually when he had come home from Laura's feeling as close to content as he thought he ever could, he pulled the case out and methodically began to pack.

That morning he had reached his usual high water mark of shirts and socks and pants, before hesitating, as he aways did, and going to work leaving the rest of his gear unpacked. He knew now that when he got home, the suitcase would be angrily emptied and stowed away for another month or so before he felt able to contemplate again the move which Laura was demanding with increasing urgency. He could not, he thought, impose on her the black moods and the nightmares which Longley had just thrust so brutally into the broad light of day.

Roz Jenkins let Mower and Thackeray into her house with a cursory nod. Her face looked puffy, there were dark circles under her eyes and her hair stood up in unkempt spikes, giving her a slightly startled air. She waved the two men from the narrow hallway into her sitting-room with a vague gesture, and as they crossed the threshold into the dim light of a room with the curtains still drawn Mower sniffed sharply and looked round for

59

the source of the herby smell which hung heavily on the stuffy air.

Roz turned on a lamp on a low table and slumped dejectedly on to one of the sofas. Beside the lamp a small brass dish containing a little oil smoked steadily and filled the room with fumes. Mower smiled grimly at Roz, quite sure that the heady oil was a disguise for a scent he – and, he suspected, she – was much more familiar with. But apart from her slightly glazed look his sharp eyes could find no more evidence for his suspicions.

Apparently oblivious to all this, Thackeray had settled himself comfortably in a chair facing Roz.

'Have you had any more thoughts about any male visitors Louise may have had?' Thackeray began.

Roz shrugged slightly. 'Not a boyfriend, but the vicar came round once or twice with hymn music.'

'The vicar? Miles Bateman?'

'That's right.' The broad face was impassive.

'You didn't think to mention his visits last time we spoke?' Thackeray said sharply.

'I'm sorry. You were asking about boyfriends. I'm sure he wasn't that. He just slipped my mind.'

Mower glanced sharply at Thackeray, wondering what else might have slipped Roz's mind, but the chief inspector turned the questioning in another direction.

'We were disturbed to hear that Jane Watson had left,' he said. 'I shall need to ask her some more questions. Have you any idea where she's gone?'

Roe shook her head emphatically and then grimaced, as though the movement had proved painful.

'I've no idea,' she said. The light was still poor but Thackeray suspected that there were tears in her eyes.

'That's a pity,' he said. 'You must understand that if someone as close as she was to a murder victim disappears, apparently voluntarily – and she was seen by someone with a ruck-sack waiting for a bus on Aysgarth Lane – then there is one very unpleasant interpretation that can be put on that.'

Roz shuddered this time and there was no doubt about the incipient tears now.

'That's crazy,' she said. 'Jane couldn't kill anyone, or any-thing, for that matter. She sits in front of the television weeping about veal calves and deer hunting and the loss of the rain forest.'

There was the unmistakable contempt in Roz's voice of the strong for the weak.

'She had hysterics a couple of weeks ago when we found a mouse in the kitchen and Louise and I wanted to kill it. She goes through a moral crisis if we swat a fly.'

'So who did kill the mouse?' Sergeant Mower asked unexpec-tedly from the other side of the room where he had taken a seat at the table with his notebook. He evidently made her start and she flashed him a look of undisguised dislike.

'Louise chased it out into the back garden,' she said. 'Louise wasn't squeamish at all. She could have been a nurse or a doctor or something like that . . .'

'Are you squeamish, Miss Jenkins?' Thackeray asked quietly.

Roz shrugged slightly helplessly. 'Not particularly,' she said. 'Not like Jane, anyway.'

'But you like looking after people, don't you? So people tell me. Did you look after Jane?' Thackeray asked.

Roz lay back against the cushions for a moment and closed her eyes, her lashes glistening wetly.

'She certainly needed it,' she said very quietly at length, with a sigh. 'So yes, I suppose I did look after her, in a way.'

'So tell me about her,' Thackeray said. 'I'm very puzzled about Jane. You see, when I asked one of my officers this morning to check at the university to find out where her home is – in case that's where she'd gone – can you guess what he was told?'

The girl nodded very slowly.

'I can guess,' she said.

'The only address she gave was this one. Isn't that rather strange?'

'She didn't want anything to do with her family,' Roz said. 'She'd left home and didn't want to be traced.'

'Any particular reason?'

'Oh, yes,' Roz said wearily. 'The best possible reason. Her father had been screwing her since she was six. Or so she says. She's having therapy of some sort. She recovered this memory,

61

says she'd blotted it out entirely. Of course, her family's gone completely bananas, denying everything. There've been the most appalling rows, apparently . . .'

'She told you all this? Why?' Thackeray asked.

'People do tell me things. I suppose I'm a good listener,' Roz said.

'A shoulder to cry on?'

'I suppose.'

'You say she didn't want to be traced,' Mower broke in again, earning himself another scowl. 'Is Watson her real name?'

'I don't think so,' Roz said.

'But you wouldn't know what her real name is?' Mower persisted and could see that Thackeray was no more surprised than he was when Roz shook her head.

'You do know that there are penalties for withholding information in a serious criminal case?' Thackeray asked coldly.

'I can't tell you what I don't know,' Roz came back sharply. 'She only told me what she wanted to tell. Not everything, by any means. I don't know what her real name was or where she came from. She was quite determined no one was going to find that out.'

'So it's unlikely she would have gone home anyway?'

'Very unlikely,' Roz said. 'I should think that's the last place she'd want to go.'

'Any other suggestions?' Thackeray asked. He reached across to the bureau beside his chair and picked up a framed photograph of Jane. 'I'll need to borrow this,' he said. He studied the portrait for a moment. 'She's not the sort of girl who looks as if she could sleep rough for very long, is she? She must have had in mind somewhere to stay. Did she have money? Enough to go to a hotel, for instance?'

'She wasn't short of cash, as far as I was aware,' Roz admitted reluctantly, looking about her like a smoker seeking a cigarette but apparently finding nothing to satisfy whatever urgent craving had seized her. She shuffled uneasily deeper into her seat.

'She never moaned about money like most people do, most students anyway,' she went on at length. 'I think she had some sort of income of her own, though I don't know where from. Certainly not from her father, that's for sure.'

'I shall want to search her room again,' Thackeray said, and as

Roz made to protest he raised a hand. 'And the rest of the house. I can get a warrant or we can do it more quickly with your agreement. Either way it has to be done.'

Roz shrugged dispiritedly and large tears began to roll unchecked down her cheeks as she slumped further into the enveloping cushions.

'You'd better get on with it then,' she said.

Laura Ackroyd pulled her coat collar up tightly against the sharp north-westerly wind which was cutting down the valley from the high Pennine hills. She followed her two companions along Canal Street, a dark, narrow cutting through the old industrial heart of Bradfield, where a few of the nineteenth-century mills and warehouses upon which its prosperity had been built still stood derelict waiting for the developers to transform them into studio apartments or town houses overlooking the oily black waters of the canal.

The couple she was following, a young man and woman in jeans and short jackets, slowed to let her catch them up.

'Come on,' the woman said. 'We've earned a cup of coffee.' She led the way to a scuffed wooden door which she opened with a key. Beyond lay a small shabby room furnished with elderly armchairs and low tables piled with tatty magazines, rather like a run-down doctor's waiting-room. The health posters on the walls, dealing with contraception, sexually transmitted diseases and Aids, reinforced the impression that this was some neglected outpost of the National Health that the marketing people had not yet got their hands on.

'Not so many customers as usual tonight,' the young woman said as she took off her jacket and switched on a tiny fan heater which whined noisily as it struggled to warm the draughty space.

'It seemed like a lot to me,' Laura said, shivering slightly and deciding to keep her coat on. 'How many do you usually see? How many prostitutes are there in a town this size, for goodness' sake?'

'Too many,' the young woman said shortly while her companion opened the bulky shoulder-bag that he had been carrying and checked the contents.

'We generally take out a couple of dozen hypodermics and five dozen packs of condoms and hand out most of them,' he said. 'We've only got rid of half that number tonight. How many would you say, Lyn?'

'A couple of dozen packs at most. I guess the police activity around Whitley Street has kept a lot of the women off the street tonight,' the young woman said, filling a kettle at the sink and plugging it in. She was fair and pink-cheeked, with an earnest, determined face and clear, untroubled blue eyes. She smiled at Laura.

'But after we've done our round we usually get a few people coming in here. There's a doctor on duty for an hour or so later on. And then a couple of the blokes do another round at half eleven. Trade perks up after the pubs close.'

She nodded at an open door beyond which lay another darkened room where Laura could make out a desk and a couple of chairs and an examination couch.

'Also volunteers, the doctors?' she asked.

'Oh, yes,' Lyn said. 'We can't pay anyone. All the money we raise goes on supplies.'

'Some of those girls should still be at school,' Laura said angrily.

'Some of them are still at school,' Lyn said, her tone matter-of-fact. 'Some of them are twelve or thirteen when they start.'

In ten years' reporting Laura thought she had seen the worst the town could throw up, but the women and girls who had slipped out of the shadows that evening to take their supplies had filled her with anger and despair.

'Jesus Christ,' she said.

'He'd have been as angry as you are,' Lyn said without any embarrassment, as if she were speaking of a friend. 'Love the sinner, hate the sin, you know?'

'So where does the money come from?' Laura asked.

Lyn glanced at her companion who was spooning instant coffee into three none too clean mugs.

'John knows more about the funding than I do,' she said.

'It comes mainly from local churches. And the Christian Union at the university is very supportive. But really Miles Bateman from St Jude's is the driving force.'

Laura looked puzzled.

'I thought he was involved in the campaign to get the prostitutes off the streets,' she said. 'I came across him the other night in Whitley Street making common cause with the Muslims. I wouldn't have thought handing out free condoms was quite his scene.'

'Well, it just shows how little you understand,' John came back sharply. 'Jesus is looking to save sinners. "Joy shall be in heaven over one sinner that repenteth."'

'Right,' Laura said, shaken.

'First you have to make contact,' Lyn said earnestly, handing Laura a mug of dark brown liquid. 'Looking after the girls' physical health leads quite naturally to concern for their spiritual health, you see. It provides the opportunity we need, right?'

'To save their souls?' Laura asked with more overt scepticism than she intended.

Lyn flushed slightly.

'If you like,' she said. With her grubby white T-shirt and ancient jeans, she made an unlikely Mother Teresa, Laura thought uncharitably, but she said no more. She knew her limitations with regard to matters of faith. She had learned her scepticism at her rationalist grandmother's knee and had found no reason to change her views even as she had grown up and away from Joyce Ackroyd's political certainties.

'If Mary Magdalene could be saved – ' John began, but what threatened to become an earnest if fruitless debate was interrupted by a clatter at the door. Sherry Maguire came in, hair in disarray in the wind which whipped through the small room like icy breath, closely followed by a slim girl, who looked half frozen in her skimpy mini-skirt and short black jacket, her face deathly pale where it was not marked by an angry bruise which ran from her temple to her cheek. Silent and shivering, she moved gratefully into the blast of warm air from the heater while Sherry nodded at the two charity workers and looked askance at Laura.

'You again?' she said, and there was no friendliness in the greeting. 'Didn't you get more than enough t' other night for your bloody paper?'

'I want to do another piece about the risk of Aids,' Laura said.

'Like laikin' in t' gutter, do you?' Sherry sneered.

'An article might help,' Laura said, although it took all her histrionic powers to put some conviction into her words.

'And give your readers a cheap thrill, an' all,' Sherry came back quickly. 'Any road, don't involve me again. I've had about as much as I can take of bloody reporters and bloody coppers for one week. Lyn, it were you I came to see,' she said, turning to the project organiser who was standing biting her lip, unsure whether or not to intervene. 'Cassy here needs somewhere to stay. She's moved out. Got thumped once too often didn't she.'

'What about the women's refuge?' Lyn said, glancing at Cassy's bruised face without much sympathy.

'They won't teck me there wi' me habit,' Cassy mumbled. 'I need a clean needle an' all.'

Lyn reached into the bag of supplies and handed the girl a couple of cellophane-wrapped syringes.

'Condoms?' she asked.

'Aye, I better 'ad. I'll not get a fix else.'

Laura watched in near despair as the girl stashed her supplies away in her shoulder-bag with a matter-of-fact acceptance of the necessities of her life. She could not, she thought, be more than sixteen years old, if that.

'Can't you give her a bed, Sherry?' John asked.

The older woman shook her head emphatically.

'No chance,' she said. 'I'd have the social round my neck if I let a junkie kip down wi' t' kids, wouldn't I? And her bloke'd soon work out where she were any road, and be round kicking t' door in. She'd not be safe wi' me.'

Laura drew a sharp breath and then hesitated, but not before Sherry had read what had briefly crossed her mind.

'Don't be daft,' she said contemptuously. 'An interview in t' *Gazette* is the last bloody thing she needs. She's not that desperate for a bed.'

'That wasn't what I was going to suggest,' Laura began, but she did not complete the sentence. There was no way they were going to believe that her offer of a bed for the night would come without strings.

'Miles will know somewhere,' John said decisively. 'He'll give her a bed at the vicarage if necessary.'

Cassy looked less than enthusiastic about that but Sherry seemed appeased.

'I'll take her over there, then, shall I?'

John glanced at a handwritten list pinned to the notice-board.

'I'll give him a bell and tell him you're coming. He's not due in here tonight.'

He ushered the two women out and shut the door again against the howling of the gale.

'How old is she?' Laura asked helplessly.

John shrugged. 'Cassy Davis? About fifteen, I should think. It's difficult to tell sometimes. If they're on heroin they look older than they really are. She's been around as long as I've been working here, which is a couple of years now.'

He picked up the phone to make his call and Laura glanced idly at the list on the board.

'We don't work every night, of course,' Lyn said by way of explanation. 'We've got a rota.' Laura looked more closely and took in the pairs of names, each one for a matching pair of male and female volunteers. One name seized her attention.

'Roz Jenkins?' she said. 'From Whitley Street.'

Lyn looked tense and nodded.

'Lord, we should have changed the list,' she whispered. 'I hope she can keep coming . . .'

'How did she get involved?' Laura asked.

'Oh, through the university,' John said, putting an arm round Lyn's shoulder. 'She's in the women's group. I'm a student too. A lot of us go to St Jude's, and that's how Lyn and I got involved. We don't exactly see eye to eye with Roz and her lot about prostitution, but she's willing to slog the streets with us so we bury our differences.'

'Louise Brownlow was a member of St Jude's, wasn't she?' Laura asked. These were evidently the murdered girl's happy clappy friends about whom Roz had been so contemptuous.

'Oh, yes, she played the guitar quite often at morning service. I think Miles recruited her and Roz on one of his missionary calls round the neighbourhood. We don't usually bother with Whitley Street because most of the residents are of a different persuasion, but we did have one go last term sometime. Louise started coming to services quite often after that. Roz was not a regular, but she came once or twice.'

'But it was Roz, not Louise, who worked here on your rota?'

'It's not surprising, is it?' John said. 'They lived surrounded by these women. It must have seemed an obvious thing to do in the circumstances.'

Laura finished her coffee, thanked John and Lyn and left the centre filled with a deep and impotent anger. Even if Cassy had agreed to be interviewed, she was not sure that the girl's seemingly desperate situation would interest Ted Grant whose resolutely tabloid evening paper became a 'family newspaper' whenever the mood took him, generally when an issue was raised he wanted no truck with.

She walked back to her car and as she put the key into the lock she froze: someone was coming quietly up behind her from the gloom of the looming derelict warehouses.

'I can't find the bleeding vicar. Did you mean it about that bed?' Cassy asked.

7

'We're going to have to go public on her unusual tastes,' Michael Thackeray said bleakly to sergeant Kevin Mower as they watched the last man on their list of half a dozen suspects walk down the corridor from the interview room. Some had gone jauntily, some dejectedly, but all, so far, unscathed by their determined questioning.

'You'll have the tabloids up the motorway foaming at the mouth, guv,' Mower said. 'They're already sniffing about wondering why we haven't arrested a boyfriend. Or at least named one. And the Asians all have solid alibis. After the arrests they went back to the Muslim centre, Ahmed and ten younger men. No knives – or none they're owning up to.'

'The press are going to get even more excited when they realise we've mislaid a girlfriend,' Thackeray said. 'No doubt they'll compute two and two into sixty-nine when I give Jane Watson's details to the *Gazette* later.'

Mower raised an eyebrow at that but he found Thackeray as inscrutable as ever. That his boss had an active love life he had no doubt; that it did anything much to light up his life he could see no firm evidence. And having been smitten himself by Laura Ackroyd's fiery charms when they first met he occasionally permitted himself a moment's carefully concealed resentment of Thackeray's apparently unappreciated good fortune.

The chief inspector was scowling out of the office window.

'I can't run a case to protect people from the attentions of the press pack,' he said eventually. 'So far my main concern has been for Louise's family, but I hear from the Foreign Office that they've found her father and he's on his way home. I'll have to tell him the truth and after that we can go public with a clear conscience.'

'You don't think there could have been a lesbian relationship with Jane?' Mower asked cautiously. 'Though that's not what got her pregnant, is it?' he added quickly, almost immediately discounting the thought.

He was aware of Thackeray's distaste for the line the inquiry was taking and he did not want to be accused of indulging his own fantasies.

'How do I know?' Thackeray said shortly. 'If you thought she was gay you should have asked Roz Jenkins when we saw her. Presumably she would have known. Do lesbians enjoy handcuffing and spanking each other?'

Mower was not sure whether the question was seriously meant or not. With Thackeray, he thought, you could never tell.

'Some do, some don't, I expect, guv,' he said. 'But we haven't got far with the blokes, have we? It doesn't look as if any of the ones we've interviewed put her in the family way.'

'Yes, well, we'll keep that under wraps a little while longer. The man who knows she was pregnant, if we find him, will almost certainly be the father of the child – and quite likely her killer, too.'

'With or without the handcuffs,' Mower muttered to himself, frustrated by the slow progress the inquiry was making. They had spent the morning interviewing six men who had previously come to police attention for their unusual sexual tastes, but without evidently moving the case one inch further forward. One of the men invited to the police station had stated flatly that he was not interested in women, however willing they were to truss him up like the turkey Mower could not help thinking he resembled. Three had produced alibis which, if confirmed, would put them many miles from Whitley Street at the time of the murder, while the other two had claimed vehemently never to have come across Louise Brownlow in their continuing quest for the satisfaction of needs which they claimed their wives would not meet.

'We'll tackle it from the other end,' Thackeray said. 'Go back to her friends and acquaintances. Above all, find Jane Watson. In the meantime we'll have a chat to the Reverend Miles Bateman and see just what Louise got up to at St Jude's. In view of her other spare-time activities, it seems a very strange way for her to have been spending her Sundays.'

'Perhaps she was looking for absolution, guv,' Mower said incautiously.

'Don't talk about what you don't understand, Kevin,' Thackeray snapped. 'Anyone who tells you forgiveness is that easy to come by is a fool.'

Laura Ackroyd tapped the word 'ends' on to the final paragraph of her feature on the students' Aids patrol and leaned back in her office chair with a sigh of satisfaction. When she was genuinely moved by a subject the words would flow with a sort of magic which no writer she knew could fully explain. Today had been one of those days and she knew without needing to be told that even Ted, whose contempt for women was only matched by his contempt for graduates, would be satisfied.

She got up from her desk stiffly and stretched, the tension draining out of her as her concentration on the task in hand relaxed. She had pinned her usually rampant copper hair up that morning with an austerity which matched her mood and, in a severe black suit and almost no make-up, she looked pale and slightly strained. She had tossed about in bed the previous night, alone and distressed more than she would admit to herself by the young girl, Cassy, whom she had put to bed in her spare room.

Her instinct to offer the battered girl a place for the night had been uncomplicated and sincere enough, and she had been shocked by the suspicion with which it had been greeted. There were times when she despised herself for apologising for belonging to what should have been an honourable trade and despised

70

even more virulently those who made the apology necessary. She should learn to live with it, or get out, she told herself. On a day like today, when she felt she had done an honest job of reporting on the depths where Cassy lived and would probably die, she knew she could not give up now.

But she had not told Cassy's story. The girl had sat shivering uncontrollably on her sofa when they reached the flat the previous evening, her teeth chattering against the rim of the mug of coffee which Laura had made for her. She was tired, she claimed, but Laura did not believe that was the whole reason for her evidently fragile state. Somehow her search for a bed at the vicarage and, undoubtedly, for a fix had proved unsuccessful and Laura had no doubt that the girl's decision to come back to her was one made in a desperation she could only guess at.

'You won't write nothing, will you?' the girl had said over and over again as imperceptibly her shivering eased and she lay back against the cushions, clutching her mug like a life-line. Her face had taken on a translucent paleness against which her bruises stood out like bloody gashes, and her eyes had receded into dark pools of misery.

'We saw Jase out there,' she confided at last in a near whisper. 'He were coming up t' street towards us. I dodged into one o' t' wrecked buildings where I sometimes do a trick and let Sherry lead 'im off. Then I saw you getting into your car and thought that were a good way out.'

'It's all right,' Laura said. 'You're very welcome to stay. And I'll write nothing you don't want me to write. I promise.'

'Aye, well, after I'm dead you can say what you like,' the girl said matter-of-factly. And before she shut her eyes in complete weariness and let Laura help her to bed she told her how her father had first raped her when she was eight years old.

Laura had watched her for a time as she slept, a ravaged arm, the veins purple and infected, flung across her face as; if to ward off whatever life had to hurl at her next. Treatment, Laura had suggested gently, only to be rebuffed fiercely. Methadone, which the doctors favoured, Cassy had said, was no treatment at all. She would rather take her chances on the street. Thankful that Thackeray had not turned up to witness an act of charity of which she knew he would not approve, Laura had turned out the light and gone to bed herself. When she got up next morning, Cassy had gone, leaving her to check guiltily that nothing had been stolen. As far as she could see, nothing had.

Laura wandered across the office to get a cup of coffee from the machine and on her way back to her desk looked idly over the picture editor's shoulder at the prints he was selecting for the day's front page. Amongst the jumble of images, two faces stood out, two young women standing on the doorstep of a Victorian terraced house, both frowning at the camera as if at some unwelcome intruder into their lives.

'Who's that?' she asked, flicking through a number of photographs of the same pair and indicating the slimmer girl, dwarfed by the bulk of Roz Jenkins.

The picture editor glanced idly at the prints.

'They're the flat-mates of the student who got knifed. Roz and Jane ... I can't remember their other names. You'll have to ask Fred. He's supposed to be doing me a caption. The skinny one is the one who's disappeared.'

'Disappeared?' Louise said. This was a new development she had not caught up with. The 'skinny one', the one she did not recognise, was the one who had caught her attention and she studied the image more carefully, even more certain now that, although she did not know the girl, she reminded her strongly of someone she did know.

'Can I keep this?' she asked, picking up a version of the picture which she knew was not usable, and the picture editor nodded, unconcerned. The crime reporter, though, who identified Roz's companion as a Jane Watson, did nothing to answer the question which was nagging Laura now like an aching tooth. She knew she had never met either of the murdered girl's house-mates until her unexpected interview with Roz. And yet somehow she recognised Jane's pale features, long blonde hair and anxious expression.

By lunchtime, at the end of a busy morning, the half-recollection which had been tormenting her had swum into focus. She picked up her battered old VW Beetle from the *Gazette*'s car park and drove quickly through the lunch-hour traffic up the hill to the Heights, inevitably known locally as Wuthering, a sixties development of gaunt flats which had quickly rotted in the wind and driving rain and was now more than half demolished.

In a tiny bungalow in the shadow of the flats lived Laura's grandmother, Joyce Ackroyd, retired, arthritic, frustrated and as fiery in her determination to build a new Jerusalem in Bradfield as she had ever been.

Laura always approached her grandmother's house with some trepidation. As she sat for some moments now in the car, gazing at the scene of desolation which had been Brontë House before the cranes and swinging demolition balls had reduced it to rubble, her mind flew to the dazzling blue and white of her father's Portuguese villa and the stony response he had given her last time she broached the subject of his mother's increasing frailty.

'She believes in t' bloody welfare state,' he had said. 'If it can't provide, then it's her own bloody fault. She'd not cope with this climate, anyway. And your mother wouldn't want her here. She couldn't cope either. You'll just have to see what can be done at home. If it's a question of money let me know.'

It had been a sterile discussion anyway, she thought bitterly, remembering how she had bitten back, with unaccustomed discretion, the angry retort which had sprung to her lips. It would not be the climate or her daughter-in-law which would defeat Joyce if she moved to live with her only son. It would be Jack Ackroyd himself, self-made, self-opinionated and self-satisfied and, which Joyce found even harder to tolerate, a millionaire who believed sincerely that money could buy any-thing, including peace of mind.

Laura got out of the car with a sigh and locked the doors carefully. It was quite possible to leave a car on this estate and find it stripped to its chassis within minutes. Joyce must have seen her pull up in the Beetle because she welcomed her granddaughter on her doorstep with open arms and a tremulous smile.

'What's wrong?' Laura asked anxiously.

'Just a bit of pain today, love. It's the damp weather. Not to worry. There's nowt to be done about it now.' Joyce's arthritis had taken her out of her beloved town council years before she had wanted to retire. Her remaining pleasures in life were the granddaughter who had inherited her looks and her temperament and her own uncanny capacity to keep in touch with every twist and turn of the political life at the town hall which she had so reluctantly let go. She let Laura help her into her favourite armchair.

'Can't the doctor give you more effective pain-killers?' Laura asked angrily.

'Trouble is they tend to addle your brain and I can't be doing with that,' Joyce said sharply, and Laura guessed that she probably did not take the ones she had been prescribed.

'Lunch?' she said. 'I brought some Marks and Sparks sarnies.'

'You shouldn't waste your money like that,' Joyce said but the complaint was no more than a token. When Laura had arrayed her spoils on plates her grandmother tucked in happily enough.

'Then you can do me a favour,' Joyce said through a mouthful of BLT.

'Of course,' Laura said.

'Take a duster round this room,' Joyce said. 'I'm getting so clumsy I'm frightened of smashing things these days.'

Laura glanced around and saw that the knick-knacks and photographs which covered every flat surface did not gleam in the way that they used to, and the pot plants on the window sill looked dry and faded.

'You need some help in the house,' she said.

'I can manage,' Joyce said. 'There's a lot worse off.'

Laura did not argue. She knew that if there was one thing more unproductive than arguing with her father it was taking on his mother. He had gone down a different path, but the Ackroyd determination had taken him there.

'So what's brought you up, any road?' Joyce asked shrewdly as they ate.

Laura smiled shamefacedly. 'Can't I just drop in for lunch without an ulterior motive?' she asked.

'Aye, but not today by the look of you.'

Laura shrugged and took the photograph she had brought from the office out of her shoulder-bag.

'D'you remember a girl I went to school with called Caroline Boulter? Lady Caroline we called her, because her father was a lord of some sort. I seem to recall you knew the family.'

Laura had been packed off to boarding school in the south of England by her father, very much against her will, so as to lose her Yorkshire accent and acquire, as he put it, some airs and graces. The first objective had been achieved in spite of herself though she very much doubted if he ever thought he had got value for money on the latter count. Laura had remained obstinately wedded to her native city, to its blunt forthrightness and her grandmother's convictions, which her businessman father had despised.

'Ernie Boulter,' Joyce said with a mischievous grin, her discomfort instantly forgotten. 'MP for one o' t' mining constituencies in South Yorkshire. I'm not sure I recall which one. Aye, I remember him, though. Came up here a few times when he was in Attlee's government to read us the riot act because we didn't like some o' t' things they were getting up to down there. Miners' MPs were on the right of the party then.'

Laura raised a quizzical eyebrow at that, but her grandmother was not to be interruped in full flow.

'He behaved like Lord Muck even then,' she said dismissively. 'Then later on they gave him a peerage and he set himself up in the Home Counties somewhere, took the Conservative whip in the Lords, became quite the country gentleman, I believe. Broke his neck riding to hounds in the end, if I remember rightly, which was no more'n he deserved by all accounts.'

Laura had absolutely no doubt that Joyce could remember absolutely rightly. Even when she was a child and the great days of the post-war Labour government were fading into history, her grandmother was living and breathing the mythology of triumphs and betrayals which she had experienced as a girl and a young woman.

'So Caroline was what? His granddaughter? She was in my class but I've lost touch now. I expect she's married with 2.2 children.'

Joyce looked at her sharply at that, seeking to confirm the note of regret she only half caught, but Laura busied herself with her sandwich and gave nothing away.

'Aye, that'd be right. The son inherited the title, I think, but I don't think he's ever been much of a politician. No doubt he turns out to vote when the Tory government calls, like the rest of the backwoods beggars, but I've never heard of him doing anything constructive about owt. Caroline must be his daughter if her father's Lord Boulter.'

'What was a Labour government doing creating hereditary peers?' Laura asked, genuinely puzzled.

'Selling their supporters down the river as usual,' Joyce snapped. 'There were no life peerages then. But they could have abolished the House of Lords in '45 if they'd put their minds to it. And the public schools and the rest of the paraphernalia of the class system. That was the golden opportunity and they let it slip through their fingers. What is it you youngsters say? Chickened out? That's exactly what they did. Chickened out!' Her regret for the revolution which never quite happened, and her contempt for those who had failed to seize the moment when a war-weary country was desperate for change, was undimmed by the passing of fifty years.

'Aye well, happen they'll abolish themselves in the end,' she said. 'If the monarchy goes, the rest'll tumble, I dare say. I just hope I'm still here to see it.'

'Come on, you're going to be here a long time yet,' Laura said, with a cheerfulness only partly feigned. There were times, though, when her grandmother had a fragility which frightened her in spite of the combative gleam in her eyes. They had always been comrades, since the days when she had trailed after Joyce sticking leaflets through letter boxes at election time, and their closeness had survived even her defection from the ranks of the committed to the battalions of the sceptical. She could not imagine the life without Joyce which was inexorably approaching.

'So how did Caroline Boulter crop up again, any road?' Joyce asked, her curiosity aroused.

Laura showed her the photograph and explained Jane Watson's closeness to the murder victim in Whitley Street and her subsequent disappearance.

'A sister, perhaps,' she hazarded.

'It'll tell you in *Who's Who* how many children he's got,' Joyce said, contemptuously. 'Or t' other one – *Debrett's Peerage*. We used to reckon we'd use that, come the revolution. They're all in there.'

Laura caught the gleam of mischief in Joyce's eyes and grinned.

'There's a very strong resemblance to Caro,' she said. 'The more I look the more I can see it.'

'You'd better find out if she's got a little sister hidden away somewhere, then, hadn't you?' Joyce said. 'Your policeman'll thank you, I dare say.'

Laura gave her grandmother an old-fashioned look. Joyce seldom pried into her private life but Laura knew that she did not wholly approve of a liaison which seemed to have progressed little over more months than she cared to count.

'Maybe,' she said non-committally, ignoring Joyce's sigh. If the old woman fancied becoming a great-grandmother, Laura would give her no encouragement, she thought. Her own feelings on that subject were too sensitive for her to explore alone in the dead of night, never mind in company in the full light of day.

Almost abstractedly she tidied up the kitchen and living-room of the tiny bungalow, dusting far more meticulously than she would ever have done in her own flat. She kissed her grandmother's parchment cheek perfunctorily and took her leave, unsure whether she was annoyed with herself or with Joyce, or perhaps with herself for being annoyed with Joyce. There were times, she thought, as she slammed her car into gear and drew away from the kerb with an angry squeal of tyres, when determined self-sufficiency hurt.

The parish church of St Jude's loomed, dark and gargantuan, over the huddled terraces of Victorian Bradfield. Its tall Gothic windows were dimmed by the grime of generations and by heavy, protective wire grilles. The once golden sandstone walls, the tracery and the buttresses were blackened by more than a century of smoke from tall mill chimneys which smoked no more. Only the faintest glimmer of refracted light gave any indication that on a wet spring evening the church was occupied.

Chief Inspector Thackeray and Sergeant Mower stood in the porch, which was lit by a single unshaded electric bulb, and listened to the rhythmic sounds of music from within.

'We can't interrupt a service, can we, guv?' Mower asked

hesitantly, deferring to his boss's superior knowledge of all things ecclesiastical. Apart from an occasional wedding and funeral, Mower did not believe that he had ever attended any form of worship in church, chapel or mosque.

Thackeray eased open the heavy oak door far enough and gently enough, he hoped, for them both to enter the church unnoticed. They were at the west end of the nave; facing them, the high altar, behind an intricately carved wooden screen, lay in almost total darkness. There were no pews and the blue plastic stacking chairs which had evidently replaced them faced south in a large semicircle at the apex of which was a simple table covered with a white cloth and adorned with a plain wooden cross.

At a lectern slightly to one side stood a man in early middle age, chubby-faced and bright-eyed, in a purple polo shirt and black jeans. He was leading the singing with arms which waved jerkily and not completely in time with his ragged choir. The congregation of mainly young people sang and swayed and waved their hands in the air, palms outstretched, to a slightly halting guitar accompaniment provided by another younger man who had perched himself on the table which Thackeray assumed served as an altar. The Reverend Miles Bateman at the lectern registered the approach of the two policemen with no more than a flicker of an eye, and continued to conduct his wraggle taggle singers to the end of a repetitive, and to Mower's ear tuneless, hymn which they evidently enjoyed hugely.

'Praise the Lord,' he said as they intoned a solemn Amen. He glanced at the intruders again. 'Perhaps, brothers and sisters, we can thank Jesus tonight that two of our shepherds have come forward to be saved.' A number of the young people turned to look in their direction and both men were struck by the dazzling smiles and bright eyes of the Reverend Bateman's flock. One young woman bustled from her chair and came towards them with arms outstretched.

'You are very, very welcome,' she said, beaming and taking Thackeray's right hand and Mower's left in hers and attempting to draw them into the semicircle of seats. Thackeray took his hand back abruptly.

'We'll wait over here for Mr Bateman to finish, thanks,' he said, turning on his heel and making for a bank of chairs tucked away in the dimly lit side aisle furthest away from the focus of the vicar's activities. Mower could feel a tension in his companion which seemed out of all proportion to the girl's innocent if misplaced enthusiasm for their immediate conversion. The two men watched as Bateman concluded his service, Mower surprised at the youth of the assembly and the intensity of their commitment to the slightly banal hymns they were singing, Thackeray disturbed by the total command the vicar evidently had over his flock.

He sat now, listening to what for him was a service of an informality bordering on the irreverent. To him the music was indistinguishable from the pop which poured from a thousand teenage stereos and as lacking in reverence. He had been brought up as a boy with the full panoply of the Latin Mass and, although he had become more or less accustomed to the vernacular which replaced it, he had never heard anything like the prayers which these young people addressed to a Jesus they seemed to regard as a personal friend and companion who was as likely to be sitting beside them on a blue plastic chair in jeans and T-shirt as watching over them from any more exalted plane.

The service had eventually drawn to a close, and after exchanging warm embraces with some of the young women who gathered around him after the blessing, Miles Bateman glanced in the direction of his reticent visitors and began to move towards them, one or two young women still hovering in his wake with puppy-like devotion.

'I was expecting you,' he said. 'But I think we'd be more private at the vicarage. Some of these folk will stay for a while to pray.' He nodded towards some of the congregation who had dragged their chairs into a circle and were sitting holding hands, eyes closed, with a look of something approaching exaltation on their faces.

Bateman led them out of the church but not to the sort of Victorian vicarage which the policemen half expected. He turned instead into the gateway of an end-of-terrace house, the same as a hundred others within a stone's throw in Whitley Street and other roads nearby. Catching their surprise perhaps, the vicar shrugged.

'The old vicarage came down years ago,' he said. 'One of those white elephants the church used to support until they worked out what they were costing them to light and heat. When the roof began to fall in they called it a day. Built a block of flats on the site. The rents probably pay my salary.'

He unlocked the door of his house and nodded them into the usual narrow hallway and then into the bay-windowed front room which obviously served as study as well as living-room. A computer stood on the desk, the walls were lined with books and tapes and videos, and most of the chairs were littered with files of documents. A plate of half-eaten sandwiches and a glass of milk stood beside an open Bible on the coffee table in front of the high wooden fireplace, and two tabby cats, startled by the visitors' approach, rubbed themselves up against Bateman's legs, miaowing in some alarm.

'Just let me put the boys out,' Bateman said, scooping up an animal in each hand and disappearing with them towards the back of the house.

'Why do these kids fall for all that stuff?' Mower asked softly as they waited for him to come back.

'Someone who's always there, forgives all your sins and tells you that whatever horrors assail you in this life it'll all be better next time? It's a seductive message,' Thackeray said. 'Particularly if you're lonely and vulnerable.'

'I'd have a cat-flap, but round here all sorts of unwanted objects tend to arrive that way if you do,' Bateman said as he came back, giving Thackeray a sidelong look, as if he had overheard some of what he had said. 'Would you like a drink?' he asked, opening a cupboard and revealing an array of bottles and glasses. 'Or is it true what they say about policemen never drinking on duty?'

Thackeray shook his head, perhaps too emphatically, and was rewarded with a look which, he was annoyed with himself for feeling, bore an ounce too much sympathy. Mower too declined. Bateman poured himself a generous measure of single malt and waved his visitors into the chairs he had hastily cleared of junk.

'There's no Mrs Bateman?' Mower asked conversationally and the clergyman shook his head.

'Never got around to it, I'm afraid,' he said. 'Jesus has kept me pretty busy.'

Thackeray winced slightly and looked away. He could not

accustom himself to the matey appropriation of Christ as a bosom friend which the Evangelicals affected.

'You fill that old church, I hear,' Mower said, aware of his colleague's discomfort. 'A lot like that have been pulled down or turned into flats where I come from.'

'Jesus fills the church,' Bateman said with a self-satisfied smile. 'But yes, there's not much chance of St Jude's being pulled down yet awhile, I'm pleased to say.'

'In spite of this being a mainly Muslim area?' Thackeray asked.

'The congregation comes from all over Bradfield,' the vicar said. 'We get a lot of students from the university. Sixth-formers. But not just that age-group, though what I aim to do is make worship relevant to a generation which wasn't brought up with the old rituals and certainties. Chanting the psalms doesn't make much sense to kids brought up on Nintendo and MTV, does it? And I don't see why one shouldn't use the vernacular for God as well as Mammon, do you? But I wouldn't want you to think I was just attracting the impressionable young with guitars and tambourines and videos.'

'What happened to the church organ?' Thackeray asked.

'The organ needed forty thousand pounds spent on it to keep it going,' Bateman said sharply. 'There were mice in the pipes and woodworm attacking the keyboard when I arrived. There are better ways of spending the church's money.'

'And Louise Brownlow played the guitar for you?' Thackeray watched intently as Bateman digested this question, but no sign of worry or alarm disturbed his bland, surprisingly youthful face and his pale blue guileless eyes held Thackeray's own assessing gaze without flinching.

'I assumed it was Louise you had come to talk about,' he said. 'A terrible tragedy. We're all devastated.'

'Tell me how you met Louise, Mr Bateman,' Thackeray said.

Bateman took a careful sip of his whisky and settled himself back in his chair.

'She simply came to church one Sunday,' he said. 'She and her friend Roz. And of course we made them welcome, as we always do when strangers turn up. Roz didn't make a habit of it, but Lou came most weeks. I got to know her quite well because it turned out she played the guitar and she agreed to stand in for one of our regular musicians occasionally. I was teaching her some of the hymn tunes.'

'Jane Watson didn't come at all, did she?' Thackeray asked. 'The other girl at Number 17?'

Bateman looked vague. 'Not as far as I'm aware,' he said. 'We have a system for picking up newcomers, making them feel at home, encouraging them to come again. She could have slipped through the net but I'd be surprised.'

And annoyed if his efficient recruitment strategies had gone awry, Mower thought to himself.

'How long ago did Louise start attending church?' Thackeray asked.

Bateman frowned slightly. 'About five, perhaps six months ago. Sometime before Christmas, because she brought her guitar to a couple of our carol services. I remember that quite clearly.'

'And where did your guitar lessons take place? Here at the vicarage? In the church?' Thackeray asked, glancing at the vicar's guitar which leaned against a bookcase in the corner of the room.

'Sometimes at church, sometimes at her place,' Bateman said easily. 'It was very informal, just fifteen minutes sometimes after a service.'

'Did you go round to her house the night she was killed?'

'No, no, of course I didn't,' Bateman said, firmly. 'I was doing some hospital visits that evening, at the Infirmary. You can check up on that easily enough, chief inspector, if you need to.'

'Do you offer the sacrament of confession in your church, Mr Bateman?' Thackeray asked, changing tack so suddenly that he was rewarded by a wary expression from Bateman.

'Some Anglicans do,' he said. 'I don't offer it myself in any formal way. I regard myself more as a counsellor than a confessor but I'm always happy to listen to parishioners . . .'

'Did you listen to Louise Brownlow? Did she tell you anything, anything at all, which you think might have a bearing on her death?'

Bateman placed his hands together under his chin and pursed his lips for a moment, as if considering how far he should go in answer to that question.

'If she did it would be confidential,' he said at length.

Mower drew a sharp breath, waiting for the explosion he was

sure would come from Thackeray, but the chief inspector gave no sign of anger beyond a slight tightening of the lips.

'You say you are not bound by the confessional as a Catholic priest would be, Mr Bateman,' he said. 'But you're certainly bound by your duty to help me find Louise's killer.' He spoke quietly, but his voice carried a breath of arctic wind, as the vicar continued to hesitate.

'She was not a happy girl,' Bateman said slowly at last. 'She was desperately worried about money. She didn't confide in me, but I got the feeling that there was boyfriend trouble. Just an impression I got.'

'So you don't require your congregation to repent publicly and give up their sinful ways at St Jude's?' Thackeray said. 'You surprise me.'

'What do you mean?'

'I thought it went with being born again,' Thackeray said. 'Don't you advise your flock at all when they're in trouble? Counselling seems an inappropriate word for tackling what used to be called sin in my church-going days. Confession and absolution was what my lot laid down.'

'I don't follow,' Bateman said, looking flushed now and draining his whisky in a single draught.

'Are you telling me that Louise didn't tell you – or that you didn't find out – that what was bothering her was far more than boyfriend trouble, as you put it? In six months of teaching her the guitar? Visiting her in her own room?'

'She told me very little,' Bateman said, angry himself now. 'She was unhappy, that's all. She was never very specific about why. And I deeply resent the accusations you seem to be making that I'm in some way responsible for what happened – or involved in some way.'

'There are all sorts of levels of responsibility,' Thackeray said. 'Some more culpable than others, as I'm sure a man in your position must know.'

'I was in no way responsible for Louise's troubles,' Bateman said firmly.

'And you had no idea that she'd been driven to desperate lengths to try to solve them? I would have thought with your contact with so many students you would have known all about what can happen to some of these girls when they're desperate for money.'

Bateman groaned slightly and shook his head.

'I know nothing about her private affairs,' he said firmly. 'Nothing at all. Louise never gave the slightest hint.'

'Do you know who the boyfriend was?' Thackeray persisted.

Bateman shook his head. 'She never talked about things like that.'

'None of the young men in the congregation? You would have noticed who she was friendly with, surely?'

'I only ever saw her with girlfriends, as far as I remember,' Bateman said. 'There was no particular boy.'

'Never mind,' Thackeray said. 'We'll find out. Forensic science can come up with all sorts of answers these days.'

Bateman looked appalled. 'You mean . . .?'

'The obvious, and other things,' Thackeray said enigmatically. 'You didn't fancy her yourself, then?'

Thackeray's question was brutal in its directness and Bateman flinched.

'As you took so much trouble over her musical education? She was a young attractive girl and you're a single man. It must have crossed your mind. It's certainly done more than cross the mind of some others in your position – a father figure, a vulnerable and impressionable young girl?'

'No!' Bateman said explosively. 'There was nothing like that between us, nothing at all. With all these young women in my congregation I have to be above suspicion in that respect. Absolutely above suspicion.'

'And there is the credibility of your campaign against prostitution to consider, isn't there?' Thackeray said unsympathetically.

'Exactly,' Bateman said eagerly. 'Another good reason to avoid any illicit liaison.'

'I think we'll leave it there, for the time being, Mr Bateman,' Thackeray said, with all the emphasis on his final cautionary phrase. Mower snapped shut his notebook and watched Bateman as he swallowed hard and attempted a smile which could only be called ingratiating.

*

When the vicar, still looking shaken, had seen them out Mower glanced judiciously at his boss as he unlocked the car door and got in.

'You were a bit hard on him, weren't you, guv?' he asked as he fastened his seat belt.

Thackeray gave him a tired smile.

'I thought we should give the Reverend Bateman plenty to think about,' he said. 'If anyone knows what was going on at 17 Whitley Street I'm sure it's him.'

'Any particular reason?' Mower asked, knowing Thackeray's dislike of hunches.

'I suppose because Roz and Jane initially never told us about the connection, that he'd been to see Louise at home. As if they wanted him out of the picture.'

'You think they were trying to protect him?'

'I don't know, but I'm quite sure someone is trying to protect someone in this case. There's no other explanation for the astonishing lack of communication they claim existed in that household,' Thackeray said sombrely.

'You don't think three females could live together without knowing each other's intimate secrets?' Mower asked mischievously. 'A bit sexist, isn't it?'

'I didn't quite say that,' Thackeray said.

But you meant it, Mower thought.

'And all that forensic stuff?' he asked, judiciously changing the subject. 'We don't have any serious forensic clue to the boyfriend, do we?'

'No, but it threw him, didn't it? Which it might do if he is the father of Louise's baby and he thinks we can use blood tests to prove it.'

8

The taxi from King's Cross swung out of the grinding, choking maelstrom of the Caledonian Road, negotiated the humps and chicanes of several complicated traffic-calming schemes, the modern equivalent of moat and drawbridge, and drew up outside the glossy royal blue front door of an early nineteenth-century terraced house in an Islington square.

Laura paid off the cabbie, almost forgetting a tip until a ferocious scowl reminded her what was expected. She stood for a moment gazing up at the white stucco façade with its gleaming, perfectly proportioned windows which gave a glimpse of swagged curtains and lamps already lit and softly glowing against the encroaching London dusk.

Trust Caro to end up somewhere like this, she thought ruefully, glancing down at her travel-crumpled jacket and summoning up an image of her own small top-floor flat, cosy enough if you didn't go in for cat-swinging as a way of life, but a million miles from this sort of *House and Garden* elegance. With a shrug, she stepped up to the front door, rang the shiny brass bell push and watched the semicircular fanlight – obviously an original feature – turn from grey to gold as a light was switched on inside.

'Laura,' said the tall young woman who opened the door. 'How lovely to see you. I'd have recognised you anywhere.'

'With my hair it's difficult to fade into the background,' Laura said wryly as she followed her old school friend into a narrow, thickly carpeted hallway, although she too would have recognised Caroline across a crowded street and saw in the flesh even more clearly the resemblance to her younger sister: the same fly-away blonde hair, the same pale face and deep-set serious eyes.

Her hostess took her coat, making small talk, and eventually ushered her up the stairs and into a first-floor drawing-room whose tall windows overlooked the street to the front of the house and a long, tree-filled garden at the back.

Caroline Everett – her married name, she had told Laura on the telephone when she had agreed, with politely veiled surprise, to see her – would have been as slim as her guest were it not for the fact that beneath a loose silky smock, in a colour which reminded Laura of a Mediterranean sky, worn over leggings, she was evidently in the late stages of pregnancy. Her hair was cut expertly to frame her thin, oval face, and her eyes, as she waved Laura into a deep armchair, were unmistakably anxious.

'When is the baby due?' Laura asked cautiously, not wanting to fall at the first fence.

'In six weeks,' Caroline said.

'The first?'

'Oh no. Giles is seven and Emily's five. They're at a birthday party in Highgate at the moment.' She looked vaguely at her watch, with a studied gesture. 'I have to fetch them at seven. It's the nanny's afternoon off. Doesn't time fly?'

Laura shook her head briefly, trying to adjust to a dozen or more years of change. Caroline Boulter had not been a close friend but in the hothouse world of a boarding school, classmates were forced into an intimacy which they might never have sought in a world where discriminations were more easily made. Caroline, she recalled, had always expected privilege and had usually been accorded it as a consequence. Laura remembered being astonished during one of her earliest holidays from school to hear her grandmother's caustic revelations about the Boulters' humble antecedents in the Yorkshire coalfields.

She had gone back to school nursing this potentially hurtful knowledge like an illicit weapon but she had never, as far as she could recall, used it. Caroline's was not an arrogant hauteur, more a sublime ignorance that anyone could be remotely tempted not to offer her the deference she regarded as her due. In the end Laura had recoiled from tipping her from her pedestal with an unusually mature combination of contempt and compassion which in retrospect she slightly regretted.

'And you?' Caroline repeated, glancing at Laura's left hand with vague sympathy.

'I don't seem to have found the right man yet. No one permanent anyway.' The conventional phrases came automatically and glossed over such a tangled web of hopes and disappointments that she moved on quickly in case Caroline pressed the point. It was not an avenue she wished explored. 'I'm very involved with my job anyway,' she said, not entirely truthfully.

'You're a journalist?' The slightest nuance of surprised distaste could possibly have been detected in Caroline's question. 'You always were the hard-working girl.'

'Working woman,' Laura corrected her without much passion. Caroline, she guessed, was a lost cause. 'And you?'

'Oh, no, not now,' Caroline said quickly. 'I did work for a while after college. For a gallery in Bond Street. But we had Giles soon after we were married and we never felt that a working mother was a good idea. Jeremy was quite strongly against it, as a matter of fact.'

'So what does Jeremy do to keep you in luxury?' Laura asked bluntly, casting an appraising eye around the softly gleaming antique furniture and the tasteful water-colours which adorned Jeremy's eau-de-nil drawing-room walls.

'A barrister,' Caroline said quickly. 'He's a QC, but he specialises in commercial cases so I don't suppose you'd have heard of him.'

'I don't suppose I would,' Laura said. 'A bit older than you, is he?' she wondered aloud.

'Oh, yes, a bit. Barristers can't marry young, you know, they earn so little when they start.' Caroline laughed nervously as if reading Laura's unspoken thought that they almost always made up for that, with knobs on, later. 'It's been a long time since Eggers, hasn't it?' she said. 'What fun we had.'

Fun was not the first word which came to mind when Laura recalled Egerton House, the private girls' school tucked away in the rolling Surrey hills where she had spent seven years of her life, most of them painful.

'I hated every minute of it,' she said. 'Until I got into the sixth form anyway. That was a bit better.'

'But why?' Caroline asked, evidently genuinely surprised.

Laura shrugged. It would take all evening, she thought, to explain why a gawky, red-headed eleven-year-old with a faintly northern accent and a boisterously and ostentatiously self-made father had been made to feel an outcast by cohorts of young Carolines with all the self-confidence and arrogance of the southern élite. And even if she took the time, she thought, Caroline still would not understand.

'Did your sister go to Egerton as well?' she asked instead.

'Jane?' Caroline asked, looking wary for a split second before she tossed the blonde hair away from her eyes and met Laura's gaze with apparent frankness. 'Yes, she did, as a matter of fact. But she's my very little sister, you know. There's nine years between us, so we'd left before Jane started at Egerton. We never overlapped. Why do you ask?'

Laura reached into her capacious bag and pulled out the

glossy black and white photograph she had purloined from the picture desk.

'This girl reminded me so much of you that I thought it must be your sister. I seemed to recall that you had one.'

Caroline took the photograph gingerly and let her hair fall over her eyes again, masking her expression.

'Where was it taken?' she asked at last, her voice slightly husky.

Laura told her.

'Yes, it's Jane,' Caroline said. 'She's lost a lot of weight again, she's very thin, but it's her. Has something happened to her?'

'Not as far as I know,' Laura said. 'But she's disappeared and the police want to talk to her.'

'Good Lord, what about?' Caroline exclaimed and Laura told her briefly about the murder at the house Jane 'Watson' had been sharing.

'Surely they don't think she killed this girl, do they?' Caroline said sharply. 'They're not going to put a photofit on the TV news or anything dreadfully embarrassing like that, are they? Jeremy would never forgive me.'

'I don't really know whether she's a suspect,' Laura said unsympathetically. 'But I do know the police aren't very keen on their key witnesses disappearing without a by-your-leave. They certainly want her back in Bradfield.'

'She's been disappearing on and off for years,' Caroline said distractedly. 'She walked out of school when she was fifteen. She was anorexic. She was depressed. You name it. She ran away more times than I can count before she finally got her A levels and began to look as though she was going to settle down. But then she ran off again. I was there with the children the weekend she finally left home, my father's home, that is. That was two years ago. I haven't seen her since.'

'That's dreadful,' Laura said, her response that of the only child who would have given anything for a brother or sister to share her childhood with.

'You don't understand,' Caroline said. 'She was much younger than I was. She was still a baby when I went away to Eggers. I hardly knew her, really. What I did know was the distress she caused my parents as she became a teenager. She was quite

89

impossible. They did everything for her, all sorts of treatment, sent her to Canada when it really looked as though she was going to starve herself to death. My mother died, you know, when Jane was sixteen and I really think that was partly the result of the worry she'd caused us all. She destroyed my mother and came close to destroying my father. Life has been a damn sight more bearable without her.'

Caroline put a hand carefully on her stomach, as if to feel her child kicking, or perhaps to calm it.

'I hope to God none of my children grows up like Jane,' she said, with feeling.

'Do you think she could have stabbed her house-mate?' Laura asked.

'I don't know what Jane's capable of,' Caroline said. 'As far as I'm concerned she's mad.'

'And you've no idea where she could have gone?'

'No idea at all. She certainly wouldn't look to me or my father for help.'

Laura sighed.

'I think you'd better brace yourself for the photographs on the TV news, then,' she said.

'Do you have to tell the police about this?' Caroline said slightly wistfully, as if she knew the answer almost before she had framed the question.

'I don't have any choice,' Laura said, knowing that even having come this far in identifying Jane Boulter without informing Michael Thackeray was not going to win her Brownie points privately or publicly. 'I can't withhold evidence from the police. Nor can you, if they come knocking on your door.'

'And I suppose you'll write about it in your bloody newspaper.' Caroline's tone suddenly became petulantly waspish.

'What I know, which isn't much,' Laura admitted.

'How can you do that?' Caroline asked. 'How can you do that to people, to anyone, let alone people you know?'

'Your sister's in the public eye, now,' Laura said. 'You didn't put her there, and nor did I. It's just something that's happened.'

'Jeremy is going to go utterly, utterly bananas,' Caroline said miserably. 'He's just started work on some big banking case. The last thing he'll want is this sort of publicity in the family.'

'Oh, I should think this will be a bit of light relief after what some bankers get up to,' Laura said unsympathetically. 'After all, at worst Jane has knocked off one individual. The City wipes out thousands at a time.'

'Still as red as your flaming hair, Laura,' Caroline said, getting to her feet angrily. 'Well, when Inspector Plod comes round I suppose I'll know who to thank, won't I?'

'If you knew where she was, would you tell the police?' Laura asked curiously.

'I'm really not sure, darling,' her school friend said.

'Ah,' Laura said softly to herself as she drew up outside her flat just before midnight and recognised the car which was parked just ahead of her. The sigh mixed pleasure, relief and anxiety in roughly equal measure. Pleasure that Michael Thackeray was waiting for her, relief that the decision when to tell him about her London expedition had been made for her, and anxiety that he would disapprove of her freelance efforts to resolve at least one of his current mysteries.

'You're very late,' he said, kissing her on the cheek and following her to the front door of the tall Victorian villa.

'Blame British Rail, or whatever it calls itself these days. The London train was half an hour late into Leeds.'

'You've been to London?' He knew better than to express too much surprise. 'I hope they pay you overtime.'

'It wasn't work,' she said opening the heavy outer door and waving him up the stairs ahead of her. Inside the front door of her top-floor flat he gave her no time to speak before taking her in his arms and kissing her more passionately.

'I've been sitting out there more than an hour waiting for you to come home,' he said. 'Am I a fool?'

'You're a fool,' she said happily.

She extricated herself from his arms, took her coat off and went into her tiny kitchen to make coffee, feeling absurdly pleased with life.

'You may not be too happy when I tell you where I've been,' she said more soberly as she carried a tray back into the living-room and took a seat opposite Thackeray, who had taken off his coat and jacket, loosened his tie and was slumped on the sofa looking, for him, unusually content.

91

He sat up suddenly, his face tightening in anxiety and his blue eyes instantly remote.

'You haven't been to London for a job interview, have you?' he asked quietly.

'No, it's not that,' she said. She looked at him speculatively. 'Would you mind so much?'

'You know I would,' he said flatly, and she instantly regretted her question.

'So are you going to tell me why you went?'

She took the by now somewhat crumpled photograph of Jane Watson and Roz Jenkins out of her bag and handed it to him.

'I thought I recognised the girl who calls herself Jane Watson,' she said.

'You know her?' Thackeray said incredulously. 'Why didn't you tell me?'

'No, I don't know her. But she reminded me very much of someone I did know, once. Someone quite a bit older but who looked exactly like that when she was seventeen or eighteen. I went to see an old school friend in London. That girl is her sister.'

She told him everything she had learned on her visit to Caroline Everett's home.

'I don't want all this Lady Jane stuff in the *Gazette* yet,' Thackeray said. 'I want to talk to her, but I don't want her frightened off, particularly if she's had psychological problems. She'll run and we'll never find her if we're not careful. Did this Everett women suggest she might be suicidal?'

Laura shrugged. 'Not really,' she said. 'Mad was the word she used. There's not much sisterly love lost there. But you'll have to talk to Ted Grant about what the *Gazette* publishes. You know I can't sit on what I've found out unless he agrees.'

'I'll talk to him in the morning. You're sure the sister doesn't know where she is?'

'I don't suppose I'm as good as you at sniffing out the truth, but I didn't think she was lying,' Laura said.

'Oh, don't underestimate your powers of persuasion, my love,' Thackeray mocked gently. 'Anyway I'll ask the Met to interview her tomorrow to make quite sure.'

'She will not like that,' Laura said feelingly.

Later, as Laura lay close to Michael Thackeray in bed, watching the smoke from his cigarette drift sluggishly to the ceiling, she shivered suddenly.

'Cold?' he asked, pulling the duvet higher to cover her naked breasts.

'Just a ghost walking,' she said. 'I was thinking of that girl on the run. She looks so young and vulnerable. Where would you go to hide if you couldn't go home?'

'The trouble with you...' Thackeray said, putting out his cigarette and sliding down the pillows to take Laura in his arms again, 'the trouble with you is you're too soft-hearted for your own good.'

Laura had a sudden vision of Cassy Davis pale, distraught face and suppressed a shudder.

'Is that all?' she asked.

'No, that's not all. You're impulsive, pig-headed, bloody-minded and irrational.'

'Move in with me,' she said.

'With all those imperfections to contend with? You must be joking.'

'A trial? Just to see if you can cope with them all full-time.'

He felt the sudden tension in her and knew she was deadly serious, and he felt the familiar cold panic seize him as it did every time she ventured to draw him further into permanence than he dared to go. He ran his hands over her body, exciting her as easily as he knew now he always could.

'Not now,' he said, smothering her protests with a kiss, and mentally slamming his suitcase shut and kicking it back under his bed. 'Not yet, Laura. Not yet.'

9

Jacquetta Price was a tall, heavy woman, her iron grey hair bushing out from her head in a massive frizz to her shoulders where it seemed to be attached by static electricity to the fluffy rainbow stripes of a sweater several sizes too small for her. Beneath the encompassing woolly brightness her bosom heaved like a mountain range being hurled to its birth by tectonic forces beyond human comprehension. Sergeant Kevin Mower followed its movement with a mesmerised fascination. Chief Inspector Thackeray, however, appeared unmoved.

'What people tell me in therapy must remain confidential, chief inspector. You have to understand that.'

'I think not,' Thackeray said flatly. 'If it came to court, Mrs Price, I don't think there's a judge in the country would regard it as anything other than contempt of court if you tried to claim confidentiality in a case as serious as this.'

Mrs Price sighed heavily and went through another convulsion, lifting herself slightly out of the depths of her deep armchair to allow her voluminous black skirts to billow in the draughts created by her movement. Mower got a fleeting impression of massive fleshy thighs bulging over the top of stockings held up by suspenders, an unusual sight he had always regarded as erotic until now. He glanced down more determinedly at his notebook to mask his disillusioned amusement. A waft of sickly sweet perfume mixed with body odour turned his expression to one of extreme distaste.

'Murder?' she said dramatically. 'You are talking seriously about murder? Talking seriously about Jane as a suspect in a murder case?' Her voice rose and cracked with a mixture of outrage and incredulity.

'By no means,' Thackeray said. 'But she is a material witness, at the very least. I must talk to her again.'

Mrs Price pursed her slightly protruding lips which were liberally and glossily painted a colour that Mower, who took an interest in such things, could only describe as puce. He wondered why she bothered when the rest of her face consisted of a series of rolls and ravines of muddy flesh which appeared to have experienced neither make-up nor even soap and water for some considerable time.

'You realise what a fragile state this girl is in?' she prevaricated.

Thackeray nodded imperceptibly. Mower could sense the distaste with which he contemplated the therapist. 'I understand she has had problems for some time.'

'Problems!' Mrs Price almost screamed. 'That's the understatement of all time.'

'Mrs Price, you really must listen to me,' Thackeray said, his voice dripping icicles. 'I need to speak to the young woman who calls herself Jane Watson. This is not negotiable. If you have any idea where she might have gone, then you must tell me. Concealing information could be regarded as obstructing the police.'

'I don't know where she is,' Jacquetta Price snapped pettishly. 'I've no idea at all. She could be anywhere. She could have thrown herself in the river, for all I know. It's not impossible. She is a fragile, fragile flower . . .' She stopped speaking suddenly, a slightly puzzled look crossing her large and generally impassive face. 'What do you mean, calls herself Jane Watson? Isn't that her name?'

'I rather thought you might have known that,' Thackeray said. 'Did she not tell you who she really is?'

'No, she didn't,' Mrs Price said, looking somewhat taken aback by her client's evidently unexpected duplicity. Breathing heavily, she hauled herself out of the depths of her armchair, crossed the room at a magisterial pace and took a brown cardboard file from the bottom shelf of the bookcase which lined one wall of her consulting room. Both Thackeray and Mower had already cast an interrogative eye over her library and absorbed the names of psychological experts they could easily recognise and passed over many more that they did not.

'Is Jane Watson a suicide risk?' Mower asked.

'Undoubtedly,' Mrs Price snapped. 'She's tried at least twice before. Quite apart from the anorexia.' She hesitated for a moment, flicking through the sheets of paper within her file, with a look of faint uncertainty now.

'You say her name isn't Watson,' she said. 'And I really believed that I had gained her confidence.'

'You mean you thought she was telling you the truth?' Thackeray said.

'Oh, I'm sure she was telling me the truth, about most things,' Mrs Price said, her confidence returning. 'She presented a classic case of repressed memory, absolutely classic.'

'Abuse?' Thackeray said, the distaste in his voice as well as his expression now.

'Such a lot is buried in these traumatic family situations, chief inspector,' Mrs Price said. 'She was beginning to remember quite nicely at our last couple of sessions.'

'Perhaps you'd better tell me what she was beginning to remember?' Thackeray said.

Jacquetta Price sat down again, wafting another gust of attar of roses around the two men, and folded podgy hands beneath the lowest of her several chins. Anorexia had clearly never been her problem, Mower thought uncharitably.

'I feel quite betrayed,' Mrs Price said thoughtfully. 'Quite betrayed that she should have persisted in a lie over something so basic as her own name.'

'We believe Jane is her own name,' Thackeray said, more gently now that it was evident that the therapist was beginning to crack. 'It's her family name she seems to have held back.'

'Yes, well, that makes a certain amount of sense. They do hide, you know,' Mrs Price said earnestly. 'They hide from themselves as well as other people, because they feel guilty about what's happened. Even when it starts in early childhood they can still believe that in some way they are to blame. They bury what's happened under layers and layers of lies, very often. That's why it takes so long to get to the bottom of it all. Jane and I had only really just begun.'

'I understood she had been coming to you for some time,' Thackeray said.

'Oh, no, chief inspector. Months, only months. That's a mere preliminary skirmish in psychotherapy, you know. Proper analysis can take years.'

'Where did you train, Mrs Price?' Mower asked sharply.

'Oh, in the States,' the therapist said firmly. 'All the best therapists train in America, you know. They're years ahead of us, years.'

Mower caught Thackeray's eye and saw reflected in it his own scepticism.

'Where exactly?' Thackeray asked.

'California. A little college in southern California,' Jacquetta Price said airily, secure in the knowledge that whatever she claimed could not be checked and that in any case it was not illegal to offer therapy without any training at all.

'So perhaps you'd better tell us just what it was that Jane Watson had begun to tell you,' Thackeray said.

'Oh, yes, well, it was all coming together.' The woman's enthusiasm was unmistaktable now. 'It was all beginning to come out. It was exactly what I expected, of course, with her history of anorexia and depression. She was a textbook case.'

'I think the details are what I need.'

Thackeray wondered whether the request sounded as forced to his listeners as it did to him. He found himself deeply reluctant to hear just how that frail, pale girl might have been used by those she should have had reason to trust.

'She began to remember what happened to her as a very small child,' she said, and her voice took on an almost child-like quality itself. 'She began to remember playing with worms. Of course I asked her what she thought the worms were and gradually she came to accept that a large worm was a penis. She cried when she remembered that and I asked her why and she said that it had hurt her. She said she thought the worm had bitten her, but of course we worked out that wasn't what had happened. We had to end that session. She was so distressed.'

'Who?' Thackeray asked, his voice harsh.

'Oh, the father, naturally,' Mrs Price said. 'It's always the father, isn't it?'

'Not always,' Thackeray said softly, so softly that Mower was not quite sure he had heard him at all.

'Does this therapist woman think she could turn violent?' Superintendent Jack Longley asked.

'She'd turned it all in on herself, she thought,' Michael Thackeray said. He was standing by the window in his office, gazing down at the town's central square which was filled with workers hurrying to catch buses outside the Victorian town hall opposite. He had left his chair to Longley, who looked hot, impatient and uncomfortably overdressed in an obviously new suit and uncharacteristically garish tie, where a purple stripe contrived to clash with the superintendent's overhanging pink chin.

'Guilt, she said. It's all about consuming guilt.' Thackeray gazed steadfastly out of the window, refusing to meet Longley's eye.

As if he doesn't know all about that, Longley thought, casting an unusually sympathetic glance at his subordinate. He carries it a bit better these days, though, I'll give the Ackroyd lass credit for that.

'Aye, well, psychology's all very well but if she can't tell you whether or not she's run amok with a carving knife what use is it all in the end?'

'She thought not,' Thackeray said. 'If there was any violence she thought it would be directed at the father. That was her theory anyway.'

Longley snorted. 'A bloody inexact science, if you ask me, psychology.'

'Even so, it might be as well to warn Lord Boulter that his daughter could be on her way to see him,' Thackeray suggested. 'He's something big in the City. And puts in an appearance in the Lords now and again.'

'Aye, have a word,' Longley said. 'Best not let him get carved into chitterlings without warning, eh?'

'Even if he does deserve it?'

'I thought you were soft on capital punishment, lad,' Longley scoffed. 'A bit of a closet pinko.'

'For murder,' Thackeray said bleakly. 'There's worse things.'

Longley looked at the younger man reflectively.

'Did you ask Ted Grant to hold back on what your bonny lass discovered about the missing girl?'

'Yes, he agreed to wait a couple of days if that would help,' Thackeray said, studiously ignoring the reference to Laura.

Longley ran a finger between his shirt collar and his neck.

'I hate these dos at County,' he said heavily. 'All dolled up just for the dubious pleasure of taking a glass of summat with the chief's missus. And lots of chat with that fool they've brought up from the Met. Human resources manager, I ask you! Do I look like a human resource, for God's sake?'

'Kevin Mower reckons they've swallowed a business manual too many down there,' Thackeray said.

'Aye, well, it doesn't seem to be improving their crime statistics much, does it? We'll be calling the villains customers next and asking them if they'd be so kind as to stay overnight in one of our single rooms with en suite facilities.' Longley subsided deeper into his chair and sighed. 'We couldn't have got it wrong about this lass, could we?' he asked, suddenly full of doubt. 'She couldn't have gone the same way as her friend and been dumped in some ditch?'

'She was seen leaving with a ruck-sack, sir,' Thackeray said mildly. 'And the more we learn about her the more likely it seems that she'd run if she thought her identity was going to be exposed. If our own inquiries don't come up with anything by the end of the week I've promised the *Gazette* a picture and a bloody good story to go with it. In the meantime I'll warn her family and ask them to get in touch if she turns up there.'

'Where's there?'

'Some village in Hampshire, apparently. And a flat in London for when the father is attending the Lords.'

'Aye, well, I'd better get off to this do, I suppose,' Longley said, raising his bulk from Thackeray's chair with an effort. 'It's a tricky one, this, if there's bloody politicians involved, even if they are the other end of the M1. Have a care, lad.'

He stood beside Thackeray at the window for a moment, looking down through the branches of cherry trees just coming into bud.

'If you made an honest woman of that Ackroyd lass, she wouldn't run rings round you like that,' he offered tentatively. 'You'd know what she was getting up to.'

'I wouldn't bank on it,' Thackeray said coldly, fighting down the irrational anger which welled up at this unwarranted intrusion into his private life.

'The trouble with you, lad, is you think you've turned to stone,' Longley said with some asperity.

'No, the trouble with me is that I know I bloody haven't,' Thackeray came back without thought. 'I've lost one wife and child. Why the hell should I risk another?'

'Aye, well, it's nowt to do with me,' Longley said mildly. 'I'm right out of order, I dare say. Forget I said a word.'

'Sir,' Thackeray said bitterly as the chief superintendent lumbered to the door and went out without a backward glance.

'Damn and blast,' he said to himself in the ensuing silence, resting his head against the cold glass of the window before spinning round and opening the office door and bellowing for his detective sergeant who was deep in conversation with a female colleague on the other side of the CID room.

'Guv?' Mower said anxiously as he came into the office and closed the door behind him, racking his brains for any reason he could have provoked Thackeray's never to be despised anger.

'Have you got any sense out of Forensics?' Thackeray asked, trying to get his breathing and thumping heart back to normal.

Mower, still watching him curiously, picked up a folder from his desk.

'I was just going to fill you in, guv, when His Nibs arrived. They've hit the jackpot. There were traces of the famous bodily fluids on the sheets. Enough for a DNA analysis if that's what we want. And they want to know if we want a blood test done on the dead girl's baby.'

'We do,' Thackeray said flatly. 'That baby has a father somewhere and I want to meet him. Any joy from the hospital?'

'Joy unconfined, guv, I reckon. The Reverend Mr Bateman does usually visit on a Tuesday evening and he did visit the Tuesday in question. But no one can recall him being around the wards much after eight o'clock. Half-past seven, one nurse reckons she saw him leaving. So he'd plenty of time to get back home before Louise Brownlow was killed.'

'And plenty of time to give her more than a guitar lesson,' Thackeray said with unaccustomed viciousness. 'I'll have that sanctimonious Jesus-freak, if it's the last thing I do.'

'Right, guv,' Mower muttered, very aware, not for the first time, that Thackeray was not a man whose wrong side he wished ever to explore. He suddenly felt quite sorry for Miles Bateman.

10

In Whitley Street, war was already threatening. The working girls had been patrolling the pavement in ones and twos since mid-afternoon, disappearing occasionally for a short time in punters' cars. But business was slow, few cars even reduced speed as women moved to the edge of the pavement displaying what they had to offer to the drivers, and by dusk a couple of burly men had hustled down asking women angrily for explanations.

By the time Laura Ackroyd arrived there were arguments in progress up and down the pavements on both sides of the street.

Looking around for a familiar face, she spotted Sherry Maguire deep in angry conversation with a uniformed policeman.

'You again,' Sherry said dismissively as Laura approached. 'Who invited you to t' party?'

'Someone rang the office and said there was going to be trouble,' Laura said. 'Surely they're not going to arrest you all again?' She glanced at the young police officer who looked away, obviously embarrassed by the question.

'Oh, no, they want our help this time,' Sherry said contemptuously. 'Bloody nerve! They only want to talk to t' punters as they drive up in case they saw owt the night that lass were killed. Only trouble wi' that is that t' bloody punters'll be half-way down Ayagarth Lane in sixty seconds when they realise what's going down.'

'We've got orders to stop cars turning into the street,' the policeman said, his tone surly now. 'There's nowt I can do about it. My sergeant just said to tell you, that's all.'

'Christ,' Sherry said. 'I think I might as well bugger off home now. What about you, Cass? We'll not turn tricks here tonight.' She turned to a figure which had been sheltering silently in the shadow of the trees beside her, head down, the collar of her leather jacket turned up.

'I was sorry you didn't stay to breakfast,' Laura said to Cassy, to Sherry's evident astonishment. 'You were very welcome.'

'Aye, well, I had to get on,' the girl mumbled uneasily.

'Have you found somewhere permanent?' Laura persisted.

Cassy shrugged. 'Aye, I'm fixed up now,' she said, moving further down the street, away from the policeman, who did not seem particularly interested in her. Laura followed slowly, not wanting to frighten the girl again.

In the shadow of the next clump of trees she stopped and allowed Laura to catch up with her.

'I want nowt to do wi' t' newspapers,' she whispered. 'I told you that.'

'Or the police?' Laura guessed, accurately to judge by the alarm which briefly flashed across the girl's face, visible even in the fitful light from the street lamps. 'You weren't here the other night, were you? You didn't get arrested with me and Sherry.'

'I came later,' Cassy said dismissively. In spite of her high collar the bruises on the side of her face were still clearly visible.

'Do the police know that?' Laura asked carefully.

'Sod them,' the girl said, glancing back to where Sherry still stood uncertainly on the edge of the pavement watching the police constable walk back towards the corner of Aysgarth Lane where the ambush had been set for the Whitley Street clients.

'I've got a proposition for you, Cassy,' Laura said tentatively.

'Oh, aye? What's that then?'

'I want to write a feature about homeless girls, prostitution, drugs ... you know, how it all happens, how it all hangs together. If you'd agree to help me I think I could get you some payment. Not a fortune or anything, but something.'

'I told you. I want nowt to do wi' reporters,' Cassy said stubbornly. She looked Laura up and down. 'The *Gazette*, isn't it? Nowt you could pay would get me fixed up for a single day, love. You haven't got the least idea, you haven't. Not a bloody clue.'

'It might help other girls,' Laura said, but Cassy just laughed, an edge of hysteria very close to the surface.

'Do you know how old I was when I went on t'street? Do you know? Do you?'

Laura shook her head helplessly.

'I were eleven,' Cassy said. 'Eleven years old. I ran away from t' children's home they put me in because my old man were getting into my bed at night, and when I went into t' home I found the big lads doing t' same bloody thing to t' little lasses. I reckoned that if that were all I were going to get I might as well get paid for it. Jesus Christ! Articles in t' bloody newspapers! What good do you think that's going to do for kids like I was? Chop men's bloody balls off if they touch kids and you might do some bloody good.'

'Think about it,' Laura said, aware of footsteps approaching quickly behind them.

'Cass!' It was Sherry, who put an arm round both of them and urged them away down the street. 'I just saw your friend up there with that bastard Hornby and another couple o' blokes. You'd best get out of sight.'

Cassy glanced back the way Sherry had come, the fear in her eyes evident even in the dim light.

'Right, I'm out o' here,' she said curtly, opening the garden gate immediately behind her and quickly disappearing inside.

'Will she be all right?' Laura asked anxiously. 'Who's her friend anyway?'

'The fellow who beat her black and blue the other night. Her minder, so called, although the only minding he does is to take every penny she earns and keep her hooked by getting her a fix when she's desperate.'

'Dear God,' Laura said. 'Is there no way out of this?'

'Oh, aye, there's ways out,' Sherry said. 'Where've you been living all your life? They're called decent jobs, and decent homes and decent parents who don't screw you – and I do mean screw you. The sort of things you take for granted. That kid was doomed before she even left primary school.'

Laura felt a wave of impotent anger threaten to overwhelm her.

'Cassy's right. An article in the *Gazette* isn't going to make much difference,' she said, her voice husky.

'No, well, we all have to do what we can. I've tried with Cass, but I reckon she's a lost cause. They'll find her dead of an overdose one night and that'll be – ' Sherry broke off, distracted by angry shouting from the other end of the street.

'Here's trouble,' she said. 'I'm off, I reckon. There'll be nowt doing round here tonight the way things are shaping up.'

Sherry turned on her spiked heels and stalked away, heading towards Aysgarth Lane, away from the crowd gesticulating angrily at the other end of the street close to St Jude's. Laura walked slowly and slightly reluctantly towards the noise of confrontation.

She found a twenty-strong group of protesters, led by the formidable combined religious thrust of Miles Bateman and Mohammed Ahmed, partly blocking the road, provoking catcalls from the women still looking for punters as far from the police as they could get and, more ominously, threats and jeers from the men who had come to support them.

The posters and placards had changed this evening, Laura noticed. Their message was not aimed this time at the women but unequivocally at their clients. 'We have your number,' said several. 'Does your wife know you're here?' asked another.

'What are you going to do? Take down the car numbers?' Laura asked one of the young women clustered around the vicar of St Jude's.

'That's right,' she said. 'Miles says if we can't get rid of the women then we may be able to drive out the kerb-crawlers.'

'The trade will only move somewhere else,' Laura said reasonably.

'Let them go and do it on the bypass or somewhere, not amongst respectable families,' the girl said firmly. 'No one wants them here.' It was the voice of impassioned certainty and Laura knew she would be wasting her breath to challenge it.

Behind them the raised voices were becoming angrier as Mohammed Ahmed tried to restrain a couple of the younger Asian men in the group. A single policeman seemed to be trying to calm things down and getting a furious response from the protesters.

'You're aiding and abetting these women, constable,' she heard Bateman say, to a firm murmur of approval from the parishioners who clustered around him – whether protectively or for protection was difficult, Laura thought, to judge. 'The local people have a right to ask them to leave. It's an illegal trade.'

'My only interest is in keeping the peace, sir,' the policeman said, trying to placate the unplacatable. He turned away to speak urgently into his radio as his words were greeted with more jeers but it was already too late. Laura did not see who threw the first punch, but within seconds the confrontation had become a mêlée as fighting broke out between some of the more hot-headed protesters and the men 'protecting' the street women. Laura ducked as one of the placards was thrown, narrowly missing her head and skittering across the roadway making the young policeman, still calling for assistance by radio, jump inelegantly out of the way.

Cautiously Laura retreated a few yards down the street and took refuge in a garden gateway as shouts from the Aysgarth Lane end indicated that the police were heading in the direction of St Jude's, several officers running ahead of a police van which switched on its blue flashing light and began to sound its siren as it approached.

Most of the crowd scattered and ran, disappearing into the side streets beside the dark hulk of the church before the police arrived. Laura saw Miles Bateman standing his ground, still surrounded by young members of his congregation, directing the officers in the direction in which, she supposed, the women and their minders had run. It would never enter his head, she thought, that he was as guilty as anyone of provoking the violence.

Intending to ask him for a comment for what looked like turning into tomorrow's front page lead, she walked slowly towards what was left of the group of demonstrators but before she got there her attention and that of everyone in the street was attracted by a piercing howl from the darkness of the churchyard a hundred yards away. There was no doubting the urgency of the cry and police, demonstrators and Laura all began to run in the same direction.

A young Asian man stood in the gateway, dark eyes staring in shocked horror as the police approached. He said something in a language no one else there understood.

'In English,' a policeman said roughly. 'What's wrong? In bloody English.'

'There's a body in there,' the young man said. 'Someone . . . I think . . . I think someone is dead.'

Chief Inspector Michael Thackeray watched impassively as the crumpled, blood-soaked remains of Jason Beardsley were zipped into a body-bag and lifted on to a stretcher. He had been an unprepossessing young man, podgy-faced, lank-haired, his fingernails thick with dirt, in spite of his designer shirt and jeans and the heavy gold jewellery which he wore around his neck. But in the harsh glare of the portable arc lights which had been erected to illuminate the gloomy churchyard and its tilting, dilapidated tombstones, death had given him a dignity which in life he had certainly never had.

Thackeray shuddered slightly as the mortuary attendant casually tucked a stray hank of hair inside the bag before pulling up the last two inches of the zip.

'I'll have a closer look at him first thing,' the pathologist Amos Atherton said, taking off his plastic gloves and throwing them into a rubbish bag. The whole area was strung about now with blue and white police tape. 'Treat all this stuff as potentially contaminated with the plague, tell your forensic lads,' he said, kicking the bag and nodding meaningfully at the pool of blood which remained as a sticky reminder of where Beardsley had fallen.

Thackeray ran a foot through the pile of detritus which had blown into the corner between the first tombstone and the gatepost with a look of distaste. Dead leaves, sweet wrappers, a couple of used condoms and a half-eaten paper of fish and chips lay in a rotting heap which had spilled over on to now well-trodden long grass between the graves.

'Apparently this was favourite place for the women to bring the punters,' he said. 'Out of sight amongst the dead.'

'Your team are going to enjoy sifting through that lot,' Atherton said.

'It looks like being a messy business all round,' Thackeray said.

'What are you thinking? One of the Asian lads?'

'Or one of the women.'

'Not an obvious crime for a woman, I shouldn't have said,' Atherton said thoughtfully. 'Three hefty blows with a knife. It'd take a strapping lass to do that. Tall, too, I should think. But I'll be able to tell you more when I've had a closer look at the wounds in the morning.'

'Not long dead, though?' Thackeray asked.

'Oh, no. His temperature had hardly dropped. About as fresh as I ever get them. A right little daisy, though to look at him you might reckon he were more of a deadly nightshade.' Atherton glanced at the tall policeman with a malicious grin. 'Given the number of bobbies you had milling about here, you should have caught the beggar red-handed.'

'Yes, I'll be asking a few questions about that, don't you fret,' Thackeray said grimly.

The pathologist lumbered off towards his car and Thackeray glanced around the murder scene reflectively. The churchyard surrounded the massive bulk of St Jude's on three sides. It had long fallen out of use as a burial ground, its space filled to overflowing with the Victorian dead whose stone and marble monuments had been left to fall and crumble amongst an overgrown jungle of yews and rhododendrons and long grass, a perfect place for forbidden pleasures of all kinds, and in summer a well-known haunt of tramps looking for a sheltered place to fall into alcoholic oblivion. Two had already been roused from an alcove at the back of the church but could offer nothing coherent about what had happened to Jason Beardsley just yards away in the darkness.

Beardsley's body had been found face down, sprawled across the last resting place of one Thomas Wright, woolcomber, and his dearly beloved wife Alice, who had both departed their respectable lives within a year in 1882. His blood had been smeared across the tilting headstone as if he had slithered down it before collapsing across the smashed parapet below, almost obscured by weeds, to die clawing handfuls of green foliage in some final agony.

As soon as it was light, Thackeray thought, the whole church-yard would have to be meticulously searched for the weapon which had killed Beardsley. A large and fairly heavy knife, had been Atherton's initial assessment, and there was no trace of such a weapon in the immediate vicinity of the body. Nor, a quick sweep of the churchyard by his officers had determined, had there been anyone else sleeping rough that night in the deep shadow of the overgrown trees and bushes.

Whitley Street was almost deserted now too, apart from the handful of uniformed officers who remained to keep idle sight-seers at bay. Thackeray had sent Sergeant Kevin Mower and his other detectives about the neighbourhood to draw up as com-plete a list as possible of all the people who had been in the street that night. In the morning the routine task of interviewing every demonstrator, every prostitute and any punters who had been identified would begin.

And Laura. Thackeray had been conscious of Laura's presence ever since he arrived on the scene but apart from a bleak acknowledgement when he got out of his car he had ignored her. He accepted that she had her job to do, just as he had his, but he admitted that he disliked it when they overlapped. He had sent Mower to interview her about what she had seen that evening, and which other witnesses she could identify. Now, he knew that she was waiting for him inside St Jude's, which Miles Bateman had opened up as a refuge, physical as much as spiritual, for anyone who needed to escape from the dark and cold and bloody horror of the churchyard.

Laura Ackroyd increasingly obsessed his waking thoughts.

When he was not with her he craved to see her like a man lost in a desert craves water, and when he was with her his heart was lifted in a way which he had thought for years was no longer possible. When he said he loved her, he meant it. When she asked for more than a casual relationship, he shied away still like a baulking horse at a looming fence. He had no confidence that he could ever make that leap.

With a sigh he turned and opened the heavy oak door of St Jude's and stepped into the dimly lit interior of the church for the second time. Laura was sitting in a blue plastic chair with her feet propped up on another, her jacket collar pulled up to her chin, her hair escaping from its clips in spiralling strands which caught the light like burnished copper, and her eyes half closed. Thackeray watched her for a moment, the weariness and distaste which had filled him in the churchyard draining away, before he walked quietly across the blue and black tiled floor and put a hand gently on her shoulder.

'You're tired,' he said. 'You shouldn't have waited.' She looked up at him with the smile and the sparkle in her grey-green eyes which reduced him to jelly.

'It's odd watching you at work,' she said. 'You seem so remote. I had to check out the change wasn't permanent.'

'You spoke to Kevin Mower?'

She nodded.

'I've done my witness bit,' she said. 'And I'll have to be doing my reporter bit first thing in the morning. In the meantime I thought I could do you.'

He laughed.

'You're shameless,' he said, pulling her to her feet and putting an arm around her. He glanced towards the high altar which was shrouded in deepest gloom.

'I don't think even the trendy Miles Bateman would tolerate that here, however great the temptation,' he said. 'Come on. Let's go home.'

Laura wondered how deliberately he had chosen that word as she followed him with a sudden surge of optimism to the door of the church.

Laura looked at the front page of the *Bradfield Gazette* and allowed herself a faint smile of satisfaction. She was, by inclination, a feature writer who took pleasure in a slower and more measured consideration of current events. But seeing her story about the previous night's murder, full of eyewitness detail and first-hand description, spread across the front page, with her own name in 14 point bold in a box in the centre column, still held its own thrill. Even more satisfactorily, it would say something to those of her colleagues who regarded 'women's issues' and therefore, by definition, women journalists as a sub-species never to be trusted amongst the slugs and snails of what they regarded as 'Real Life'.

'Fancy yourself as our crime reporter now, do you?' Fred Powers, the chief sub, asked sourly, coming up quietly behind her. 'Pity there wasn't room for a nice little politically correct résumé of the poor bloody victim's deprived childhood, isn't it? Good riddance, I say. And more power to the vigilantes. It's time that area was cleaned up.'

The news that Beardsley had been in the street to mind some of the working girls had mysteriously leaked out of police headquarters to the editor's office while Laura had been pounding out her story at eight o'clock that morning. Thackeray, she acknowledged wryly, had said nothing about the victim's profession when they had returned to her flat the previous night. Not that he had said much at all, she recalled with still lingering satisfaction.

'I wouldn't have thought you'd relish the idea of travelling much further to get a bit on the side at your age,' Laura said kindly and Powers flushed, the dislike which was always there in his eyes hardening for a moment into something worse, before he stalked across the office to his own desk, scowling.

Laura felt the pleasure she had taken in her small triumph drain away, leaving a bitter taste in her mouth. It was lunchtime and she logged off her computer terminal wondering for a moment if Thackeray would be free before dismissing the idea as absurd. With two murders on his mind he might not be free again for weeks, she thought, and wondered, not for the first time, whether in the end their two incompatible careers might not drive them apart more certainly than the determined distance he mostly kept.

Her phone rang and she picked it up desultorily, the morning's frantic effort to meet her deadline leaving her drained. A voice she did not know asked if that was Laura Ackroyd and she hesitated for a moment before admitting her identity, instinctively disliking a tone which succeeded in being masculine, peremptory and arrogant in a single question.

'Boulter, here, Miss Ackroyd,' the voice continued. 'Caroline's father. I understand you were inquiring about my second daughter Jane? Is that right?'

'Yes, I was,' Laura said faintly. 'So are the police, I think.'

'Yes, I'll deal with them. It's you I wanted to talk to,' Lord Boulter said. 'I happen to be in Yorkshire this afternoon. Can we meet?'

'I suppose so,' Laura said without enthusiasm. 'I'll have to clear it with my editor.'

'Lunch,' Boulter said flatly. 'D'you know the Deepcliffe Hall Hotel? Near Arnedale.'

'Yes, I know it,' Laura said. Only too well, she thought, recalling a disastrous dinner she had shared there with her erstwhile live-in lover at the acrimonious end of their affair.

'One o'clock,' Boulter said and hung up, leaving no time for further discussion. Laura stared at the phone, aching to ignore the summons, but knowing that her insatiable curiosity would not let her. Damn the man, she thought.

Her editor, Ted Grant, grunted non-committally when she popped her head round his office door to ask for an extended lunch-hour. His watery blue eyes in a ruddy face veined with purple like some Technicolor cheese were no friendlier than they ever were in spite of her morning's exertions. Grant was an editor of the old school who believed women should know their place, which was emphatically not on the front page, the sports pages, the business pages nor in any position more elevated than that of feature writer.

'Can't you keep your love life for after hours?' he said. 'Just because you get the front page lead doesn't mean you can run rings round the bloody job.'

'It's nothing to do with my love life and there may be a story in it,' she said, restraining the urge to slam the door on him and walk out of the office for good.

'Aye, well, see there is if you're a minute later than half two,' Grant conceded reluctantly. 'There's still Friday's features to get sorted, don't forget.'

Half an hour later Laura drove into the broad gravelled drive of Deepcliffe Hall, a long low manor house with mullioned windows which had recently been converted into a country house hotel. She parked her ageing Beetle carefully in a car park full of sleek BMWs and Jags and grinned at the contrast unapologetically. If there was one lesson both her father and her grandmother had taught her, from their deeply antagonistic points of view, it was that an Ackroyd was as good as the next man – or woman. Neither envy nor deference came easily.

She glanced in the rear-view mirror and took in a creamy oval face, the copper hair neatly burnished and fastened back, bright eyes and lips enhanced with the merest touch of lipstick to match the deep rose silk shirt she had gone home to put on for the occasion. She was not dissatisfied with what she saw.

Nor, she sensed, was Lord Boulter as he rose with an unashamedly appreciative look from the deep armchair in the entrance lobby where he had been reading the *Financial Times.*

'It was good of you to come,' he conceded, the voice carefully modulated, deep and unequivocally Home Counties, as he led her quickly into the adjacent dining-room.

He was a tall man, his iron grey hair receding slightly above a face which combined a square-jawed determination with an air of deep-seated anxiety in the fine lines around the light blue eyes and the rather sensual mouth. Laura did not warm to Lord Boulter any more in the flesh than she had on the telephone. He was a powerful man used to getting his own way and would, she guessed, be ungrateful if in one's debt, vindictive if crossed. If his daughter Jane had run away and left him she had probably had good cause, Laura thought.

Settled at a window table with a view across velvet lawns dotted with trees and drifts of spring flowers, Laura allowed herself to be steered towards asparagus, followed by salmon *en croute* with a chilled white wine. She was, she reminded herself firmly, here to listen to this man, however overbearing his manner.

'You must be wondering why I asked you here,' Boulter said eventually as they waited for their first course.

Laura inclined her head in what she hoped might be construed as gracious consent to that proposition.

'You haven't written anything about my daughter Jane in your newspaper yet, have you?'

'No, the police asked us to hold back for a few days,' Laura said truthfully enough.

'And then?'

'And then I'll write about what I found out when I went to see Caroline.'

'And if I asked you not to?' Boulter said, his anger increasingly apparent now and his face becoming more flushed than would have been accounted for by the whisky he had ordered as an aperitif.

'I would take advice from my editor, who would take advice from the police,' Laura said coldly. 'What you're asking isn't in my power to give you. It's out of my hands.'

Boulter absorbed this, staring intently at the plate of asparagus which the waitress had placed in front of him. He nodded impatiently as she poured butter sauce over the tips for him, and preceded to pick up and eat the succulent spears hungrily before he spoke again. With slightly less eagerness, Laura followed suit. Boulter, she could see, was not a man who would confide easily. If she were to gain anything useful from this meeting she would have to be patient and not force the pace. As if reading her thoughts, Boulter pushed his plate away and smiled at Laura slightly wolfishly.

'What you don't realise,' he said quietly, watching the neighbouring diners out of the corner of his eye to make sure that they could not overhear, 'is that my younger daughter Jane is mad, clinically and quite possibly certifiably mad. She's already destroyed her mother and now she thinks she's found a way to destroy me.'

'By committing murder?' Laura asked incredulously, keeping her own voice down to match Boulter's.

'No, of course not,' Boulter came back quickly. 'She couldn't kill anyone. Not directly. Certainly not with a knife. Her methods are much more insidious. She foments guilt, that girl. Her mother died of guilt, blaming herself for Jane's behaviour until eventually she became ill.'

'Jane had anorexia?'

'That's what the doctors called it. I called it a sheer pig-headed refusal to eat. To make us all suffer.' Boulter spoke now in jerky sentences, the emotion barely contained beneath his normal façade of civilised urbanity. He was, Laura thought, a man in deep trouble.

'I don't think anorexia is as easy as that,' she said carefully.

'That's what the bloody therapist who called me said,' Boulter snarled.

'Jane's therapist contacted you?' This was the first Laura had heard of a therapist but the news did not surprise her after what Caroline had said about her sister's history.

'She rang me to tell me Jane had run away and that I couldn't get away with anything because Jane had told her everything that had happened and she had passed it on to the police.'

'And what did she mean by that?' Laura asked, realising that this was the crux of Boulter's own manic anxiety.

'She said Jane remembered being interfered with as a child. Jane had already hinted as much last time she was home. But this woman was quite unequivocal. She's saying she was abused. By me!' Boulter almost choked and earned some curious looks from fellow diners at nearby tables. With an effort he controlled his breathing and took a mouthful of wine, rolling it around his mouth slowly as if the motion would calm his jangled nerves.

'You're saying that the therapist is claiming that Jane has recovered some memories that had been lost, buried in her past? It's widely believed that this does come out in therapy,' Laura said quietly. 'There's a lot of evidence in America.'

'And a lot of evidence that these so-called memories can be false,' Boulter said furiously. 'I've never laid a finger on my daughter, either of my daughters. The very idea disgusts and revolts me, as it would any normal father. This therapist has put the idea into Jane's head. I've tried to stop all this, but now Jane has vanished, the police are involved and it's running out of control.'

Boulter paused to contain another wave of fury which threatened to overwhelm him. They sat in silence as the waitress brought salmon and served them vegetables, but as Laura picked up her fork she realised that she had lost what little appetite she had arrived with.

'You know what this could do to me, don't you?' Boulter asked when the waitress had moved away. 'Publicity, possibly even criminal charges if she persists with her story. I could be destroyed.'

'Why are you telling me all this, Lord Boulter?' Laura asked. 'I'm not clear how I fit in.'

'Because I want you to be warned. When Jane turns up, as I expect she will if the police are determined to find her, I want the press to know that this "abuse" is a tissue of lies, that I deny it totally and absolutely. And that if so much as a breath of it appears in print I'll sue for libel. I'll take any newspaper which prints this garbage for every penny they've got.'

'I suppose it could do you considerable damage,' Laura admitted. She thought back to the entry in *Who's Who* she had consulted to check her suspicion that Caroline Boulter had a younger sister. Lord Boulter had wide business interests in the City of London and had been a junior government spokesman in the House of Lords. 'In business or in politics?' she asked, as much to let him know that she was not as ill informed as she suspected he assumed a local newspaper reporter would be as because she really thought it mattered.

'Both,' Boulter said flatly. 'Damage so considerable that no newspaper in its right mind would publish such a suggestion. My son-in-law estimates that libel damages of a million would be reckoned on the low side.'

'You want me to pass that message on to my editor, I take it,' Laura said.

'To whoever you think needs to know,' Boulter said. 'The London media I can deal with myself. But I don't want a piddling little paper like the *Bradfield Gazette* throwing spanners into my affairs by not realising what dangerous waters they're swimming in.'

Laura suppressed a smile as she digested the jumble of metaphors, folded up her napkin, put it on the table between them and stood up.

'Thank you for the offer of lunch,' she said. 'I seem to have lost my appetite. My grandmother knew your father, you know. A bit like knowing Lloyd George, I understand, as far as lost leaders are concerned. I'll tell her I met you and that you seem to be continuing the disappointing family tradition.'

She was conscious of silence and curious eyes watching her progress across the dining-room to the door and could hear Boulter's heavy breathing recede as a politely astonished hubbub took over. She did not look back. She had better not accept any more invitations to Deepcliffe Hall, she thought, as she got into her car. She seldom seemed to get much beyond the first mouthful of their exquisite and extremely expensive cuisine.

Chief Inspector Michael Thackeray sat in his office in shirt-sleeves facing a rubicund and contented Superintendent Jack Longley, who had evidently lunched well. Thackeray wished he shared his boss's confidence that the explosive tangle of violence which had enmeshed such a small part of the town as Whitley Street could be unravelled as easily as he seemed to assume.

'So how far have you got?' Longley asked, shifting his bulk to allow his belly more room to expand in the cramped office chair.

'I've got a team talking to the Asian community, including two Punjabi-speaking officers. Mohammed Ahmed is already complaining that we're harassing the young men who were out on the demo with him last night. I've got another team interviewing the church members who were with Miles Bateman. They're mostly delayed adolescents who seem to think he's some sort of Messiah, but we have to suppose that they'll tell the truth, at least. And Kevin Mower is talking to all the prostitutes and minders we've been able to trace.'

'And the victim was pimping?'

'Oh, yes, there's no doubt about that. He's known, got form, been inside twice, once for dealing in heroin,' Thackeray said.

'So if it wasn't for the demo you'd likely be looking for an aggrieved tart, or another pimp, or another dealer with a grudge?'

Thackeray shrugged his assent.

'If it weren't for the demo,' he said. 'And the fact that there was another stabbing within the week in a house only yards away.'

'You think they could be connected?' Longley asked sharply. 'What are you suggesting? A serial killer who doesn't care what sex his victims are?' The superintendent did not hide his scepticism.

'I was wondering more if one of the locals Bateman and Ahmed have stirred up hasn't got carried away, started some sort of crusade...' Thackeray trailed off, uncharacteristically unsure of himself as he met frank incredulity in Longley's rheumy blue eyes.

'What does Amos Atherton say in his PM report?' Langley asked.

'He doesn't say anything much,' Thackeray confessed. 'The knife wounds are similar, that's all. We've not found a weapon, so we've nothing definite to go on. I've had everything out of that churchyard short of opening up the graves and asking the dead what they saw. So far all we've come up with is a skip-load of garden rubbish, a bucketful of used condoms and enough cola cans and silver foil to keep *Blue Peter* going till next Christmas. Except the mummies and daddies wouldn't think much of the games they were being used for. None of which is any help at all.'

'Pimping and prostitution are dangerous trades. The drug trade down there makes them even more dangerous. Chances are its sheer coincidence that the two of them got knocked off the same week,' Longley said. 'I shouldn't indulge any fantasies about a double murder if I were you, Michael. It'll be the tedious police work which comes up with the solutions, as usual. With so many people about, someone will have seen Beardsley in that churchyard before he died, you'll see. And you'll probably find that the Brownlow girl made a mistake with one of her clients. Even the professionals do that now and again, and she was a rank amateur. It's only in America you get fundamentalists taking guns and knives to folk they don't like. Not in Bradfield.'

'You're probably right,' Thackeray conceded. 'I'm not thinking straight. I had a late night.'

'On duty, I hope,' Longley said jovially, lumbering to his feet.

'And off,' Thackeray admitted with a faint smile.

'Aye, I saw the Ackroyd lass had been on the job last night,' Longley said, enjoying Thackeray's evident discomfiture. 'Don't get involved in too much pillow talk with a reporter, will you?'

Before Thackeray could think of a suitably diplomatic reply to that his door inched open and Sergeant Mower put his head round.

'Come in, Kevin, I'm just going,' Longley said expansively.

'Sir,' Mower said, coming properly into the room. 'I just thought you ought to know, guv,' he addressed Thackeray. 'I had a session with Sherry Maguire. You know she said she saw someone going into 17 Whitley Street the night Louise Brownlow was killed? She thinks she saw the same man again last night on the demo. She recognised him – or she recognised the coat he was wearing that night. She'd have recognised him sooner but it wasn't his usual gear, she says.'

'What did I tell you?' Longley said over his shoulder to Thackeray. 'Someone always sees summat they never even think they've seen. So who was it, lad? Don't keep us waiting like a bloody Agatha Christie novel.'

'It was Miles Bateman, sir. The vicar of St Jude's.'

'Right,' Thackeray said. 'I've been wanting another word with the Reverend Bateman. I think the time is ripe to bring him in.'

12

Miles Bateman came into the interview room in a dark suit and his clerical collar. He had insisted on changing out of casual clothes, Kevin Mower told Thackeray in the bleak corridor lined with anonymous interview room doors, before agreeing to accompany the sergeant to the police station. With old-fashioned courtesy he stood up as the sergeant came back into the interview room with the chief inspector. On a chair beside him was a dark-coloured duffel coat which he reached for and fingered nervously as the two officers came in.

'Sergeant Mower tells me that I can be of some further assistance,' he said.

'I think you can, Mr Bateman,' Thackeray said. 'Do, please, sit down.'

'Am I under arrest, Chief Inspector?'

'No, merely helping me with my inquiries,' Thackeray said shortly. 'You are free to leave at any time.'

Bateman nodded and did as he was told. He looked pale and strained above the unusual formality of his collar, and he seemed to be having some difficulty in keeping his hands under control. Every now and again they jerked involuntarily.

'I invited you here because I don't think you have been entirely frank with me,' Thackeray said at length.

Bateman shrugged slightly.

'I can't think how that might be,' he said. 'I think I've been as helpful as I could be.'

'I'd like you to tell me a little more about your relationship with Louise Brownlow,' Thackeray said. 'You said that she first came to St Jude's before Christmas. How long was it before she decided that she would like to play the guitar for your services? Quite quickly, I assume?'

'She was keen, yes. She brought her guitar in quite soon, I think, but she didn't know a lot of our more popular hymns. She'd been brought up at school on something antediluvian like *Ancient and Modern*. And she wasn't a good sight-reader so I was helping her out. The boy who's been our mainstay, musically speaking, is leaving Bradfield soon, so I was keen to find a replacement. Louise seemed ideal.'

'So whose idea was it for you to visit her at home?'

Bateman hesitated for a moment.

'We found the church a bit cold,' he said at last.

Mower gaped slightly at the apparent naïvety.

'And I didn't think it was quite suitable for her to keep coming to the vicarage all the time. People might have got the wrong idea,' Bateman went on, evidently oblivious of the impression he was creating.

Thackeray looked at Bateman long and hard, and with the deepest scepticism.

'So how often did you visit her at Number 17?' he asked at length. 'To teach her the guitar.' The pause was deliberate and the implication plain and Bateman flushed slightly.

'I don't remember exactly,' he said. 'It must have been four or five times, I suppose, since Christmas.'

'In her room?'

'Well, yes, there was no alternative really. It was a big bed-sit. She entertained all her friends there.'

'So we're talking about sessions in her room every couple of weeks? Not more often than that? Not once a week, perhaps?'

'No, no, I don't think as often as that. But I really wasn't counting.'

'Would she have been counting, Mr Bateman?' Thackeray asked. 'Do you think she looked forward to your visits, to your lessons? I get the impression that quite a lot of the young women at your services are very – how shall we put it? – attached to you. Was Louise one of the girls who felt that way?'

'I really don't know, Inspector. I think she was pleased to be playing at our services. She seemed to enjoy it. There was nothing more to it than that.'

Bateman appeared almost to have settled down now to the pattern of question and answer which he seemed so far to have found unthreatening. It was not a situation Mower thought would continue much longer.

'I do have a problem with what you're telling me, Mr Bateman,' Thackeray said, a hint of menace creeping into his voice.

'A problem?' the vicar asked faintly.

'I find it puzzling that a man who says he's concerned about his reputation, so concerned that he did not like inviting a young woman to his own house, should be quite happy to visit a house where that same young woman was carrying on a trade as a prostitute.'

Bateman's hands jerked from the table top on to his lap and back apparently without any volition on his part, his eyes took on a startled expression and he let out his breath in a gentle hiss between clenched teeth.

'She wasn't a . . . you can't say a thing like that . . .' Bateman seemed to find some difficulty in pronouncing the word Thackeray had flung at him.

'Oh, I don't think there's much doubt about what she was, Mr Bateman, and I think you knew. It's becoming quite common amongst students these days, I'm told. But what is even more puzzling is the fact that a young woman who found it morally acceptable to earn money in that way seems also to have become a pillar of your church. You have to see my difficulty and why I

119

find it hard not to believe that the link between you and Louise Brownlow was a bit more – shall we say – physical than implied by the provision of a little guitar tuition. In which case I can understand why you found the church a bit on the chilly side. Were you one of Louise Brownlow's clients, Mr Bateman?'

Thackeray's attack was overtly contemptuous and Bateman paled visibly. Two small red spots appeared on his prominent round cheeks and he seemed to be having difficulty drawing breath for a moment.

'No,' he said at length. 'I was not.'

'But you knew what she was doing?'

'No, no,' Bateman banged clenched fists on the table in front of him for emphasis but his eyes were those of the rabbit mesmerised by the approaching stoat.

'She told you, didn't she?' Thackeray asked quietly. 'She told you as her confessor, though you don't like that title, do you? But your function was the same.'

'No, no,' Bateman said again, although the conviction was draining from him and he began to slump against the table like a deflated paper bag.

'She told you,' Thackeray insisted. 'She must have told you.'

'She told me,' Bateman agreed faintly. 'I tried to persuade her to stop.'

'And she wouldn't?'

'Wouldn't, couldn't . . . one or the other.'

'Did you know Louise kept a diary, Mr Bateman?' Sergeant Mower broke in.

Bateman swung round in his chair to face him.

'No, I didn't know that,' he said, obviously horrified by the idea.

'Just appointments, appointments with initials, we were sorry to discover. Not an intimate record of what she was up to, if that's what's worrying you. But it does record your visits, you know. At least an MB who makes regular appearances. Not on a regular evening each week but at least once each week. Sometimes more.'

'I must have lost count,' Bateman said miserably. 'I didn't think it was as often as that.'

'Why did you go round there so often?' Thackeray asked. 'Was it purely as the girl's minister, purely to try to get her back on track? Or was there something else?'

Bateman looked at the chief inspector with something like hatred in his pale eyes.

'It wasn't purely for anything, Mr Thackeray,' he said with unexpected vehemence. 'As you've been trying to prove ever since I walked into this room. I wasn't interested in the handcuffs and whips and things she kept for her clients. I'm not perverted in that way. But yes, I was interested in Louise. I was infatuated with her, if you must know, rather than the other way round. I couldn't keep away.'

'You slept with her?' Thackeray's voice was very quiet now. 'You realise, of course, that if I arrest you I'm entitled to take DNA samples – with or without your consent – don't you? If you had sex in that room it won't be very difficult to prove.'

Bateman swallowed hard and shrugged again hopelessly.

'Yes, I slept with her, when I could persuade her to come to bed with me.'

'Did you pay her for her services?'

'Jesus God, no, I didn't, you bastard,' Bateman suddenly shrieked. 'I loved the little whore, you fool. Don't you understand that? I loved her.'

There were tears in Bateman's eyes now but Mower knew that Thackeray had not finished and would not back off until he had. He felt almost sorry for Bateman.

'Were you the father of her child?' Thackeray asked.

Bateman shrugged.

'I don't know,' he said faintly. 'I expect so.'

'Did she tell you that you were? Did she threaten you in some way? Is that why you killed her?'

'All she threatened was to have an abortion,' Bateman said with a shudder. 'I tried to persuade her not to do that. If I was interested in saving the life of a child I'd hardly kill the mother, Chief Inspector. I'm not your murderer, God help me.'

'You said you didn't generally visit on Tuesday evenings, the evening you go hospital visiting at the Infirmary?' Mower broke in suddenly, harking back to Louise's diary and taking Bateman by surprise. 'But your initials are there for that Tuesday.'

'Yes – no – I mean, no, not on Tuesdays, not that Tuesday. I was at the hospital.'

Thackeray leaned back in his seat for a moment, his face impassive and his eyes very cold and blue.

121

'I don't believe you, Mr Bateman,' he said quietly again. 'I don't think you are telling me the truth, in spite of your cloth, which you've gone out of your way to emphasise today, and in spite of what you've already admitted.'

'I don't know what you mean,' Bateman said.

'Oh, come on, Mr Bateman, you know exactly what I mean. Whatever you are, you're not a fool.' Thackeray's contempt was biting.

'I don't know what you mean,' Bateman said again, burying his hands on his lap beneath the table.

'Then let's start again, Mr Bateman,' Thackeray said patiently. 'Let's take it a step at a time. You are a middle-aged professional man and Louise was an attractive young girl and you were visiting her at her house on a regular basis simply, you said, to teach her the guitar, but now, you admit, to get into bed with her at any available opportunity.'

'It began quite innocently. I *was* teaching her the guitar,' Bateman said, his face closed and stubborn now. 'One thing led to another.'

As it does, you poor bugger, Mower thought to himself, glad that he had never had to face Thackeray in his avenging angel mode. There was no compassion for the vicar in the chief inspector's face as he closed for the kill.

'But you're asking us to believe that you tried to persuade her to have this child? As a student? With no visible means of support?' Thackeray asked, not attempting to disguise the incredulity in his voice.

'Abortion is a sin,' Bateman said flatly. 'I offered to help her in any way she needed if she carried the child to term.'

'Did you offer to marry her, Mr Bateman?' Thackeray pressed.

'Yes, I did,' he said.

'And she turned you down?'

'Yes, she did.' Bateman's voice faltered now, and he kept his eyes down, twisting his hands frantically beneath the table.

'And that was on your last visit, was it? On the night she died?'

'Last visit?'

'The visit you made after you'd returned from the hospital on the night she died,' Thackeray said implacably.

'I didn't – ' Bateman began but the chief inspector did not allow him time to finish.

'Oh, yes, you did, Mr Bateman. You were seen going into that house that night. I'm sure you remember what you were wearing?'

Bateman's eyes flashed to the duffel coat beside him and back again to his hands. He hardly needed to admit the connection.

'You were wearing the same coat last night at the demonstration in Whitley Street,' Thackeray said, and Bateman nodded.

'I have a witness who recognised you when she saw you again. You visited Louise on that Tuesday night and I think you lost patience with her in the end and killed her.'

'No,' Bateman said. 'No, no, no.'

'So what did happen when you saw her?'

'We argued about the baby again. Quarrelled if you like. But she was alive when I left her. I swear she was alive. I could no more kill Louise than I could kill my own mother. She was carrying my child, for God's sake. Don't you understand what that means?'

Mower knew that he did not imagine the look of pain which flickered briefly across Thaekeray's face at that and was gone as if it had never been.

'And that is your current version of the truth, is it?' Thackeray asked. 'For a man of God you seem to take a remarkably cavalier view of what the word means.'

'It is the truth,' Bateman said, panic not far away. 'I was afaid of what you would think, what conclusions you would jump to. And I was right, wasn't I? You do think I killed her. I lied and so I'm guilty, that's what it comes down to, isn't it?'

'Not quite, Mr Bateman,' Thaekeray said wearily. 'But it does make finding the truth a great deal harder if people who claim to be innocent deliberately deceive us. Anyway, I think we're all a bit clearer about what happened that evening, are we not? I'll want to talk to you again, but for the moment you can go.'

'You're not arresting me?' Batten said incredulously, licking dry lips.

'Not just now, Mr Bateman,' Thackeray said dismissively. 'But don't go anywhere without letting me know.'

'Laura,' Chief Inspector Thackeray did not quite call out the name but the sharpness of his exclamation brought a knowing smile to Kevin Mower's lips as they hesitated in the gateway to 17 Whitley Street. It was just getting dark and the street lights were flickering into life, casting their inadequate orange glow along the tree-lined road.

In the shadows at the far end they could make out a group of Asian men in traditional dress beginning their now ritual patrol. Closer at hand a couple of women stood unobtrusively under the trees, watching warily. Cars were few and none slowed down, the presence of the two policemen, even in plain clothes, still a sufficient deterrent to all but the most determined kerb-crawlers.

'She looks as though she's heading for the vicarage,' Thackeray said, momentarily nonplussed at the sight of Laura Ackroyd heading determinedly away from them, past the vigilantes, towards the dark bulk of St Jude's.

'Can't you stop her, guv?' Mower suggested edgily. 'If you want him to stew, you can do without the *Gazette* nosing about.' One day, he thought, without too much sympathy, Laura Ack-royd was going to land her lover in serious trouble.

'There'll be worse than the *Gazette* nosing about tomorrow, by all accounts,' Thackeray said gloomily. 'The press office has been fielding calls from the London papers. We've been lucky so far but it looks as though the whole thing is going to blow up in our faces.'

'Catch up with her, guv,' Mower suggested. 'I'll make a start with Roz Jenkins and you can join me.'

'Give me ten minutes,' Thackeray said, striding off in Laura's wake, leaving the sergeant with his hand on the gate to Number 17 and a sardonic smile on his face.

In fact he did not catch up with Laura until she was already retreating down the vicarage path. The house behind her was in complete darkness and she had obviously failed to get any reply to her ringing on the door bell. She took a moment to recognise the dark figure which approached from the shadow of the overgrown laburnum tree overhanging the vicarage gate.

'Overtime?' he asked, seized by a moment's panic as he always was when he saw how her face lit up as she recognised him.

'And you?' she said, glancing around to see if anyone could see them before brushing his cheek with a fleeting kiss. 'We mustn't keep meeting like this.'

'You're looking for Miles Bateman?' he asked, carefully disguising the anxiety that prompted the question. The *Gazette* should not know yet, he thought, that the vicar had spent several hours at the police station that afternoon.

'I'm still trying to get to grips with the whole prostitution thing for my features,' she said easily, setting his mind at least partly at rest. 'I wanted to ask him a bit more about his campaign and his Aids centre. They don't really seem to add up, do they? I couldn't get hold of him by phone earlier so I thought I'd call in on him on my way home. I didn't think you'd be free till late.'

'No, it's not very likely,' Thackeray said.

Laura shrugged and turned her face away to hide the momentary disappointment. What must it be like, she wondered, to be attached to a man who worked nine-to-five. She would, she concluded almost as quickly as the thought crossed her mind, be bored within a week. She turned back to Thackeray with a smile which made him catch his breath.

'So I'll just see if he's over in the church. There seem to be some lights on over there,' she said easily.

They both looked towards the brooding bulk of St Jude's, where a faint glow behind the tall windows indicated some sort of activity inside.

'I'll walk over with you,' Thackeray said.

'That's uncommonly protective of you, Chief Inspector,' Laura mocked gently. 'So far I've been in more danger in Whitley Street from your over-attentive colleagues than from anyone else. Remember?'

'How could I forget when you keep on reminding me?' he said. 'Can't we call that a day?'

'If you're sure he's been sorted out.'

'He's been sorted out,' Thackeray said shortly.

St Jude's churchyard lay in deep shadow, lit only by the faint light in the church porch, the police cordon gone now that every available scrap of evidence had been scraped from the muddy ground. But as they approached the door Laura and Thackeray were surprised to see two figures sitting on one of the low stone table-top tombs, clutching each other in evident distress.

'Can we help?' Thackeray asked as they approached. The two

young women looked up. Both were in tears and neither seemed inclined to explain themselves to two strangers.

'I'm looking for the vicar,' Laura said. 'Do you know if he's around?'

This innocent question seemed to distress the girls, teenagers of little more than school age, she thought, who clung to each other even more closely, the tears which ran freely down their cheeks glistening in the faint light from the porch.

'Has something happened to Mr Bateman?' Thackeray asked sharply, suddenly made anxious by the girls' reaction.

The older of the two tossed a veil of soft hair away from her face and stared at the two strangers.

'Not happened, no,' she said. 'He was in church with us. Just a prayer service. We come every evening if we can. And he said he had something to tell us.'

'What did he tell you?' Thackeray asked, alert now with a tension which Laura could sense even in the half-light which obscured his face. 'What exactly happened?'

The directness of the question seemed to calm the older girl, although her companion continued to sob quietly, leaning against her friend's shoulder, her hands still clasped across her face.

'He said he was leaving St Jude's,' she said. 'That he couldn't lead our services any more. That he wasn't worthy of us . . .'

'Oh, that's so awful, so untrue,' the younger girl whispered through her tears. 'Miles is such a wonderful man.'

'Did he say where he was going?' Thackeray said, his voice harsh against the soft sobbing and the gentle sough of the wind in the trees above them. 'Did he say when he was going?'

'No, no, that wasn't what he was talking about. You don't understand,' the girl said. 'He was confessing his sins. Telling us about a girl he knew who he'd done things with, wicked things, he said, impure things, leading her into sin when he should have been leading her into the light, leading her to Jesus. Oh God, I don't believe it. It can't be true. He's such a good man.'

'And the service is over? He's gone now?' Thackeray's tone was urgent now and Laura guessed that his interest in Miles Bateman was a seriously professional one, the sin he suspected him of the most mortal of all.

126

'He was still in the church praying when we came out,' the girl said. 'We were about the last to leave. We wanted to stay with him but we couldn't bear it any longer and I don't think he really wanted anyone there any more.'

Thackeray looked around briefly and took stock. The rest of the churchyard appeared deserted. The handful of vigilantes who had been patrolling nearby had moved further down Whitley Street.

'I'm a police officer,' he said gently to the two girls. 'I want you to stay here until I come back. I'll need to talk to you again. Do you understand?'

The girls nodded dumbly, clearly only half comprehending the implications of what he was saying.

'If you like,' the older girl said.

'Laura,' Thackeray said. 'Mower's down the street but I daren't risk fetching him. There isn't time. Will you come with me? I need a witness. He won't fight but he might run.'

Laura nodded, suddenly seized by a sense of deep foreboding. She followed Thackeray to the church door which creaked open noisily and they looked inside. St Jude's was much as Thackeray remembered it, the circle of cheap plastic chairs in place but unoccupied now, the high Gothic arches of the chancel and transepts rising into almost total darkness, the gilded high altar the merest glimmer in the surrounding gloom beyond the choir screen.

'Mr Bateman, are you there?' Thackeray called firmly, casting an eye around the perimeter of the church looking for doors behind which the vicar might be concealed, but the light was so poor that it was difficult to make out with certainty anything beyond the pool of yellow light from the lamps dangling on long thin flexes above the main circle of chairs.

'He's not here,' Laura whispered, feeling diminished by the huge, cold, echoing emptiness which faced them.

'I'm sure he is,' Thackeray said. 'He wouldn't have left the church lit up and unlocked. Not in this neighbourhood. Not even if he was planning to run.'

They stood for a moment simply listening to a silence made more intense by the sheer height of dark space above them. Suddenly it was broken, thunderously, by a single booming clang as a bell swung once, like the crack of doom, and then filled the air with its dying resonance like swarms of angry bees fading away on a summer day.

'Jesus Christ,' Thackeray said with uncharacteristic vehemence. 'What the hell was that?'

Outside they could hear the chatter of startled birds, flung from their roosts by the commotion, a single high-pitched scream and then, further away, the excited chatter of voices drawn by the booming bell.

'Where's the belfry?' Laura said helplessly. Behind them the door creaked open again and the two girls who had been in the churchyard hurried into the church, hair dishevelled and swollen eyes wide with anxiety.

'The bell tower's out of bounds,' the older girl said. 'It's dangerous, condemned. Miles warned us never to go near – '

'Where's the door?' Thackeray said, shaking her arm roughly.

She looked around the church wildly for a moment before pointing towards the west end, which lay in almost total darkness.

'The spire is up there,' she said vaguely.

'Are there no decent lights in this bloody place?' Thackeray said. 'It's impossible to see anything properly.'

'I think there are more,' the girl said, turning back towards the door. 'I think I've seen switches.'

Ignoring her, Thackeray strode across the nave, his footfalls echoing off the worn tiles, towards the west end of the church where, even in the gloom, it was possible to see at close quarters that part of the structure was roped off, enclosing thick stone walls in which a wooden door, displaying a crooked Keep Out notice, stood very slightly ajar.

As he approached, with Laura close behind him, someone found a light switch and filled the whole church with a pale golden glow, hardly strong enough to read a hymn book by but at least adequate to allow them to see where they were going. From within the bell tower there was a crack, as if wood had splintered, and Laura felt a small stab of fear. Thackeray pushed the door open and recoiled slightly as a sharp musty smell hit them in the face.

'Bats,' he said succinctly.

It took a second or two for him to accustom himself to the gloom beyond the door.

'Oh, Christ,' he said for the second time that evening as he recognised the slim form of the Reverend Miles Bateman hanging apparently lifeless, just a few feet in front of him, from one of the bell pulls which dangled from the darkness of the belfry above. The vicar's neck was stretched taut above his black shirt, the white of his clerical collar torn almost off to form an obscene question mark behind a face suffused with blood.

'Laura, help!' he said. 'I'll take his weight. See if you can loosen the rope.'

Feverishly Laura struggled with the heavy coils which Bateman had wrapped around his neck while Thackeray held the limp body clear. It seemed to Laura that it would take hours to pull the rope loose with shaking fingers and breaking nails. Thackeray did not urge her on but she was half aware of his increasingly laboured breathing and half of other sounds, rattling and creaking, in the roof above them.

'What is it?' she asked with growing alarm as the noise grew and became more insistent and a thin mist of tiny particles began to drizzle down on them.

'Keep going,' Thackeray said. 'We have to get him out.'

Laura glanced upwards and wished she hadn't as the rain of dust and grit grew thicker and filled her eyes, half blinding her. To her astonishment she thought she caught a glimpse of indigo sky and a star where no star should be visible.

'We've got to get out,' she said, her fingers slipping off the rope for the tenth time.

'We can't leave him,' Thackeray insisted, ignoring an ominous crack and a rattling clatter from above.

With a grunting heave he lifted Bateman's limp body over his shoulder, freeing one hand to help Laura with the rope.

'It's off,' she said at last as the bell pull fell free under their combined and frantic efforts.

'Now get out of here quickly,' Thackeray said. Between them they manhandled Miles Bateman roughly through the narrow doorway as the cracking sounds above them increased in intensity and the rain of dust became thicker and chunks of stone and masonry began to fall.

'Out!' Thackeray shouted to the two girls and several other bystanders who were waiting for them in the body of the church. 'Get out! The roof in there's coming down. Get out of the church.'

Blindly the little group scuttled from the church door into the porch as an explosive crash behind them confirmed their fears and a cloud of dust and debris pursued them into the chilly air of the churchyard. Even in the dim light from the street the slow, almost elegant collapse of the spire of St Jude's and its supporting bell tower into the body of the church was an awesome sight. But, leaning anxiously over the limp form of Miles Bateman, Laura and Thackeray were hardly aware of the deafening commotion behind them or of the rain of dust and splinters of stone and slate which showered them.

'Is he alive?' Laura asked.

'Yes, I think so,' Thackeray said, his voice hoarse. Very deliberately in the dim light he crouched over Bateman and started mouth to mouth resuscitation and slowly Laura could see that the unconscious vicar was beginning to breathe of his own volition. Surrounded now by crowds of curious onlookers who had been drawn to the scene of the catastrophe by the thunderous noise, Thackeray eventually sat back on his heels and wiped a filthy hand across his forehead.

'Has someone sent for an ambulance?' he asked wearily.

'On its way, guv,' said Sergeant Mower breathlessly, pushing his way through the crowds. 'Are you OK?'

'We're fine,' Laura said, though the hand which was resting lightly on Thackeray's shoulder was trembling.

Thackeray stood up, his face grim under the film of sweat and dirt.

'Take over here, Sergeant,' he said quietly. 'I'll get Laura home and see you back at HQ later. Another thirty seconds and we'd have been under that lot.' He nodded at the pile of rubble which had been the west end of St Jude's.

He drew Laura and the sergeant out of earshot of the onlookers.

'I want a watch on Bateman at the hospital,' he said to Mower. 'He tried to top himself.'

'Right, guv,' Mower said impassively.

Thackeray steered Laura out of the churchyard and slowly up the road to where she had parked her car as the flashing lights of emergency vehicles began to swerve down Whitley Street. She handed him the keys without complaint when he offered to drive and said little as they headed up the hill out of the town to her flat.

'That was a bit close,' she said soberly as he pulled up in the quiet street of Victorian villas where she lived.

'Too close,' he said. 'I'm sorry, Laura. I shouldn't have taken you in there with me. That was my job, not yours. And my fault too. It was unforgivable. You could have been killed.'

'What do you mean, your fault?' she asked, puzzled. 'You were very determined to get him out. I thought he was already dead.'

Thackeray looked bleakly down the quiet street.

'I couldn't leave him there,' he said. 'I'd driven him that far. I needed to know I hadn't killed him.'

Laura sat silently for a moment trying to digest what Thackeray had said.

'You're too hard on yourself, Michael,' she said at last. 'If anything drove Bateman to that bell tower it was his own guilt.'

'Maybe. But that's not what the girl said, is it? He told them he'd slept with Louise, not that he'd stabbed her. I pushed him hard because I thought he was guilty of the murder but perhaps I got it wrong.'

'You're not infallible,' she said. 'You're allowed to get it wrong sometimes.'

'Not that wrong. And not to drag you into danger to satisfy my professional pride – '

'Michael, I wasn't dragged,' Laura said firmly. 'I went with you because I wanted to help. We did help. We saved his life. You couldn't have done that on your own.'

She kissed him on the cheek gently.

'I need a shower, and I need to sleep,' she said. 'Leave my car at the office, stop tormenting yourself and call me tomorrow. Don't forget you did me a favour tonight by landing me with a bloody good story. I'll be Ted Grant's blue-eyed babe again in the morning, you'll see.'

Thackeray watched as she went in through the front door before he let in the clutch and pulled away from the kerb. She could be as irrepressibly cheerful as he could be determinedly morose, he knew, but this time he thought that she was deceiving herself more than him. In the cold light of morning she would realise what an unforgivable risk he had asked her to take.

As he drove carefully down the hill back towards the bright lights of the town in the valley below, some words of a poem drifted into his mind.

'Yet each man kills the thing he loves . . .'

He could not remember the poet but the sentiment suited him well enough. He had, by his own reckoning, done exactly that once and tonight had come perilously close to doing the same thing again.

'God help me,' he muttered to himself as he pulled Laura's car into a parking space in the *Gazette* car park, though the belief the phrase implied had long gone. If he had been too hard on Bateman, he thought, it was because in some respects he envied him his faith.

13

'Come on, girl, get your bloody finger out!'

Grant was breathing heavily at Laura's shoulder as her fingers flew over the keys. It was eight thirty the next morning and she felt deathly tired and distinctly hung-over, although her only night-cap had been a virginal cup of cocoa taken alone before she had washed the dust and debris out of her hair under the shower and fallen distractedly into bed to hug her pillow inconsolably in the absence of the body she craved.

'Do we know how the vicar is?' she asked over her shoulder.

'Still out cold,' Grant said unsympathetically. 'Hospital's saying nowt worth printing, police are saying nowt worth printing, so it's all down to you. "How I saved trapped vicar's life in church disaster." You'll get your offer from the *Globe* yet, if you carry on like this.'

'Trapped is hardly the word,' Laura muttered incautiously. 'And he certainly didn't want his life saved.'

'Aye, well, we'll lay off the suicide attempt for today. Takes the edge off the story, that does,' Grant said. 'Today we want a heroine, and the Reverend can't be ungrateful if he's unconscious, can he? As luck would have it the police are saying nowt about that, either.'

'I'll look a fool if he dies and it comes out we found him hanging from the bell rope,' Laura prevaricated. She often felt unhappy at Ted Grant's somewhat cavalier attitude to the truth but seldom as uneasy as she did now.

'Entangled in the bell ropes. That's all you need to say. And if we need to justify it later, then we were saving everybody's feelings while the Reverend hovered between life and death – or heaven and hell in his case, I suppose. Now come on, Laura. We want this wrapped up before the London lads get up the M1. And if they want interviews with you for tomorrow morning I don't want a single detail that hasn't appeared in the *Gazette* first. Understood?'

'Understood,' Laura said.

'Right. Fred's doing a side bar on how a dangerous structure could come down without warning like that. If it hadn't dropped straight through the roof we could have had a major calamity up there with houses demolished and God knows what instead of just a wrecked church. Pity really. It would've kept us going for months, that would, with inquests and inquiries and compensation rows.'

'Miracle escape for Whitley Street?' Laura asked sarcastically. 'I wouldn't be surprised if someone didn't see a vision, though I shouldn't think the Virgin Mary feels particularly at home there these days.'

She had intended her comments ironically but there was no irony in Ted Grant's soul.

'A miracle,' he muttered, moving quickly back to his own office. 'I wonder if we could stand that up.'

Doggedly she completed her story, signed off and leaned back wearily in her chair. She felt much worse this morning than she had done the previous night when the risk she had run in the doomed church had impinged far more heavily on Thackeray than it had on her. But in the cold grey light of morning, wakened at six thirty by an anxious call from her grandmother who had heard her name mentioned on the early morning local radio news, she felt sick and shaken by delayed shock.

Joyce Ackroyd had been only half convinced, she knew, by her assurances that she had not been in any real danger the previous night. She would be even less reassured when she saw the first edition of the *Gazette*, as she surely would by the middle of the afternoon. Seasoned old political campaigners like her grandmother, who had honed her claws to a steely brightness over many years, never lost the ability to tease out the truth from the sort of kindly evasion and subterfuge Laura had offered her before dawn. She would have to go to see her before the day was out to make her peace with an offering of something more nearly approaching the truth, she decided.

And she was perturbed, as Thackeray had known she would be, by the risk he had undoubtedly taken with both their lives. She had underplayed it in her story, suggesting that there had been a decent interval between their exit from the tower and its collapse. But the memory of how close they had come to death dismayed her more than she would admit.

She sighed as the phone on her desk rang again. It was David Mendelson, the Crown prosecutor who had married Laura's best friend Vicky soon after they had all been at university together. It was at David and Vicky's house she had met a policeman who had become, to the Mendelsons' minds, an unsatisfactory part of her life only because an apparently less than permanent one.

'Are you OK?' David asked without preamble. 'I've had Vicky on the phone from her mother's three times already because she couldn't get through to you yourself. She's down there with the children for a few days. She heard something on the news . . .'

'I'm fine,' Laura said, though evidently without sufficient conviction to completely reassure him.

'Really?'

'Really. Give me Vicky's number and I'll call her.'

He did as he was asked but made no effort to hang up although Laura knew that if anyone led an even more frantic professional life than a senior policeman it was a prosecutor.

'I hear on the grapevine that the vicar was not exactly trapped in that tower by accident,' he said at length

Laura smiled faintly. She knew all about the legal grapevine. 'Not by accident,' she said cautiously. There was silence at the other end.

'Let's hope for Michael's sake he doesn't pop his clogs then,' David said.

Laura drew a sharp breath. 'Why?'

'It doesn't look good to lose your prime suspect like that,' David said. 'Never goes down well, even if he leaves a full confession behind. And I gather this one didn't. Justice isn't seen to be done if the accused gets off the hook that way.'

'That's crap,' Laura said.

'Succinct as ever,' David said, laughing. 'But it's unfortunately true. Don't you remember how cheated people felt when Fred West killed himself in gaol before he could be tried? It won't do Michael's career much good if it comes out he had him in for questioning and then let him go, and it turns out he was guilty all along.'

'That's very unfair,' Laura said hotly.

'Laura, Laura, you never learn. Who said anything about life being fair?'

'I have to go now, David,' Laura lied. 'I'll call Vicky.' She hung up ungraciously, feeling the tears of tiredness and frustration prickle the back of her eyes. I hope the grapevine withers and rots, she muttered into her coffee cup, knowing she was blaming the messenger in exactly the way she hated when the blame for some tragedy she had reported was flung at her.

She glanced at the phone again and shrugged. She had learned by experience that the call she wanted to make would founder in a welter of empty promises by third parties to pass on messages and get back to her very soon. In any case what she really craved, world enough and time with Thackeray to talk, to be silent, to make love, was as likely today as a trip to the moon.

'Come on, girl, don't just sit there. What about a follow-up for tomorrow?' Ted Grant's voice broke in harshly.

'What about One Hundred Easy Ways to Bring the Roof Down?' she suggested irritably.

Ted looked at her with watery eyes filled with dislike.

'One day I'll swing for you, girl,' he said, turning on his heel and slamming his office door behind him, leaving her to wonder whether his singularly inappropriate threat was an accident or not.

*

'We've got the Asian community playing hell about Christian steeples coming down around their ears, we've got the bishop doing his nut about a church he seems to think we demolished on purpose, we've the civil liberties lobby up in arms about innocent motorists being harassed as they go about their lawful occasions in Whitley Street, we've half the whores in the town claiming restraint of trade and now you tell me that the prime suspect who says you drove him to top himself probably wasn't a suspect at all. Can anything else go wrong with this case, I ask myself? Or are we at rock bottom here? Because if we're not, Michael, I think you'd better think seriously about a job in the Outer bloody Hebrides – or Outer bloody Mongolia, if you've any gift for languages. Because as far as the chief constable's concerned we're up to our necks in the sticky stuff.'

Michael Thackeray stood with his back to the window in Superintendent Jack Longley's office, looking far more relaxed than he felt. He knew that Longley's tirade would wear itself out and be followed by a more rational consideration of the difficulties he had himself spent half a sleepless night trying to resolve.

Which was not to underestimate the mess they found themselves in. He had arrived at his office early, to find Sergeant Mower already there fielding a stream of calls which brought uniformly bad news.

'Still unconscious, guv. They're doing tests,' was the verdict he had obtained on the vicar of St Jude's from the Bradfield Infirmary just across the road from the central police station.

"I was surprised when he started breathing again last night,' Thackeray admitted gloomily. 'I thought we'd lost him then.'

'Why bother when they want to go?' Mower asked. 'I went out with a nurse once who reckoned it wasn't worth the trouble.'

The phone had rung again saving Thackeray from even attempting to explain why, in the dust and confusion of the previous night, he had desperately wanted the breath he was forcing into Miles Bateman's sluggish lungs to bring him back from what looked like certain death. It seemed now, though, as if his and Laura's efforts might have been in vain.

'He was out to get you personally, guv,' the sergeant said, gloomily terminating the third call he had taken. 'That was the bishop's secretary. The bishop has had the same letter you've got there on your desk, ranting on about undue pressure, bullying tactics, and his own blameless conduct – apart from the sex, of course – and he reckons that was OK because he wanted to marry the girl. But as she's dead and you've ruined his reputation with your unjustified suspicions, he says he's decided to end it all because he can't see any way he can continue his ministry with young people. I wonder who else he's sent a copy to.'

That question was quickly answered by the internal call from Longley which had summoned Thackeray peremptorily his office. Both the superintendent and the chief constable had apparently also been vouchsafed a copy of Bateman's ubiquitous, and as it had turned out premature, farewell to the world.

Longley sat at his desk, his fury eventually dissipated, waiting for some reaction from the younger man. At the back of his mind were the niggling doubts he had had about Thackeray when he had arrived in Bradfield. As far as Longley had been concerned, Thackeray's ten-year-old reputation for thoroughness had barely been tarnished by those fading reports of a younger, more ambitious sergeant, a high-flyer of whom great things had been expected, who had come within a whisker of self-destruction.

Had that long-buried, almost forgotten younger Thackeray come back to haunt him, after more than a year in which he had been more than satisfied that he had made a good choice in his DCI, Longley wondered. He now hoped, with a real concern for the man he had grown to trust as well as for his own position, that his confidence had not, as the chief constable had angrily suggested that morning, been seriously misplaced.

'I don't think I was any harder on Bateman than I would have been with any other person I was interviewing about a brutal murder, sir,' Thackeray said quietly at length. 'He'd lied about his movements that night. He'd lied about his relationship to the girl. I needed those issues cleared up.'

'You went by the book?'

'I went by the book.' Thackeray carefully controlled his fury that the question should even be asked.

'No threats while the tape recorder was turned off? You didn't let your dislike of churchmen get to you? You're sure?' Longley persisted, knowing enough of Thackeray's past to understand that hypocrisy of the sort Bateman had been guilty of would earn Thackeray's bitter contempt. 'Prejudice comes in all shapes and sizes.'

'I treated him fairly, sir,' Thackeray insisted, still apparently without heat. 'Every word I said to him is recorded. You can listen to the tapes.'

'I need to tell the chief that I'm happy with the way you interviewed him,' Longley said unapologetically. He had every intention of listening to the tapes.

'Sir,' Thackeray said, only the tension around his jaw giving any indication of his feelings.

'There's just one good thing in all this mess,' Longley conceded. 'The bastard doesn't seem to have sent any of his whinging letters to the press. We've not had any inquiries from that quarter yet.'

Thackeray smiled faintly. His, in Longley's view, much too close relationship with one representative of the press was a constant source of potential friction between them.

'It'll only be a matter of time before it leaks,' he predicted. 'And no, of course I won't tell Laura Ackroyd about the letters. I'm not that eager to become the subject of one of Ted Grant's excoriating leaders on police incompetence or worse, thanks.'

'Any road, you think you were wrong now? You've gone off the Reverend Bateman as your prime suspect? So what changed?'

'Two things,' Thackeray said. 'Firstly his letter. It's full of a lot of breast-beating about how he took advantage of the girl, and how he was no longer fit to be the spiritual leader of his congregation, all that nonsense. But he doesn't confess to the murder. And according to the girls who were at the prayer meeting, he didn't confess to killing Louise then either.'

'Half a confession's no good, you're saying?' Longley said, interested in spite of his other anxieties.

'Half a confession, I think, fits if he'd every intention of hanging himself within the hour and accusing me of hounding an innocent man,' Thackeray said. 'But that would be a pretty futile gesture if he thought I would prove he did it quite quickly anyway after he was dead. But it's not just that. We were on our way to Number 17 last night when I decided to go to the church instead. Mower saw Roz Jenkins briefly, and the girl she's taken

138

in as a new lodger, Cassy Davis. Cassy said she was in Whitley Street that night after the other prostitutes had been arrested and the street had been virtually cleared. She's on the game herself, Mower thinks. Says he's seen her before. Be that as it may, she says she saw a man going into Number 17 at about nine thirty. That's after Bateman says he left and long after Sherry Maguire saw him arrive.'

'Could she describe him?' Langley asked.

'Tall, she thought. In a short jacket. Definitely not Miles Bateman anyway.'

'You're saying that Louise had more than one visitor that night?' Longley asked.

'I'm not saying anything yet. But it's a new line of inquiry which is worth following up.'

'Aye, well, you'd best get following, lad, if you know what's good for you. Just now your name's mud at County so you'd best start looking for a quick result. Keep me posted, right?'

'Sir,' Thackeray said.

He took the stairs back into his office slowly, giving himself time to think before he faced the curious gaze of his detectives in the CID room and even more particularly the sharp eyes of Kevin Mower. He had, he knew, the reputation around the nick of being a cold bastard, and that the incident with Bateman, however unjustified the vicar's complaints, would reinforce that view. He allowed himself a grim smile as he opened his office door. He had learned the hardest possible way to hide his feelings, he thought, and he now seemed to have succeeded beyond his wildest expectations. There was irony in that, but a sort of safety too.

Mower glanced up from his desk as the DCI came in looking more unruffled by his unexpected interview with the superintendent than the sergeant thought he had any right to be.

'Do you want the good news or the bad, guv?' he asked, with what passed with him for a sympathetic smile.

'Don't mess me about, Sergeant,' Thackeray snapped.

Mower shrugged almost imperceptibly.

'Laura rang,' he said. 'Said to tell you that you feature on the front page of the *Gazette* as last night's hero.'

'That's the good news?' Thackeray asked heavily.

'The other's worse,' Mower warned. 'The hospital says that Miles Bateman is on a life support machine. They don't hold out much hope.'

'Well, if it gets out that I'm supposed to have bullied him to an early grave I'll metamorphose from hero to villain within the day, won't I?' Thackeray said dismissively.

'Looks like it, guv.'

'Well, you can never believe what you read in the papers, they say. So let's forget last night, shall we? What I want this morning is to see Cassy Davis. It seems to me she's been a bit slow coming forward, so let's find out why, shall we? Would you like to ask her to come down for a chat? Nicely?'

Mower had no sooner left than Thackeray's phone rang and the desk sergeant a floor below reported that a Mohammed Ahmed was demanding to see him. Reluctantly Thackeray concluded that he dare not risk adding racism to the list of sins HQ seemed to be marking up against his name, and took the stairs to the front office two at a time to dissipate his irritation.

Ahmed was standing stiffly by the counter, with an overcoat over his white *shalwar kameez* and a scarf muffled around his neck although to Thackeray the day seemed warm. In his hands he clutched a Tesco carrier bag tightly. When he spoke it was apparent he had a heavy cold.

'What can I do for you?' Thackeray asked ungraciously.

'Knives,' Ahmed said hoarsely. 'The night of the murder in the churchyard, your officers were asking most searchingly about knives.'

'The murder was committed with a knife. We've not been able to find the weapon yet. I've no doubt my officers will continue to ask about knives until we do.' Thackeray tried hard to keep his impatience in check. He was startled when Ahmed turned round, tipped up his carrier bag and spilled half a dozen assorted knives and daggers across the wooden counter behind them.

'I have told my people many times that when they come out on Whitley Street they are not to bring any weapons. I think they obey me. But last night I asked them all to bring me any knives they keep at home. These are they.'

'I'm grateful, Mr Ahmed,' Thackeray said shortly. 'I'll be even more grateful if you can tell me exactly who gave you each one of these.' He signalled to the desk sergeant who was staring at the arsenal on his desk with appalled fascination. 'Evidence bags, George,' Thackeray said. 'And labels.'

'You have officers who believe that every young Asian man carries a weapon,' Ahmed said heavily. 'You have officers who, when they have been questioning young Asian men, make it clear that they think they must be guilty of this crime. And perhaps of the murder of the young woman as well.'

'If you take angry people on to the street you run the risk that the anger will turn to violence,' Thackeray said.

'I know that, sir,' Ahmed said quickly. 'Which is why I have brought you the knives. I can give you the names of each of the owners, but not yet.' He held up a hand imperiously as Thackeray opened his mouth to object. 'I trust you, Mr Thackeray, but I have to say that I am almost alone in that. If you do your forensics and find that one of these weapons is your murderer's then I will tell you. Only then.'

'You are very close to impeding my inquiry, Mr Ahmed,' Thackeray said angrily.

'Close,' Ahmed agreed. 'But not impeding, I think. I wish you well in your inquiry, chief inspector. But I hope sincerely you will not find the evidence you seek here.'

Folding the Tesco bag carefully and putting it into his coat pocket, Mohammed Ahmed turned on his heel and left.

14

In the event, Cassy Davis got to Kevin Mower before Kevin Mower got to her. She arrived at the central police station just before lunchtime, dressed in jeans and a baggy sweatshirt, her eyes puffy and red with tears, her face still streaked with blue and yellow bruises, accompanied by Roz Jenkins who was exuding righteous indignation.

'We want to see the person in charge,' Roz said to the desk sergeant, a fatherly-looking man who surveyed her abundant figure and assertive features with disinterest.

'Oh, yes, miss,' he said, oblivious of the offence he caused his listener by so simple a greeting. 'And what would that be about, then?'

Cassy gave a convulsive shudder and burst into tears while Roz looked around the reception area, where a couple of depressed looking women sat on plastic chairs.

'We want to make a complaint,' she said emphatically. 'But in private, if you don't mind.'

'A complaint about what, miss?' the sergeant asked without enthusiasm.

'About one of your bloody officers,' Roz said loudly, raising a flicker of interest in the two women behind her and galvanising the startled sergeant at last to attention.

The exact nature of Cassy's complaint sent Michael Thackeray hurrying down the stairs again to the soft interview room driven by a cold and so far undirected fury. He found Cassy sitting red-eyed and shuddering between Roz, who was holding her hand, and Detective Constable Val Ridley who looked as grim-faced as he felt himself.

'A word, Val,' Thackeray said, nodding her out into the corridor.

'Exactly what's she alleging?' he asked.

'Just about everything short of rape,' Val Ridley said flatly.

'Dear God, he can't have been with her more than ten minutes.'

DC Ridley smiled a crooked smile.

'Ten seconds is long enough for some, sir. They don't bother with foreplay if they're that eager.'

'Is that a generalisation or a comment on Mower's performance in particular?' Thackeray asked.

Val flushed faintly. 'Just a generalisation,' she said.

'Right. I want the other woman out of there. Take her down to the canteen and get a WPC to give her a cup of tea. And I want this girl's record. Mower said this morning he thought she was on the game. Check it out for me. Then we'll listen to what she has to say.'

Val Ridley made as if to speak again but evidently thought better of it. Thackeray pounced just the same.

'Let's get one thing straight, Val, before we start, shall we? Whatever Cassy Davis is, I personally will take her complaint just as seriously as if we had the Virgin Mary in that interview room. Understood? And if it stands up I'll personally see Kevin Mower gets the book thrown at him. If she's lying I'll throw the book at her.'

'Nobody threw the book at John Franks,' Val said mutinously.

'That complaint was withdrawn,' Thackeray said shortly. 'Perhaps it shouldn't have been but it was, and that was the end of it.'

While Val Ridley set about the tasks he had set her he went to the control room and asked them to contact DS Mower.

'Come in, Kevin,' he said shortly, aware of the operators' intense curiosity. 'We've got some problems here.'

He walked very slowly back to the interview room, as reluctant as he had ever been to talk to a complainant. Few at the station were unaware of Kevin Mower's reputation as a womaniser. It had passed from canteen gossip into folklore as he had worked his way around every attractive female colleague who would give him the time of day.

It was not a trait which Thackeray found particularly attractive. He was too much of a puritan for that. But he had until now regarded Mower's rake's progress with little more than amused concern, the occasional alarm bell ringing only when his amorous interest brushed too close to a witness or a suspect for comfort. His impression had always been that when the going got dangerous Mower had a way of drawing back from the brink of disaster, always more concerned for his career prospects than sex when it came to the crunch. Could he really have got his sergeant so wrong? Thackeray wondered. If he had, it said little for his judgement of character and the inevitable recriminations from above would touch him as well as the libidinous Mower.

Cassy Davis was sitting where he had left her, twisting a paper tissue in her hands until it began to shred and fall to the floor. A uniformed WPC sat beside her. The room was stuffy and the tension in the faces of both the young women palpable. Thackeray took off his jacket and loosened his tie, before taking a low chair immediately opposite Cassy. She looked frail and waif-like, her blonde hair straggly and unkempt, her pale eyes disappearing into dark sockets.

'How old are you, Cassy?' Thackeray asked.

'Seventeen,' the girl said sharply and Thackeray knew that she was well aware of the implication of his first question. He guessed that nothing he could say would persuade her to admit to being under age. They would have to find out some other way. Val Ridley came into the room behind him and handed him a brief computer print-out. Cassy Davis had no convictions, but police intelligence had her listed as a known prostitute and heroin addict. There was no indication of a date of birth.

'Right,' Thackeray said. 'I'm going to ask these two women officers to take you through what happened when Sergeant Mower came to Roz Jenkins' house yesterday evening. Take your time. There's no hurry. When you've been over it with them, they'll help you write a statement which you must sign. Do you understand?'

The girl nodded and with her head low, and her voice faltering, told her story.

She had answered the door to Mower, she said, because Roz was taking a shower. He had said he would wait for Roz so she invited him into the kitchen and offered him coffee, which he accepted. While they were waiting he had asked her if she had been in Whitley Street the night Louise was killed and she had said that she had been, from about nine o'clock, when the street had been deserted, except for a tall, well-built man she had seen going into one of the houses. She had thought later that it had been Number 17, but she was nervous of the police and had not found the courage to contact them. She had not seen the man, or anyone else, come out of the house, and by ten o'clock had been away with a punter and had not gone back.

Kevin Mower had said she shouldn't be nervous of the police and at that point he had put his arm round her and told her that a lot of coppers had good relations with the girls on the street. Cassy stopped at that point and gave Val Ridley a despairing look.

'Did you encourage him, when he made that suggestion?' she asked.

'No, I didn't. I didn't want owt to do with him,' the girl said fiercely.

'And you told him that?'

'Yes, I moved away from him and told him to leave me alone.'

'But he didn't?'

'He said that wasn't very friendly, and he could do a lot for me, keep me out of trouble and that.'

144

'And then?'

'Then he came on strong, started kissing me, got his hands under my T-shirt. I wasn't wearing a bra, so he made the most of that.'

'What else were you wearing?'

'Jeans, these jeans.' She stroked a hand over the denim nervously.

'He didn't undo your jeans?'

'He was fumbling about but he didn't get the chance to unzip owt. Roz came in and found him at it, and he backed off then and said sorry.'

'But you think he would have forced you to have intercourse if you hadn't been interrupted?' Val Ridley persisted.

'Of course he bloody would. He was out of control, wasn't he? It's not as if I don't see it often enough.'

'What you're alleging, Cassy, is that a police officer is guilty of a serious sexual assault,' DC Ridley said carefully. 'Are you absolutely sure about what you've just told me?'

'Of course I am,' the girl said. 'I wouldn't be here else, would I?' She was shaking now and tiny beads of sweat glistened on her forehead.

'And you gave him no encouragement? You didn't want him to touch you?'

'No, I bloody didn't,' the girl said emphatically.

'And Roz Jenkins will back you up?'

'Well, I know you're not going to believe me, don't I? Roz came in and saw him at it. Then there was this bloody great crash outside, and we all went out to see what had happened, then your bloody mate ran off down the street to the church.'

Val Ridley glanced at Thackeray who had sat listening impassively to the girl's testimony.

'Take statements from Miss Davis and Miss Jenkins,' he said, getting up slowly from his seat. 'I'm going to see Mr Longley.'

Sergeant Kevin Mower went up the stairs to Superintendent Jack Longley's office with a sense of deep foreboding. Too many of his colleagues had been avoiding his eye since he got back to the office for him to have any illusions that his summons upstairs meant anything less than big trouble.

He found Longley at his desk with a look in his eyes that confirmed his worst fears while Thackeray, standing rigidly by the office window, gave absolutely no acknowledgement of the sergeant's arrival at all.

Longley's colour was high, but he spoke quietly, all emotion strictly under control, his normally jovial features a rigid mask.

'Sergeant, I have to caution you that you have the right to remain silent . . .'

The colour drained from Mower's face as he listened to Longley and his eyes widened in horror. He flashed a desperate look of appeal at Thackeray but got absolutely no response. At the second attempt, he managed to get out a single word hoarsely.

'Why?' Adding almost as an afterthought an even more indistinct and desperate, 'Sir?'

'I've had a complaint about your behaviour at 17 Whitley Street yesterday evening,' Longley said. 'Do you have anything you want to say about what happened between you and Cassy Davis?'

Mower swallowed hard.

'Cassy Davis? Nothing happened between me and Cassy Davis, sir. I asked her some questions, that's all. I reported everything to Mr Thackeray. What does she say happened, for God's sake?'

'She claims you subjected her to a serious sexual assault and would have gone further if you'd had the chance. And Roz Jenkins confirms that she came into the room and found you at it.'

Longley's brutal accusation seemed to hit Mower like a blow and he said nothing as he tried to regain control of his breathing.

'No way, sir,' he said at length. 'I never laid a finger on her. I don't need to go touching up pathetic wrecks like Cassy Davis for kicks. Chances are she's HIV positive, for God's sake. If that's what she's saying, she's lying. And if her friend's backing her up, she's lying too.'

'So you deny the allegation completely?' Longley asked.

'Deny it, sir? It's fucking laughable,' Mower came back, angry now.

'I have enough evidence to charge you with indecent assault,' Longley said flatly.

'On the word of that scheming little tom?' Mower objected forcefully.

'She's just as entitled to the protection of the law as any other woman,' Thackeray broke in suddenly, with scathing contempt. 'But when push comes to shove, you don't really believe that any more than John Franks does, do you, Kevin? And if you don't believe it, then there's nothing much to stop you getting your hands up any bit of skirt you think should be on free offer, is there? One of the perks of the job?'

If Mower had appeared shocked at Longley's initial accusation, Thackeray's attack knocked the confidence out of him completely.

'I thought you knew me better than that, guv,' he said very quietly. Thackeray turned away to look out of the window at the rain-lashed square below, without replying.

'Do you intend to charge me, sir?' Mower asked Longley, without much hope.

'For the moment I intend to suspend you from duty, pending further inquiries,' Longley said. 'I'll let you know when I want to talk to you again and take a formal statement. I'll take your warrant card now.'

'Sir,' Mower said. He reached inside his Italian jacket and handed the card to Longley, although his eyes were still on Thackeray, desperately seeking some reassurance from that quarter though all that was visible of the chief inspector's face was his clenched jaw. Mower's shoulders slumped as he turned to go.

When the door had closed behind him, Thackeray threw himself into a chair and ran a hand wearily though his dark hair.

'So what do you think?' Longley asked irritably.

'I think one of them should be working for the Royal Shakespeare Company but I'm damned if I know which one,' Thackeray said. 'They're neither of them innocent, in any true sense of the word, and one of them is lying their socks off.'

'Tell me about the girl,' Longley said.

'She's very young, though I'm not sure how young, she's on the game, she's a junkie – in urgent need of a fix most of the time, by the look of her – and as unstable as hell. But if the Jenkins woman backs her story . . .' Thackeray shrugged with unusual uncertainty.

'In court it would be a tart's word against a copper's,' Longley said.

'These days juries are more likely to believe a prostitute,' Thackeray said. 'And she's got some corroboration, which is unusual. The CPS will go for it and he'll go down.'

'But you don't believe he did it, do you?'

'I don't want to believe it, which isn't the same thing,' Thackeray said heavily.

'So why would the girl lie?'

'Apart from sheer bloody vindictiveness, I haven't the faintest idea,' Thackeray said. 'But if you give me some time, I'll try to find out.'

Laura Ackroyd pushed the sugar across the table to Roz Jenkins who stirred three heaped spoonfuls into her cappuccino.

'You won't let on who told you about this?' Roz asked cautiously, her face a curious mixture of circumspection and glee, her eyes shining with excitement.

'Of course not,' Laura said. Roz had turned up at the *Gazette* just as she was finishing work for the day, offering 'a good story', and Laura had led the way to a coffee bar across the road from the newspaper building, aware that the flushed, sweating figure in reception was labouring under strong emotion. It was only when she had consumed an enormous slice of coffee and walnut cake that Roz began to talk.

'One of the policemen in the murder investigation has been done for sexual assault. He came to my house to talk to me, and got involved with another of the witnesses,' Roz said, the words tumbling out breathlessly. Laura looked at her in astonishment and then took a sharp breath as the full humiliation of the evening she had been arrested came back to her.

'You mean he tried it on again?' she asked.

'Again?' Roz said, surprised. 'You mean the bastard's done it before?'

'Oh, yes,' Laura said. 'From what I hear he makes quite a habit of it. I can personally vouch for that.'

'I thought the *Gazette* should know,' Roz said. 'After I took Cassy home, I rang the police station again and they said he'd been suspended but not charged. It sounds to me as if they're going to try to cover the whole thing up, and they might get away with it because she's not exactly a virgin is she . . .'

'Cassy Davis? The young girl I met at the Aids centre? Are we talking about the same girl? You said she was staying with you?'

'Yes, that'll be Cassy, if that's where you met her. I took her in to get her away from the bastard who's been beating her up – not something the police are interested in, of course. Miles Bateman brought her round yesterday morning because he knew I had a spare room. There's a little box room at the back with a spare bed in it. I've given her that.'

'She stayed at my place for a night but she'd gone when I got up the next morning. I was worried sick about her.' Laura hesitated, recalling her own desperate anxiety about the frail girl she had sheltered. 'She only looks about fifteen.'

'She *is* only about fifteen,' Roz said angrily.

'So she's under the age of consent?'

'I suppose so. Not that it makes much difference to the way she earns her living,' Roz said.

'You disapprove?' Laura asked.

'Of course I bloody disapprove of kids of that age prostituting themselves,' Roz said indignantly. 'Not that she's had much choice, from what she says. Even so, she's still got the right to say no, and he wasn't having any of it when I walked in on them, with his hands up her T-shirt and his fancy pants undone.'

'If she's so young the police can't ignore what happened this time,' Laura said slowly.

Roz drained her coffee and wiped her lips with the back of her hand.

'That's what I thought,' she said, with a slightly complacent smile. 'But they've not charged him yet. Will you do something about it?' she asked urgently. 'In the paper, I mean?'

'Yes, I should think so,' Laura said. 'If he's not been charged in the morning we can certainly chase it up. It's outrageous if he's going to get away with it again. The man's a menace.'

'Most men are,' Roz said with deliberate venom as she got up to go.

Laura paid the bill and sat for a moment, wondering whether she could have done more to help the fragile, terrified waif she had impulsively taken in that night. Roz Jenkins evidently had no inhibitions on that score. She seemed to collect hard cases like

149

some people collect stray cats, with no hesitation and boundless enthusiasm. And if that was what it took to get John Franks his just deserts, good luck to her, Laura concluded.

She was about to leave the café when a tall man in his mid-thirties with short, cropped hair, a broad square-jawed, not unattractive face and calculating grey eyes hesitated for a moment at her table.

'Are you Laura?' he asked. 'Laura Ackroyd? They told me at the *Gazette* I might find you here.'

Laura continued to pull her coat on as she eyed the newcomer in a crumpled suit and green Barbour without much enthusiasm.

'And you are?' she asked.

'Bill Brady of the *Globe*.' The stranger took off his jacket and hung it over the back of a chair before sinking into the seat opposite Laura with all the confidence of an old acquaintance. 'Vince Newsom told me to contact you when I got up here. He thought you'd be able to give me a few leads. Vince said he knew you pretty well and was sure you'd be happy to help a mate of his.'

Vince Newsom had never been short on presumption, Laura thought angrily as she studied this unwelcome messenger from the past and increasingly disliked what she saw. Vince had clearly not changed much since she had thrown him out either.

'Vince and I split up more than two years ago,' she said, standing up. 'And I don't think we parted friends.'

'Oh, I think he still thinks a lot of you,' Brady said easily, 'though he's a bit preoccupied with some little black tart who claims she's a model at the moment.'

'I'm very happy for him,' Laura said sourly, sitting back down again on the very edge of her chair.

'Oh, come on, Laura. A more mature man's your style, surely. Let me get you another drink, will you, and you can think about the best place to let me buy you dinner later,' Brady offered, with a self-satisfied smile which clearly did not anticipate rejection.

'I don't think so,' Laura said, wondering whether Vince had suggested that she might be open to offers or that she was already involved with a more mature man. With Vince, either or both was quite possible.

'Well, skip dinner,' Brady said, evidently unconcerned at his rebuff. 'There'll be something in it for you anyway if you fill me in on this vicar in a coma story. The *Globe*'s nothing if not generous where good information's concerned.'

'Everything I know about that I wrote in the *Gazette*,' Laura said firmly, buttoning up her coat and getting to her feet again. 'And anything else I find out I'll also be writing in the *Gazette*. That's what they pay me for.'

'Oh, come on, Laura,' Brady interjected. 'You didn't even mention in your piece this afternoon that he'd tried to hang himself. The boyfriend asked you to ease up on that, did he?'

Laura sat down again abruptly, shaken both by the confirmation that Brady knew far too much about her private life and by the implication that she might have let Thackeray influence her work.

'My editor, actually,' she said coldly. 'It'll all come out at the inquest anyway.'

'Bateman's dead?' Brady asked excitedly.

'No,' Laura snapped. 'Not as far as I know. But it looks unlikely he'll survive.'

'Well, it'll come out in my story tomorrow morning, sweety, I promise you,' Brady said. 'And in half a dozen others, I dare say. It didn't take me long to find out it was a suicide bid.'

Brady signalled to a waitress and pulled out a small tape recorder.

'So come on, Laura. Tell me about the vicar and this girl they think he murdered. We got this weird letter from Bateman claiming he'd been harassed by the cops. I was going to come up to have a sniff at that but the news-desk were a bit iffy. On the whole they don't like knocking the boys in blue. We're big on lawran' order this month.'

'Something's sacred, is it?' Laura asked.

'Yeah, well, vicars are fair game, but on the whole coppers who speed justice along with an informal thump or two get an understanding blind eye turned. Within reason, of course. If your very close friend actually strung him up himself even my boss might raise an eyebrow, you know?'

Brady patted Laura's hand and she was surprised at the revulsion the action sparked, but he did not give her time to order her outrage into any coherent complaint before he went on.

151

'The reason they let me come up was what happened next. We got an even weirder fax of some pictures of Louise Brownlow. A bit blurred in transmission but if they show what we think they show and we can find the originals she wasn't just having it off with the vicar. She was well into much more interesting fun and games. And maybe the vicar was, too, which would explain why he was so keen to make a sharp exit. And that's something else no one's been letting on about, isn't it? As far as the public's concerned, Louise Brownlow is little Miss Innocent Student. The pics got the desk really horny and I was on the M1 by lunchtime. Not just a bonking vicar but a kinky bonking vicar! So come on. What's it all about? What are the police up to? Have we really got the mother of all vicar and tart stories here, or is someone having us on?'

'Sod off, Brady,' Laura said, as she finally got to her feet and turned away in disgust, aware as she swept out, cheeks flaming, that Bill Brady had collapsed into helpless laughter as he began to punch numbers into his mobile phone.

Vicky Mendelson opened her front door to Chief Inspector Thackeray with a bawling baby on one arm and a tea-towel in her other hand. A strong smell of burning wafted out of the house behind her and her expression was as harassed as Thackeray had ever seen it.

'Oh, Michael, I'm sorry, come in,' she said, brushing her daughter's silky copper hair distractedly away from an obviously feverish face with the tea-towel.

'If it's not a good moment . . .' Thackeray said hesitantly. 'I wanted to see David briefly . . .'

'He's bathing the boys upstairs. He'll be down in a couple of minutes,' Vicky said, obviously becoming more agitated as the burning smell grew stronger. 'Here, hold the baby for a minute while I see to the supper.' She thrust the still sobbing child into Thackeray's arms and disappeared into the smoky kitchen, her soft brown hair adrift, flapping the tea-towel in front of her to clear the air.

Thackeray kicked the front door closed with a faint shrug and with mixed emotions turned his attention to the writhing bundle which had been thrust into his arms. Naomi Laura, eleven months old, chubby, red-faced and furious, gazed at him with wide unblinking brown eyes for no more than a second before resuming her raucous complaint. To add to the cacophony the fire alarm on the wall at the foot of the stairs chose that moment to begin an ear-piercing shrieking which redoubled Naomi's howls and brought David Mendelson to the top of the stairs in obvious consternation.

'Is Vicky coping or are we really ablaze?' he asked with a grin when he saw Thackeray.

'I think she's coping,' Thackeray said.

'I'll be down in a minute, Michael, if you can hold the fort with Naomi.' With that he disappeared again in the direction of the bathroom from which shrieks of childish laughter could be heard.

Thackeray hoisted the screaming baby on to his shoulder, with her wet and unnaturally hot cheek against his own, and carried her into the sitting-room where both noise and smoke were less fierce. With a half-remembered action, he stroked her back rhythmically as he walked the sobbing child up and down the room until eventually her screams diminished to sobs and the sobs to moans and at last even her residual shuddering ceased. Very gently he glanced at her to confirm that she was indeed asleep before he sank carefully on to a sofa and relaxed just enough not to disturb her. Only then did he find time to address the turmoil into which holding Naomi's small, warm and slightly damp body had thrown him.

Vicky came bustling back into the room full of apologies.

'She's teething and I took my eyes off the supper to pick her up and let the blasted potatoes boil dry,' she said. 'Let me get you a drink. Fruit juice? Mineral water? What would you like?' She ran a hand through her hair and fell suddenly silent, aware of her guest's unnatural stillness. 'You got her to sleep,' she said softly. 'You haven't forgotten how?'

'It's not something I imagine you ever forget,' Thackeray said. Of his few friends in Bradfield, Vicky and David Mendelson were the ones he had learned to trust most and the ones in whom he had confided a little, though by no means all, about his family. Vicky sat down beside him and gently took her daughter from him, oblivious to the pang of loss even that natural action caused him.

153

'You know Laura wants children, don't you?' she said. 'She's much more career-oriented than I ever was, but she does want children. I've seen it in her eyes.'

'I know,' Thackeray said dully, looking away.

'I'm sorry. I shouldn't interfere,' Vicky said. 'But she's my best friend . . .'

'I know,' Thackeray said again. He wanted to scream and shout at the unfairness of life, though years of iron self-discipline had made such a reaction impossible even were it thinkable in response to Vicky's concern. Vicky gazed at him across her daughter's red curls, which threatened to rival Laura's own, and saw from Thackeray's closed and impassive face that she had already gone as far as she dared. With some relief she heard footfalls on the stairs.

'Here's David,' she said, unnecessarily.

Her husband came into the room, hot and flushed from his bath-time games, but a look of serious interrogation in his eyes. Embarrassed, Vicky left the room with her sleeping daughter without another word.

'A quick word? I have to get back,' Thackeray said. 'Off the record?

David nodded and waved him into his small study across the hall.

'It's Kevin Mower,' Thackeray said. 'He's got himself into a mess I can't see any way out of.'

15

Thackeray found DC Val Ridley waiting outside his office the next morning with an expression on her face which he could not read.

'Have you seen the *Globe*, sir?' she asked.

'It's not my first choice over breakfast,' Thackeray said. 'Puts me off my cornflakes. What's in it?'

Val pulled the paper from the bundle of files under her arm and handed it to him. The headline said it all. 'Suicide vicar link to butchered student.'

'Shit,' Thackeray said with unusual venom. He waved Ridley into his office and spread the paper on his desk to read the tabloid's story more easily.

'How the hell did they get hold of that?' he asked, even more furiously, as he absorbed the carefully worded paragraph which juxtaposed the theory that Miles Bateman's suicide attempt might have been caused by police harassment of a bereaved man with the fact that DCI Michael Thackeray was in charge of the investigation into Bateman's girlfriend's death.

Later that morning the press caused him even more serious concern. He looked at the three paragraphs on the front page of the *Gazette*'s first edition with disbelief and the by-line with embarrassment. He picked up the phone and punched in Longley's internal number only to be told by his secretary that the superintendent had gone to County HQ for a management conference. That would put him in a bad mood for the rest of the week, Thackeray thought bitterly, particularly as he would be right on hand to take any flak coming from the chief constable's office about the *Globe*'s front page lead. This was a day, Thackeray thought, when any conscientious policeman might be entitled to ask himself if newspapers served any useful purpose in the fight against crime.

'Would you give Mr Longley a message? Tell him that I haven't spoken to Miss Ackroyd since the day before yesterday?' he asked the superintendent's secretary, with only the faintest twinge of conscience.

His back covered upstairs, he called the *Gazette* and was put straight through to Laura.

'You're very well informed,' he said without preamble. 'But not quite as well informed as you think you are.'

'Michael, you can't cover these things up,' she said, less than surprised at the call or the chilly tone of voice at the other end. She had known that the police would not be pleased to find that Cassy's accusation had leaked out so promptly. 'That bastard's had it coming to him. You told me he'd been warned off. I shouldn't have let you fob me off so easily the first time when he got his wandering hands on me.'

'You really don't know, do you?' Thackeray said almost sympathetically. 'I know you won't tell me who leaked the story, though I can guess, but I have to suppose that you made some

155

effort to check it for accuracy. Who did you talk to at County HQ?'

If Laura was irritated by his sarcasm she did not allow her feelings to reach him.

'I spoke to the press office. They didn't deny it.'

'But they didn't tell you who the officer was?' Thackeray asked with increasing asperity.

'I put Franks' name to them, but they wouldn't confirm it. They said there'd be a statement if he was charged. Obviously, I couldn't use the name without confirmation.'

'You'd have cost the *Gazette* an arm and a leg in libel damages if you had,' Thackeray said.

There was silence at the other end and less confidence in Laura's tone when she replied.

'What do you mean?'

'I mean the man who's been suspended is not John Franks.'

He felt almost sorry for her now as the silence at the other end lengthened.

'Then who?' she asked finally.

'You know I'm not going to tell you that, Laura,' he said. 'Not on the record, off the record, or any other way.'

Laura gazed at her own dim reflection in her blank computer screen, pulled a face at herself, and wondered how she could have jumped to so seriously erroneous a conclusion. She knew as well as Thackeray did that her job would have been on the line if she had used Franks' name. She dredged through her memory of her conversation with the ravenous Roz Jenkins the previous evening and an appalling thought struck her.

'I'm not going to like this, am I?' she asked. 'Is it someone I know a lot better than John Franks?'

'No comment,' Thackeray said, and there was no doubt in her mind that he meant exactly what he said.

'Michael, tell me it's not Kevin Mower,' Laura said feeling faintly sick. 'Please?'

'I can't, Laura.'

'So it is him,' she whispered, shaken. 'I don't believe it. He couldn't. He wouldn't. You can't think that.'

'Laura, these are serious allegations. They're being investigated. What I believe isn't the least bit relevant.'

'You can help him, surely?' she said angrily.

156

'No,' Thackeray said. 'I don't think I can. And David Mendelson doesn't think I can either.'

Laura worked through the afternoon in a daze of unhappiness and unfocused anger and drove home hardly aware of the rush-hour traffic through which she mechanically manoeuvred her Beetle, eye and hand responding to the outside world but her mind elsewhere. She parked under the trees outside her house and sat for a moment, gazing unseeingly at the cherry blossom which was just beginning to turn the avenue an unsuitably romantic pale pink.

She had told no one in the office about the unjustified assumption she had made when she had written her story early that morning. What Ted Grant would never know he could never grieve over, she thought, but she was bitterly aware that she had come as close as she had ever done professionally to making a very expensive mistake. She had let emotion cloud her judgement and she found it difficult to even begin to forgive herself.

Nor had she told anyone about a phone call which had broken the tedium of a quiet afternoon. Caroline Everett had not bothered to identify herself. She had assumed, rightly, that her voice was familiar enough to Laura after years of after-hours giggles and confidences in the dormitory to need no introduction.

'I had a call from my sister,' she said. 'She wants to meet you. Are you interested?'

'Of course,' Laura said. 'But the police will be even more interested.'

'She wants nothing to do with them, not at the moment anyway,' Caroline said. 'I think she wants you to be a sort of go-between. She's very scared, though I think she knows they'll catch up with her in the end. Will you meet her?'

'Yes, of course,' Laura said, stifling a thousand misgivings.

'I'll call you to tell you where and when,' Caroline said. 'Give me your home number so I don't have to ring you at the office again. I'll get back to you.'

Laura had hung up still unsure whether she had committed herself to a good story or to a criminal act, though she had little doubt where Michael Thackeray's judgement would fall.

She was startled out of her self-absorption by a tap on the car

157

window at her shoulder. Kevin Mower stood on the pavement, dressed in jeans and black designer shirt, though unshaven and uncharacteristically unkempt. She picked up her bag and opened the door.

'Can we talk?' he said hesitantly, as if expecting a rebuff.

Laura shrugged.

'I don't know what good it will do,' she said. 'Michael's already furious with me for writing about the case this morning.'

'Please, Laura,' Mower said. 'My job's on the line here.'

He doesn't know how close I came to tipping mine right over the edge, she thought.

'You'd better come in,' she said, leading the way to the front door and putting her key in the lock.

He followed her silently up the three flights of stairs to her attic flat and slumped heavily on to the sofa when she waved him into the living room. The self-confidence seemed to have drained out of him, she thought, and with it had gone the boyish charm. He looked tired, haggard and years older than she had ever seen him look before.

'At least you trust me enough to invite me in,' he said bitterly. 'I thought after what you wrote this morning you'd written me off too. You may have been trying to be objective but the contempt showed through.'

'One way and another I don't seem to have made a very good fist at that story,' she said. 'I assumed this morning that the suspended officer was John Franks. That'll teach me to jump to conclusions. You look as though you need a drink.'

She went into the kitchen for ice, poured them both a vodka and tonic and put the glasses on the coffee table. It was odd, she thought, how even now she felt she could relax with Kevin Mower more easily sometimes than with Michael Thackeray with whom what was left unsaid laid traps and minefields at every turn.

'So you'd better tell me that the second conclusion I jumped to – that you didn't do it – was the right one,' she said encouragingly.

He looked at her for a moment as if trying to absorb what she had said and allowed himself the glimmer of a smile.

'Thanks, Laura,' he said. But the momentary relief in his dark eyes was instantly replaced with anxiety. 'I didn't do it, I promise you, but with two of them claiming I did I'm going to swing for it anyway.'

He told her exactly what Cassy Davis and Roz Jenkins were alleging and as she listened the pit of her own stomach seemed to clench itself into an iron ball. Yet she still believed him, partly because of the sheer outraged misery with which he told her the story and partly because, although she knew his susceptibility to an attractive woman, she had never glimpsed in him the calculated lust it would take to grab for free what he could so easily have paid for if he had felt like it without, she was sure, a moral scruple or a second thought.

'Why should they lie?' she asked at length.

'I don't know. I've spent all day and all night trying to work it out and apart from sheer bloody malice I can't think of any sane reason for it. Can you write something in the *Gazette* giving my side of the story? I don't see why they should get away with this unchallenged.'

'Is that sensible?' Laura asked. 'So far you've not been named publicly. Why put your neck in the noose before you have to? Haven't you got a solicitor? You'd be better taking a lawyer's advice than mine.'

'Yes, I know all that. I came to you because once they charge me you can't print anything, can you?' Mower said bitterly. 'I'll be in limbo, possibly even in gaol until the trial.'

'Surely they wouldn't remand you in custody,' Laura said, appalled.

'It depends what they decide to throw at me, doesn't it? It depends on the exact charge and I dare say the Crown Prosecution Service will be so bloody delighted with a sex charge where there's some corroboration they'll throw the book at me. And magistrates take a delight in jumping on wayward coppers from a great height, don't they?'

There was near panic in Mower's eyes.

'Help me, Laura,' he said. 'Please. Write something, talk to Mike Thackeray, anything. Please.'

Laura looked at him helplessly.

'Michael won't listen to me,' she said with absolute certainty. 'He'd be furious if I tried to interfere.'

'Yeah, right,' Mower said, looking away. 'I shouldn't have come, should I?'

Laura poured more vodka on to the ice in his empty glass with a sigh.

'You must see it's difficult,' she said.

'Right,' he said again.

'We are talking about the same girl, aren't we?' Laura asked thoughtfully. 'A thin, waif-like creature, badly bruised about the face, looks as though she should still be at school?'

'She probably should, though she claims she's seventeen. But if she's not, it will just make it worse for me if it comes to court. How come you know her?' Mower asked without enthusiasm.

'I've run into her twice, once at the Aids centre and then again the other night, the night of the stabbing in the churchyard. She was in Whitley Street with Sherry Maguire. I tried to persuade her to give me some background for a feature but she wasn't interested. In fact she got quite abusive but I couldn't make up my mind who she was more frightened of, the police or her minder.' Laura had decided that on the whole it was wiser not to tell Mower, any more than Thackeray, that she had given Cassy Davis a night's lodging. She had learned from experience that confidences shared with the sergeant did not always remain confidences for long if he could see some advantage in disclosure.

Mower held out his glass for another refill. Laura picked up the vodka bottle reluctantly.

'Are you sure?' she asked. 'Don't go near Michael when you're pissed.'

'The sainted Michael Thackeray can be a puritanical pain in the arse,' Mower said, putting a splash of tonic into his vodka and draining the glass in one. 'Prosit!' He looked at her with the beginning of a faint spark of interest in his eyes. 'You were saying? Cassy has a minder, has she? That I didn't know.'

'Had, I think, was the operative word. The impression I got was that he had thumped her once too often and she had run away from him. That's why she was looking for somewhere to stay, and why Roz Jenkins took her in. Then, that night on the street, Sherry said something about her "friend" being there with someone else – Hardy, Huby, Hornby? Does that mean anything to you?'

'Matt Hornby. He was there that night. He runs some of the girls. But it wasn't him she was scared of.' Mower had hauled himself upright now and was taking a serious interest in the conversation again. 'There were at least three pimps there that night, Hornby, a man called Smith and Jason Beardsley.'

'The man who was stabbed?'

'Precisely,' Mower said. But then he shrugged and flung himself back again in his seat disconsolately. 'But so what? It doesn't explain why two women are prepared to lie in their teeth to set me up. There's just no logical explanation for that as far as I can see.'

'This is a vicious, horrible case,' Laura said. 'So far I've been arrested, been narrowly missed by a collapsing church steeple, come within an inch of involving the *Gazette* in a libel action and been threatened by a peer of the realm. And I'm only trying to report what's going on.'

'Who was the peer of the realm?' Mower asked, without much interest.

'Lord Boulter. Jane Watson's father.'

'Oh, him,' Mower said dismissively. 'What did he want? He doesn't know where his daughter is. We asked him.'

'You meet three kinds of people in my job,' Laura said. 'The majority, who are quite happy to talk about what we want to write about, those who want to twist your arm to get something into the paper . . .'

'Like me, you mean?' Mower asked. Laura ignored him, not sure she liked him in self-pitying mode.

'. . . and those who want to twist your arm to keep something out. Lord Boulter came into the third category and is prepared to bully anyone who tries to thwart him.'

'So what does he want kept out of the *Gazette*?' Mower asked.

Laura told him.

'Jane's told him about these memories she's supposed to have recovered, has she? I bet that didn't go down too well.'

'Not well at all,' Laura said drily. 'Lords a-leaping have got nothing on Lord Boulter.'

'But you assured him his reputation was safe in your hands, did you?'

'You're joking. I told him to talk to my editor,' Laura said dismissively.

'Yes, well, it'll all be out in the open tomorrow probably. Last I heard, they'd decided at County to put out a national appeal for little Lady Jane Boulter, our missing witness. Once her picture's in the national papers nothing will be sacred. Your mates on the tabloids will wheedle the dirt out of someone even if we say nothing.'

Laura drew a sharp breath. Mower could not know how likely that was with Bill Brady cruising round Bradfield like a hungry shark. Caroline had promised to call back when she heard from Jane. She had no way of contacting her sister directly, she had said, although Laura was not sure that she believed her. For Jane's sake, Laura hoped that she got back in touch soon.

Mower stood up abruptly, as if making up his mind about something.

'Thanks for the drink, Laura,' he said. 'And the moral support.'

'I'm not sure either has done you much good,' she said, as she saw him to the door. 'Don't do anything silly, Kevin, will you?'

'Would I?' he asked, without conviction.

Laura knew within the hour that Mower had done precisely that, and quickly, when Thackeray arrived on her doorstep demanding to be let in so curtly that she almost refused.

'Laura, you're not being straight with me,' he said without preamble when he reached the door of the flat.

'What do you mean?' she asked, playing for time.

'I mean I've just had Kevin Mower on the phone, and even allowing for the fact that he sounded drunk and is undoubtedly worried sick, he said you'd told him so many things that I should have known about that I could barely believe it.'

'Michael, I've hardly seen you to talk to for days – '

'I'm dealing with two murders, Laura . . .'

For a moment they stared at each other in a state of near incomprehension, like strangers hesitating face to face on a crowded pavement, wondering which way to turn. Laura shrugged uneasily.

'I know, you're busy, it's understandable, I try not to make demands, but we've hardly spoken since the church disaster,' she said.

'I wasn't sure you'd want to see me when you'd had a chance to think about what happened at St Jude's,' he said.

162

'Oh, Michael,' she said. 'There are times when you behave like a fool.'

'And there are times when I don't know whose side you're on,' he came back quickly.

'I've got my own job to do. I don't think I've turned up anything which is material to your case. If I had, I would have told you,' she said.

'You had lunch with Lord Boulter!'

'Yes, he invited me out so that he could threaten the *Gazette* with a writ if anything about his daughter leaked out. But you knew all that already. He said her therapist had already talked to the police. That's why he was so worried, I assumed. He thought it would get out that way, through the police, which is not an unfair assumption in the circumstances, is it?'

Thackeray did not deign to respond to that gibe.

'You spoke to Cassy Davis,' he said accusingly.

'I didn't know you were interested in Cassy Davis, Michael,' Laura protested. 'I was trying to write a feature about prostitution, for God's sake. It's right at the top of the news agenda at the moment, Ted Grant's panting for juicy details from the mean streets of Bradfield – in case you hadn't noticed.'

'It'll go even higher up the agenda if it was her pimp that was stabbed,' Thackeray said.

'Oh, God,' she said, the fire going out of her eyes and her face losing its flush of anger as she took in the implication of that. She ran a hand through her cloud of copper hair distractedly. 'Jase,' she said. 'I remember now, she said she saw Jase. You think Beardsley was her minder? You don't think she stabbed him, surely?'

'I've no evidence for that yet,' Thackeray said. 'I'm going to have to talk to Cassy Davis. But even if she denies it, there were more than fifty people in Whitley Street that night and when we've finished interviewing all of them I'll be very surprised if we haven't turned up something to implicate someone – quite possibly Cassy. If Beardsley was the man who beat her black and blue that could be motive enough, wouldn't you say? No doubt she'd claim provocation, and no one's sure how far that defence stretches these days.'

'The only good thing about that would be that it would let Kevin off the hook, surely?' Laura said.

163

'Maybe,' Thackeray said coldly. 'You shouldn't have talked to Kevin, Laura. You should have kept out of it.'

Laura flung herself on to the sofa, in the corner where Mower himself had been sitting just an hour before. They had now got, she realised, to the real reason for Thackeray's irritation, the fact that once again, inadvertently, she had stepped on to his territory.

'I can't cut myself off as easily as that,' she objected. 'I like Kevin Mower. I've always liked him. He came round here to see me. I couldn't turn him away. If I can help him I will.'

Thackeray took in the obstinate set of her chin and the determination in her eyes and sighed inwardly. She could, he thought, be completely infuriating.

'There's nothing either of us can do,' he said more gently, sitting down beside her. 'It's out of my hands. The decisions will be taken by the CPS and the chief constable.'

Laura nodded and took his hand.

'I do have one confession to make, chief inspector,' she said giving him her best, and not very convincing, shot at an ingenuous smile. 'I was going to tell you anyway when Caro called back, but perhaps you'd better know now.'

'Caro? Caroline?' Thackeray said sharply. 'The other Boulter sister?'

Laura told him about the call she had taken at the office.

'You should have told me straight away,' he said coldly.

'She had to wait for Jane to contact her. There didn't seem much point,' Laura said.

'And she hasn't called back?'

'Not yet, no. I gave her this number so she could get me this evening if she had any news.'

'I'll want to talk to your Lady Caroline,' Thackeray said grimly. 'And we'll record the call. You can arrange a meeting with Jane so we can pick her up.'

'I knew you'd say that,' Laura said, almost inaudibly. She looked away, letting her hair fall across her face to hide the expression in her eyes.

'She's a murder suspect, Laura,' Thackeray said.

'Yes, I know, you're quite right, you can't do anything else. So why do I still hate it?'

164

'Because I'm asking you to lie and to cheat,' he said flatly. 'And because sometimes that's necessary in my job – just as it is in yours, in a good cause. Come on, Laura, you're not so naïve as to think it's not the right thing to do.'

'No,' she said resignedly, leaning back against the cushions and closing her eyes. 'I don't suppose I am.'

Thackeray watched her silently for a moment, desperate to take her in his arms, but he knew in her present mood she would resist. In the end she opened her eyes and gave him a slightly shamefaced smile.

'Of course you're right. Aren't you always right?' she said. 'What do you want to do? Bring in some of your yobs to tap the phone?'

'No, nothing so sophisticated. Your answer phone will do,' he said. 'I don't suppose it'll be a long call.'

She laughed. 'It's not as if I belong to a profession which you could even begin to call ethical, is it? You do know that a weasel from the *Globe* is sniffing around town looking for all the dirt he can get on Miles Bateman and Louise Brownlow, and on you, don't you?'

'Bill Brady? The reporter who wrote the *Globe*'s story this morning?'

'That's the one. He was offering me all sorts of inducements earlier for a trawl through the Bradfield dirt. Dinner at a restaurant of my choice – and bed, no doubt to follow, if I'd accepted. Even hard cash, when I proved less than anxious for more of his company.'

Thackeray leaned back and closed his eyes for a moment.

'There are things going on in this case which I don't even begin to understand,' he said. 'If Bateman dies the accusations that I pushed him to suicide are going to surface, and it's simply not true. But he's spread the poison far and wide, too far probably for any damage limitation I can mount.'

'He sent something to the *Globe*,' Laura said.

'Yes, I guessed he might have done. His suicide note seems to have gone the rounds and my reputation's going down the pan with it.'

She put her arm round him and massaged the tension in his neck.

165

'The *Globe*'s got something more on Louise, too,' she said. 'Some faxed photographs of her in very compromising circumstances. Brady reckons she must have been on the game.'

'Photographs?' Thackeray sat up again, alert. 'Where the hell did they come from? Did he say?'

'Faxed from a print shop in the town centre. No other identification, he said, though I wouldn't swear he was telling me the truth.'

'I think I'll be having a serious talk with your Mr Brady tomorrow,' Thackeray said. 'And if he feels he's being harassed, then that's just tough.'

'Was she?' Laura asked. 'On the game, I mean?'

'Off the record?' Thackeray said with a faint smile. 'Yes, I'm afraid she was.'

'If you've got it, sell it,' Laura whispered. 'It's no way to run a life, is it? Those poor kids.' It was not just Louise she was thinking of. Cassy's pale face and desperate eyes still haunted her.

'Have you ever paid for it?' she asked abruptly.

Thackeray looked at her sombrely for a moment before he shook his head.

'I've been lucky,' he said. 'And when there was no one special, I never felt I could pay for what should be freely given.'

'I'm glad . . .' she said softly.

'So what now?' she asked at length.

'For now, we'll just have to wait for your friend Caroline to call.'

'And in the meantime?' she persisted.

'In the meantime?'

She took his hand and pulled him into a position in which she could more easily satisfy her urge to kiss him hungrily.

'Am I forgiven then?' he asked, after some time.

'I told you, there's nothing to forgive,' she said.

He sighed.

'There's always something to forgive,' he said.

16

'So, are you happy with your promotion?' Chief Inspector Thackeray asked Acting Detective Sergeant Val Ridley the next morning, finding her already comfortably settled at Mower's desk when he arrived.

'I'm very happy, but I'm not sure many of the lads in the canteen are, boss,' she said, giving him a sideways glance as he hung up his coat. She looked neat and collected in a dark trouser suit, her short fair hair brushed back more severely than usual as if in honour of a solemn occasion, her pale face enlivened only by the faintest trace of lipstick and by the bright blue eyes which seldom gave much away. She had worked closely with Thackeray before and he respected her intelligence and perseverance but their relationship was not a particularly warm one. He did not think that Val Ridley warmed to many people.

'The lads can work for it, the same as you,' Thackeray said. He could remember a time when he had walked into a canteen day after day to be met with at best a contemptuous silence, at worst an audible murmer of abuse. 'Ignore them,' he said. 'They'll get used to it.'

'Just so long as I'm not just a token,' she said shortly. 'I'd not want that.'

'If I hadn't wanted you in the job, you can rest assured I wouldn't have asked for you,' Thackeray said, controlling his faint irritation. 'Whatever his faults, Kevin Mower's an effective copper and a token replacement is not what I'm looking for. This case is too bloody complex and too bloody sensitive for that.'

Ridley looked at him for a moment and then permitted herself a faint smile.

'Thanks,' she said.

'So what do you make of it, Val?' he asked, waving a slightly weary hand at the growing pile of files and computer print-outs on his desk and hers. 'Are we getting anywhere, or is someone running rings around us?'

'It seems to me that there are too many loose ends still to make any sense of it. We need to talk to Jane Boulter and find out why she ran, boss. The press office called, by the way, to ask if you still want to release more details to the papers this morning?'

'Ah, no, I don't,' Thakeray said quickly. 'There's been a bit of progress there. I know exactly where Lady Jane is going to be this evening, and we're going to be there to see her, so we'll hold back a bit on Louise's extra-mural activities until we see what Jane has to say.'

Val looked at him curiously. She had been in the office since seven thirty and had seen no sign of that development in any of the reports on her desk. She said nothing but her expression demanded an explanation.

'She made contact with the *Gazette* and asked for a meeting,' Thakeray said, surprised at his own reluctance to pass the information on. His private life was inevitably less private than he would like, but Val Ridley had never given the slightest hint what she thought about that, if she gave it any thought at all.

'They passed the information on to me direct,' he said, evasively.

'Ah,' Val said, an acknowledgement which combined understanding with discretion. 'Is she in Bradfield after all?'

'No, she's going to be at her sister's cottage in Derbyshire at six this evening. You're on for an evening in the country, I take it?'

'Wild horses wouldn't keep me away,' she said. 'There's another break this morning, too. Amos Atherton reckons that the stab wounds sustained by Louise Brownlow and Jason Beardsley could have been made by the same weapon. Not one hundred per cent certain, but a high likelihood.'

'I'm not sure whether that's a break or a complication. If anything, it implies a link between the two victims which we haven't got the least evidence for so far.'

'Except an interest in prostitution,' Val said. 'Or in drugs.'

'Which in the normal course of events might mean that one of them might have killed the other. But why should someone kill them both? Unless there really is a religious nutter out there – and there's no sign of that. Forensics have come up with nothing on the knives Ahmed brought in. So your local Islamic fundamentalist looks unlikely.'

'The Infirmary says Miles Bateman is still unconscious,' she said sombrely. 'There's no change in his condition.'

'You've been busy,' Thackeray acknowledged gratefully, although the news only increased his sense of foreboding about the outcome of the case. Bateman's fate hung over him like a threatening cloud, adding to his general sense of dissatisfaction with the direction of his life. He had stayed late with Laura and then gone doggedly back to his own flat to shave and change by seven, ignoring the suitcase which still peeped out from under his neatly made bed.

'Is there anything useful from the statements taken the night Beardsley was killed?' he asked, pushing both Bateman and Laura determinedly to the back of his mind again.

'A lot of people busy covering their own backs. No one who saw him except as part of the general crowd. Or no one who admits to it, anyway. He seems to have been with Matt Hornby and Jim Smith most of the time before he left them half-way down Whitley Street saying he was going to the Fox for a pint before closing time. No one saw him after that – or if they did they're not saying. When you cross-check the statements, just about everyone was on the street that night, all the usual women, their minders, all the protesters – the Asians, the kids from St Jude's, the lot. But no one apparently saw anything suspicious until the body was found.'

'Someone will have seen something, even if they don't know they did yet,' Thackeray said with more confidence in the infallibility of police methods than he really felt. 'Anyway, I think you and I'll have another go at the women this morning. For one thing, I'd like to know a bit more about young Cassy Davis. Someone must know where she came from, how old she is, and what motivates her.'

'Covering Kevin's back, are we, boss?' Val asked carefully.

'I've told you my attitude to that allegation, sergeant,' Thackeray said. 'Do I take it you reckon he's guilty?'

'He's a randy bastard,' she said, reluctantly. 'And he wouldn't be the first copper to regard favours from prostitutes as one of the perks of the job.'

'Even if the girl was unwilling?'

'Perhaps he's run out of willing WPCs,' she said waspishly.

169

For a moment their eyes met and Thackeray suddenly understood Val Ridley's ambivalence, before she looked away, embarrassed.

'I'm sorry,' he said. Beyond being aware that she was single he knew nothing of her private life and had never for a moment suspected that she fancied Kevin Mower. Was there any female of his acquaintance who didn't, he wondered sourly, including on occasion even Laura herself.

They were interrupted by Superintendent Jack Longley who threw open Thackeray's office door with scant ceremony and flung a copy of a newspaper on to the chief inspector's desk. Longley's colour was high and he seemed to have difficulty in getting his words out coherently.

'Have you seen this beggar?' he asked at last.

Thackeray straightened out the crumpled copy of the *Globe*, which showed every evidence of having been screwed into a ball, flung across the room and quite possibly stamped on before being delivered so peremptorily to his office. As he looked at the banner headline he felt his own anger rise.

'I was afraid something like that might happen,' he said. 'I was intending to have a word with the man from the *Globe*. I knew he was sniffing around in the gutter.'

He felt rather than saw Val Ridley move to his side, read what he had just read and draw a sharp breath. She knew as well as he did that although she had done ninety per cent of her homework that morning this time she had missed the ten per cent that really mattered.

The *Globe*'s front page spelled out in lurid detail the 'doomed romance' of the tragic vicar and 'little Miss Whiplash', the murdered pregnant student who had been 'on the game to make ends meet'. A slightly blurred but recognisable photograph of the two sitting entwined on a bed made sure that little or nothing was left to the reader's imagination.

'Where the hell did they get all that?' Longley asked in a strangled tone. 'It must be a leak from here. No one else had all that detail. And what about the photograph? Did we know that there were pictures of them together?'

'No, we didn't, or not until late last night, anyway, when I got a hint,' Thackeray said sharply. 'Bill Brady, the *Globe* reporter, was on my list of people to talk to this morning.'

He studied the front page intently, not wanting to meet the look of interrogation in Longley's eyes which he knew the superintendent would not pursue while Val Ridley was present.

'It looks as if it's been taken in the girl's bedroom,' Thackeray said. 'Presumably Bateman had the print and someone's passed it to the *Globe* with malicious intent. We found no photographs in Louise's room. And an even more interesting question is who was behind the camera taking shots of the two of them, and why? One of her house-mates, at a guess, but which one? Both of them swore they knew nothing about her boyfriends.'

The phone rang and Val Ridley picked it up quickly.

'It's the front office, boss,' she said to Thackeray quietly. 'A Mr Stephen Brownlow has just arrived off an early flight from London.'

'Louise's father?' Longley asked.

'Yes, sir, and he doesn't seem best pleased, the sergeant says. He's clutching a copy of this morning's *Globe*.'

'That's all we bloody need,' Longley said. 'Have him taken up to my office and you, Michael, can say a prayer to whatever saint's responsible for pouring oil on troubled waters. We're going to need a miracle here if we're going to get away without a sacrificial roasting from some pompous begger set in authority over us.'

Watching Superintendent Jack Longley grovel was an unusual sight which Michael Thackeray stowed away in the dark reaches of his mind to be savoured at a later date. Stephen Brownlow had walked into the superintendent's office, six foot four of broad, tanned, fit muscularity for all his grey hair and seamed face, and he had demanded nothing less than total submission.

'I know where I was to blame,' Brownlow said flatly. 'And my God, I'll suffer for that for the rest of my life. I wasn't there when my daughter needed me, and that's unforgivable. But this!' He slammed his copy of the *Globe* on to Longley's desk with a force which raised dust where none apparently existed. 'This is gross! This is my daughter plastered all over this front page! This could only have come from the police. There's nowhere else. In Saudi I'd have you publicly flogged and you'd bloody deserve every last lash of it.'

He glowered without distinction at Thackeray, standing impassively in his customary place against Longley's window sill, and at the superintendent himself, who had half risen at his desk when Brownlow came into the room but had sunk back into his chair now, apparently deflated, as the bereaved father's tirade continued. Anyone who did not know him as well as Thackeray did might have concluded that Longley was lost for words after this scathing assault. But the pause was a pregnant one, and gave nothing away.

'I'm very sorry, Mr Brownlow,' Longley said at length with evident self-restraint. 'We do our best to keep this sort of muck out of the papers, but sometimes we don't succeed. It's not what we wanted, I can assure you. In this case, we were not aware of the existence of these photographs.'

'So you don't know who's been blabbing to the press, then?' Brownlow snapped.

'No, I don't, but we'll find out,' Longley said, with menace in his voice. 'And if I discover that any of my officers has been in touch with the *Globe*, believe me, they won't know what's hit 'em. Now I'd be very grateful if you'd just sit down and give us the benefit of your counsel. I'm sure you're just as anxious for us to find out who killed your daughter as we are.'

Brownlow subsided into a chair with ill grace and Thackeray could see that underneath the deep tan he looked strained and tense. He watched him with real sympathy in his eyes. If Brownlow had loved his daughter even half as much as he had loved his son he knew the depth of the abyss of grief and guilt and remorse into which the man had plunged and the near impossibility of ever clawing a way out.

'How long is it since you saw your daughter, Mr Brownlow?' Thackeray asked quietly. This was his case, and Longley had already indicated that he did not wish to interfere in that. 'Have you been abroad for long?'

Whether it was courtesy or unspoken compassion which disarmed Brownlow was not obvious. He gradually seemed to shrink in his chair as the purpose of the meeting overcame his outrage, and the full horror of what had happened overwhelmed him again as Thackeray guessed it must have overwhelmed him throughout the interminable flight back from Riyadh.

'Four years,' he said curtly. 'My wife and I divorced when Lou was fifteen. It hadn't been a happy marriage. My work took me away too much. I've not seen Louise since.'

'We've not been able to trace your wife,' Thackeray said. 'There were no letters in Louise's room from her mother. Not even an address which appeared likely.'

'She's remarried,' Brownlow said. 'She lives in California. I don't even know if she and Lou were still in touch.'

'Did you not know that Louise had come to university in Bradfield, Mr Brownlow? Apparently without a grant, or any visible means of support?'

Brownlow reddened slightly and looked down at hands which seemed to be gnarled with outdoor work, not quite in keeping with his expensive, lightweight suit and silk tie.

'She sent me some forms to fill in,' he said, not meeting Thackeray's eyes. 'For her grant. I thought, why the hell should I pay for her after all this time? What's it got to do with me? I never sent them back.'

There was a heavy silence for a moment as all three men absorbed the enormity of the consequences of that moment of thoughtless spite a continent away.

'You didn't hear from her after that?'

'No,' Brownlow said.

'Do you have other children, Mr Brownlow?' Thackeray asked gently.

'A son. My wife took him to California with her. The oil industry's a hard master. Doesn't leave you much chance of a family life. There are compensations,' he added, as much, it appeared, to convince himself as his listeners.

I wonder what they are, Thackeray thought to himself, as Brownlow turned away again to stare bleakly out of the window at the overcast Bradfield sky.

'Mr Brownlow, is there owt you can tell us about your daughter which might shed any light on the situation she seems to have got herself into here?' Longley asked heavily.

'She never even seemed to like boys when I left. She seemed to be a bit of a late developer. Went round with a girl called Sally, a real pair of gigglers, always whispering together in corners, you know how girls are?' Brownlow paused and gazed at the copy of the *Globe* still lying where he had thrown it on Longley's desk. 'Is all this true, then? In the paper? She was earning money as a tart?'

'I'm afraid it looks as though it is, Mr Brownlow. I'm sorry,' Longley said.

'Jesus Christ,' Brownlow said, suddenly burying his head in his hands, his shoulders shaking. 'If I get my hands on the bastard who did this, I'll fucking kill him. Hanging would be too good . . . Is it this vicar fellow? Did he kill her?'

'There's no evidence for that at this stage,' Thackeray said quickly.

'Where's the bastard now?'

'In intensive care,' Thackeray said carefully. 'He tried to kill himself.'

'But she was doing what with him? Some sort of kinky sex?' Brownlow's revulsion was palpable.

'We're not sure,' Thackeray said. 'She was undoubtedly having an affair with Miles Bateman and he's probably the father of the child she was carrying. But he denies harming her. In fact he claims that he wanted to marry her.'

'Lou always said she'd never get married,' Brownlow said, very quietly. 'Sally came from an unhappy home as well and they used to say they'd stay together for always, and not have anything to do with men. As I say, when I left she was very immature. Just a silly girl, really. A silly, very pretty little girl.'

Brownlow stopped, deflated now and shrunken in his chair, all the aggression draining away as the full horror of what had happened overcame him again. Thackeray had seen it before: the first reaction to tragedy a wild anger, lashing out in all directions, only later followed by a collapse into grief.

'My little girl,' Brownlow said. 'Can I see her?'

'We can arrange that, Mr Brownlow,' Longley said. 'You'll be staying in Bradfield?'

'I've booked into the Clarendon,' Brownlow said.

'Aye, you'll be comfortable enough there,' Longley said. 'We may need to talk to you again.'

'Just find the bastard who did it, will you,' Brownlow said hoarsely. 'That's all I ask. It's not too much, is it?'

17

Sherry Maguire opened her front door to Chief Inspector Thackeray and acting DS Val Ridley with a scowl. It was mid-morning and she was wearing bright yellow rubber gloves which she wiped on her jeans as she let the police in. Her face was bare of make-up and her peroxide blonde hair stood in a tumbled bird's nest around her head.

'I haven't much time,' she said. 'I've got to pick t' kids up from school and take them to t' dentist.'

'Still coping, are you, then, Sherry?' Val Ridley asked with evident scepticism at this evidence of motherly duty and concern.

'Yes, I bloody am, thanks very much,' Sherry said, waving her visitors into the living-room. 'No thanks to you lot. How's a girl supposed to make a living with all this going on in t' streets?'

Thackeray lowered himself into an armchair while Val did an ostentatious perambulation around the small, tidy room, looking at the two school photographs on the mantelpiece and the pile of children's books on a low table next to the TV.

'Still keeping the social services at bay, then?'

'What is this?' Sherry appealed, ignoring the policewoman's sarcasm and speaking directly to Thackeray. 'I've told you everything I can about what's going on in Whitley Street. I can't tell you owt more.' She rounded on Val Ridley angrily. 'And leave my kids out of it, will you, you snotty-nosed cow?'

'It's your kids I worry about,' Val said, ignoring Michael Thackeray's warning look. 'What sort of a future will they have when they find out how you make your living?'

'I reckon they'll be bloody grateful,' Sherry said fiercely. 'I can earn more in one night on t' game than social security'd give me for a week. Two nights and I'm quids up on any job I can get round here. This way they're better off and I get to spend more time with them, so I don't reckon they're so badly off, thanks.'

'Till you're the one who gets raped, or knifed, or worse,' Val

Ridley said quietly, turning away. Thackeray wondered why she took Sherry's situation so personally.

'Look, what's this all about?' Sherry said impatiently to Thackeray. 'Tell this silly bitch to leave it out, will you? Where's that good-looking lad who came last time, any road?'

Thackeray and Ridley exchanged a glance before Thackeray spoke.

'He's temporarily out of action,' he said. 'He was more friendly than DS Ridley, was he?'

'Civil, any road.'

'Not too friendly?' Thackeray asked with deliberation.

Sherry looked at him, her eyes narrowed.

'As friendly as that beggar Franks, you mean? No, not that friendly. It were t' other one, a young lad, who seemed a bit overcome by my charms, as a matter o' fact.' She smiled complacently at the memory. 'But that weren't what you came about, was it?'

'We thought you might be able to remember a bit more about the nights of the two murders, now you've had time to think about it,' Thackeray said mildly. 'You don't mind, surely? You can't be very happy that there's someone with a knife out there with what looks like a grudge against prostitutes.'

'So she was on the game an' all, was she, that lass?' Sherry said, pulling off her gloves and sitting down opposite Thackeray, looking shaken. The bright morning light cruelly exposed the fine lines around her eyes and the dark circles underneath. 'I guessed it must be summat like that, all those blokes going in and out. It didn't make sense, did it?'

'Did you go back to Whitley Street later that night, after you were bailed?' Thackeray asked.

'No, I didn't. It didn't seem worth the bother.'

'So you were there quite a short time that evening?'

'I didn't turn a single trick, if that's what you're asking. Had to pay my sitter, though, just the same, didn't I?' She frowned at the memory of an evening's lost business.

'Any more thoughts about the man you say you saw going into Number 17? You said at first you didn't recognise him. Then you claimed it was Miles Bateman, the vicar. Are you still quite sure about that?'

'I wasn't at first,' Sherry said. 'I told you. It were right dark.

176

But then I saw him again in the same coat, and it just clicked it were him, summat about the way he had the collar turned up . . .'

'You're quite sure?' Val Ridley asked.

Sherry looked at her blankly for a moment.

'Oh aye, I were sure when I saw him again, in t' same place. The right sort of height and build, an' all, even though I couldn't see his face that first night. A right sly one he turned out to be, didn't he? Shouting the odds at us on t' street and then creeping off for a bit on t' side wi' that poor lass. Did he kill her, then? Is that what this is all about?'

'We've no evidence for that,' Thackeray said sharply. 'But we are interested in everyone's movements in Whitley Street that night. Did you see him – or anyone else – come out of the house later, before the police raid?'

'No, I'm sorry, I can't honestly say I saw owt else before your bloody vans turned up,' Sherry said. 'I'd like to help, God knows. No one deserves to die like that. But I can't tell you owt else.'

'What about the night Jason Beardsley was stabbed? Did you see him at all that night?' Thackeray asked.

'Aye, I did. He were with Jim Smith down t' far end near the church. I told Cassy he were there.'

'Cassy Davis? Why did you tell her about Beardsley?' Thackeray asked sharply, catching sight at last of confirmation of the connection he had suspected between the dead man and the young prostitute.

'He were her minder, weren't he? Didn't you know?' Sherry gazed at the two police officers wide-eyed.

'You're sure?' Thackeray said sharply.

'Of course I'm bloody sure. It's not a secret, is it? She came to me looking for somewhere to kip when she left him. She were living with Jason for months, but he's a violent beggar and when he hit her once too often she left him. The vicar found her a room at Number 17, but no one was supposed to know that in case Jason found out and went round there to sort her out. He didn't like losing his girls, didn't Jason. Any road, I warned Cass he were about, so she went back inside sharpish.'

'You're sure she went in?' Thackeray asked. 'Did you see where she went?'

'Well, she went into t' gate of Number 17. I didn't actually see her go in t' front door, but where else would she have gone? That reporter woman were there. She'll tell you.'

Sherry paused as the implication of what Thackeray was asking sank in.

'Oh, Christ,' she said. 'She couldn't have killed him. You can't think that. Have you seen Jason Beardsley? Yes, you must have done. Even dead you'd see he were a big bloke, were Jason, and he were right handy with his fists. There's not many blokes will take Jason on, and Cassy'd blow away in a puff o' wind. There's no way she could have killed him. She wouldn't have gone anywhere near him, that night or any other night. He scared the living daylights out of her, did Jason.'

Thackeray ignored Sherry's protestations.

'Not even if she needed a fix? I take it Jason would have been supplying her with whatever she was using?'

'I know nowt about supplying,' Sherry said quickly.

'But you know that's how pimps like Beardsley control their girls?' Thackeray persisted.

'Aye, well, that's nowt to do wi' me,' Sherry said. 'I'm not so daft as to touch drugs. For one thing, junkies have to charge less. Some o' t' punters won't go wi' junkies. They think they've all got Aids.'

'Surely you could tell if the girl needed a fix that night?' Thackeray said impatiently, ignoring Sherry's shrewd and pretty accurate assessment of market forces on the street.

'I didn't notice,' Sherry said, evasively.

'And you didn't see her again that night?'

'No, I bloody didn't,' Sherry said flatly. 'As far as I know she went indoors, like she said she would. So can I get on wi' my jobs, now, please? I told you I've got to go out.'

'Do you know anyone else who might have wanted Jason Beardsley dead?' Thackeray persisted.

Shelley looked at him pityingly.

'Just about any girl who's ever had owt to do wi' him,' she said. 'But if you think I'm giving you a list of names you've got another think coming. Whoever stabbed him did the world a favour. You never locked Jason up when he were alive. He's not worth locking anyone up for now he's dead.'

178

18

Honeysuckle Cottage, stone-faced, slate-roofed and plain, stood in a tiny garden crammed with spring flowers, beaten down by a relentless, drifting rain. Laura had no confidence once she left the motorway south of Sheffield that her school-friend's apparently vague directions would lead her to the remote Peak village of Hilton, little more than a squat church, a pub and a scatter of cottages in the lee of the fells. But she found her way to the Everetts' country retreat without difficulty.

She had agreed with Thackeray that she would arrive at the rendezvous with Jane Boulter and her sister at six. Thackeray would arrive soon afterwards to insist that the missing girl return to Bradfield to face the questions the police wanted answered concerning Louise Brownlow's death.

But Laura had determined to assuage her uneasy conscience by driving down to Derbyshire early. It was a decision which she knew would annoy Michael but that, she had decided as she agonised through an almost sleepless night when Jane Boulter and Cassy Davis became ever more hopelessly confused in her mind, was a chance she would have to take.

She manoeuvred her Beetle on to the grass verge so as not to block the narrow lane and sat back to take stock. She had left Bradfield in a ferment, swinging between unease at deceiving Thackeray and dissatisfaction with her job.

She had not yet forgiven Ted Grant for exposing her to humiliation and worse on her reluctant trawl of the red light district on the night of Louise Brownlow's murder. Now he had compounded his crime by refusing to consider the questions which were on everyone's lips since the sudden death and disaster which had been visited on Whitley Street and St Jude's.

Grudgingly he had let her go up to the university that lunchtime to a meeting to discuss women students' safety on the streets. The room had been packed and sweaty, the arguments raucous as feminists clashed with fundamentalists, libertarians with puritans, and the temperature, emotional and physical, soared.

She had not been surprised when Ted dismissed the idea of a feature on prostitutes' rights out of hand. 'They'll be wanting it on t' National Health next,' he had growled. 'This is a bloody family newspaper.'

'When it suits you,' she had muttered darkly under her breath, not wanting to provoke him into backing out of the agreement he had made to let her leave early.

But in retrospect what bothered her more than her fruitless day was the brief encounter she had had with Roz Jenkins who had been in the thick of the students' debate, flushed and angry as she left, with hair on end and eyes blazing.

'You didn't get much joy there,' she murmured, almost sympathetically.

'Well, what d'you expect?' Roz said. 'Most of them are in bed with the enemy most nights of the week.'

'And you're not?' Laura asked curiously.

'You don't have to sleep with men,' Roz said. 'In the end it's always women who pay, isn't it, whether you call it love or marriage or a commercial transaction?' As she had flounced away like a galleon in full sail Laura found herself wondering who Roz did sleep with if she didn't sleep with men. Now, as she sat outside the cottage where Jane Boulter had taken refuge, one obvious answer presented itself.

Disliking that avenue of thought intensely, she switched off the engine and took stock. A five-barred gate at the side of the cottage led into a gravelled yard which half concealed a distinctly unrural BMW and a Range Rover too clean to have had much truck with country roads. There was, she was extremely relieved to see, no sign of the police.

Her motives for arriving at the cottage early were, she admitted to herself, mixed. She still felt guilty at having betrayed the Boulter sisters to the police. Arriving first would at least give her time to prepare the girl for the ordeal to come and to apologise to her – a nice scruple perhaps, she thought wryly, but her own.

But there was more to it than that. Laura had carefully checked her tape recorder before she left Bradfield. She saw no reason, when push came to shove, why the police should deprive her of an interview which could either be used in the *Gazette* tomorrow or, if the evening ended with Jane's arrest, which she did not seriously regard as likely, could be hoarded as useful background material for when a trial was eventually concluded. She knew Ted Grant would have no hesitation in publishing that, whether it turned out to be suitable family fare or not. I love you dearly, Michael Thackeray, Laura said to herself as she got out of the car, but I don't see why I should have to sacrifice an exclusive interview for you.

The cottage smelt cold and dank when Laura's knock was answered by Caroline Everett, who held the door ajar with a look of complete surprise.

'I didn't expect you so soon,' she said. 'I thought we said six o'clock.'

'You did,' Laura said, shivering slightly as the downpour soaked through her light jacket. The afternoon had been dry when she left Bradfield.

'Actually Jane has changed her plans, changed her mind. I tried to phone you,' Caroline said evasively, not shifting her firm grip on the door.

'Oh, come on, Caro,' Laura protested. 'I've come a long way at your invitation. Don't mess me about now.'

'Well, things are different now,' Caroline persisted. 'My father's here. It's a family thing. We really don't want to talk to you.'

'I want to hear that from your sister,' Laura said firmly. The argument might have continued indefinitely if Jane Boulter herself had not suddenly appeared behind her sister, and pulled her away from the door with surprising force considering her slightness and Caroline's pregnant bulk. The resemblance between the two sisters was astonishing, Laura thought, in spite of Caroline's careful make-up and coiffure, and Jane's pale, pinched expression.

'Let her in,' Jane said, and grudgingly Caroline complied.

'If you write a word in that rotten paper of yours, I'll kill you,' she hissed as Laura pushed past her with difficulty into a small gloomy hallway which smelled of damp dogs.

'You're not going to be able to protect her, you know,' Laura said. 'And much better the Bradfield *Gazette* than the *Globe*. They've already got a reporter up here, and the other London papers won't be far behind. They're the real wolves. I'm just a pussy cat.'

181

Jane had disappeared through one of the two low wooden doors which led off the hall and beyond which Laura could hear an angry, muted conversation. Caroline waved Laura under the low wooden lintel into what would have been a comfortable farmhouse kitchen, with open fireplace, stone-flagged floor and sagging chintzy chairs, if it had not been for the chill, actual and emotional, within.

Jane Boulter had taken a chair opposite her father at the pine table, a pale, wan figure dressed in jeans and a grubby T-shirt which looked only child-sized and yet still hung off her slight frame. She wrapped her arms around herself for warmth and did not even glance up as Laura and Caroline followed her into the ill-lit room. Lord Boulter's fury, though, was scarcely veiled.

'I told you not to let anyone in,' he said to his older daughter. 'And I told you, Miss Ackroyd, that we've nothing to say to the press.'

'I came at Jane's invitation,' Laura said mildly. 'If she's changed her mind about talking to me, then I'm sure she can tell me that herself.'

Boulter poked a savage finger at his younger daughter across the table, but she merely shrugged, gazing down determinedly, avoiding everyone's gaze behind a veil of blonde hair.

'Jane is ill,' Boulter declared as the silence became embarrassing. 'I'm here to persuade her to go back to hospital for some more treatment. She's already agreed to go voluntarily.'

'Only because you said you'd have me sectioned if I didn't,' Jane Boulter said suddenly and surprisingly fiercely from behind the hair. Laura had no doubt that it was quite within Lord Boulter's capabilities to try to have his daughter compulsorily detained in a mental hospital if she refused to go of her own free will.

'Another reason I came early,' Laura said carefully, 'was to warn you that the police have found out about this meeting and are also on their way to talk to Jane.'

She had the appalled attention of all three of the Boulters now, their blue eyes unnervingly alike as they glared at her in unison. If anything could bring the shattered family together it was the threat posed by the police as much as by the press.

'You stupid cow,' Boulter said furiously and for a second

Laura was about to object when she realised that the epithet was directed at Caroline. 'You should never have brought her back up here.'

Caroline opened her mouth to protest angrily but Jane pre-empted her.

'She didn't bring me,' she said, again speaking far more firmly than Laura had expected from her dejected appearance. 'I came on my own. I knew where Caroline hides the spare key to the cottage. I've been here ever since I left Bradfield.'

'So how did you get here, Lord Boulter?' Laura asked, suddenly tired of being used as a pawn in a game she only half understood.

Boulter looked at Caroline for a moment but did not reply.

'Caroline told him to come,' Jane said, her voice full of contempt. 'She thought I needed to discuss things with him.'

'And don't you?' Laura asked.

'No, I bloody don't,' Jane said. 'He's the last person I want to discuss anything with, ever. He just wants to see me locked up.'

'Jane, this is all a fantasy,' Boulter said, a note of near desperate pleading in his voice now. 'You're imagining it all. It's part of your illness – or else that so-called therapist has been putting these dreadful ideas into your head. I swear to you, what you're alleging . . .' He almost choked, quite unable to put into words what she was alleging.

Jane gazed at him with calm contempt.

'I know what I know,' she said.

'But whatever you know, you don't have to talk about it publicly,' Caroline broke in. 'It will destroy Dad. You know it will.'

'Like he's destroyed me, you mean?' Jane asked. 'Don't talk to me about destroying people, Caroline. My therapist says that you probably knew what was going on. You and Mother must have done. And you could have stopped it. And now all you're really concerned about is your precious husband's reputation. You don't want dear Jeremy involved in any of this, do you? That's why you got Dad to come up here. You thought he'd be able to bully me better than you could yourself.'

Caroline sat down abruptly beside her father at the table and put her head in her hands.

'My God, Jane,' she said. 'You're evil!'

'Child abuse is pretty evil,' Jane said. 'So is setting a private detective on your own daughter, and he's admitted that.'

'A private detective?' Laura exclaimed, astonished.

'I was trying to trace my daughter,' Boulter snapped. 'What's wrong with that? I was concerned for her safety, for God's sake. I haven't seen her for over a year.'

'And I didn't want to see you now,' Jane said, on the edge of hysteria. 'I was tricked into meeting you here.'

Where the family conflagration would have ended Laura never knew because just as Boulter opened his mouth to speak again there was a heavy knock on the front door of the cottage, and he closed it again abruptly, a look of panic replacing the anger which had suffused it.

'Is that the police?' he asked.

As none of the Boulters seemed inclined to move, Laura went to the window and looked out. She recognised the figure on the doorstep attempting to shelter from the now driving rain with his coat collar turned up and a newspaper held over his head.

'No,' she said quietly. 'It's worse than that. It's a man called Bill Brady. He works for the *Globe* and he's not someone I'd inflict on my worst enemy.'

'How the hell did he find out about this place?' Boulter hissed in a furious whisper.

'I don't know,' Laura said helplessly. 'I promise you it wasn't from me. But his links with the police seem pretty good, so I expect he prised it out of them somehow.'

'I won't talk to him. I won't talk to anybody,' Jane said, thoroughly frightened now.

'You're going to have to talk to the police,' Laura said. 'They're not going to give up on this until they're sure you didn't kill Louise Brownlow.'

'Kill her?' Jane said, aghast and shivering in panic. 'Of course I didn't kill her.'

Laura glanced around the cottage kitchen.

'Where does that go to?' she asked, nodding towards a door beside the fireplace, with its cold, inhospitable Aga. She wondered how Jane had been keeping warm if she really had been at the cottage for several days, as she claimed.

'Into the back garden,' Caroline said.

'Can you keep Brady occupied long enough for me to get Jane away in my car?' she asked.

'Where to?' Boulter demanded, belligerently. 'I'm not having her disappear again.'

'Back to Bradfield,' Laura said flatly. 'I'll help you dodge Brady, but I'm not going to help you run away from the police.' There were more reasons why she would not do that than this fractured family could guess, she thought.

Jane nodded firmly. 'I'm not going to have any peace, am I, if I keep on running?'

'I don't think so,' Laura said. 'Not from yourself or Inspector Thackeray.' Peace with her father, she thought, she might never find again.

The banging on the front door began again with renewed vigour as Jane put on a coat and followed Laura out of the back of the house, leaving her father and sister still sitting at the kitchen table, looking stunned.

They waited for a moment in the rain beside the blue BMW parked in the gravel yard until they heard the front door open and the sound of voices recede before they crept around the blind end wall of the cottage and into Laura's Beetle.

'Wait a moment,' Laura said, getting out of the car again. Brady had left a black Escort convertible parked awkwardly on the verge behind her and she smiled as she looked inside and saw that he had left his keys in the ignition, more confident than she had been of country rectitude. She reached for them, locked the car up securely and threw the keys over the stone wall into the field, where a couple of sodden sheep bleated in protest at the intrusion.

'Give my love to Vince,'' she said blithely as she started up her engine and drove smartly away with Jane slumped dejectdly, but safely, in the seat beside her.

Acting DS Val Ridley watched the speedometer glide imperceptibly over the limit as she drove back towards Bradfield up an almost deserted mid-evening motorway. Chief Inspector Thackeray, she knew, had more on his mind than her driving. He sat in the passenger seat, gazing away from her out of the window at the scattered lights of the South Yorkshire countryside as she left the glare of Sheffield's lights behind and swooped over the undulating curves and hills of the near defunct coalfield.

She could remember travelling this road as a child and being awed, as her father's clapped-out old car racketed above the city on the Tinsley viaduct, by the roaring flames of furnaces and swirling clouds of crimson smoke which turned night into fiery day. If hell existed, she had thought, and her parents assured her it did, then Sheffield at night must be what it looked like.

It had all gone now, just as the pits which had fed the furnaces had been capped and left to fill with water. The city had been reduced to a ghost of its former self, its fiery heart burned out. And the surrounding countryside offered a bleak landscape of villages stripped of their reason for existence, decaying homes for defeated people like Val's own father and uncles, redundant, retired, desperate and despairing or dead. She put her foot hard down on the accelerator, pursued by the bitter memories which drove her.

Michael Thackeray's mood was more positive, and the cause of his still simmering anger more transparent. They had arrived at Hilton just before six to find an incandescent and very wet Bill Brady standing in the pouring rain outside Caroline Everett's cottage trying to open the door of a car parked awkwardly on the grass verge. He was attacking the lock with a thin screwdriver which bent to breaking point under the stress of his assault. He was being watched from one of the cottage windows by Caroline Everett herself who was not bothering to conceal her amused satisfaction at the reporter's discomfiture.

'Is this your car, sir?' Val Ridley asked solicitously as she got out of the unmarked police car which she had drawn up close behind the locked Escort.

'What's it to you?' Brady asked, giving the screwdriver a vicious twist and cursing roundly as it skidded across the black paintwork leaving a jagged scratch.

Val flashed her warrant card at him while Thackeray stood back watching, a faint smile on his face. He had a good idea who Brady was and was not displeased to see him suffering for his unwelcome presence there.

'Well, if it's not yours there might be a question of criminal damage, the way you're going on,' she said.

186

'Of course it's mine,' Brady snarled. 'I've lost my keys and I've locked my bloody mobile phone in there too and those bastards in the cottage would only let me make one call to the RAC. I could have sworn I left it unlocked. I can't understand how I could have lost the keys anyway between here and the front door. They say these kids can unlock a car in less than thirty seconds but I'm buggered if I know how to do it.'

'Not by brute force anyway,' Val Ridley said. 'You do have your driving licence on you, do you, sir?' she persisted, in her most icily polite traffic cop manner.

'That's in there, too,' Brady said. 'In the bloody glove box. Look, I'm Bill Brady from the *Globe*. I came here to interview someone, probably the same person you're here to interview. I parked behind a green VW and when I came out the VW had gone and my car was locked. I could swear I didn't lock it so what the hell's going on round here? That's the question you ought to be asking, officer, not hassling me when I've got enough hassle going already.'

'And did you get your interview?' Michael Thackeray suddenly asked, sharply enough to make Brady jump.

'No, I bloody didn't,' he said, abandoning his frantic attack on the car door lock and looking at Thackeray properly for the first time. 'Inspector Thackeray, isn't it? Perhaps you can tell me what's going on round here, and where Lady Jane Boulter is. She's more elusive than Lord Lucan, that bloody girl. Is she your prime suspect, inspector, or are we all wasting our time on this blasted heath or what?'

'Your time is your own problem, Mr Brady, but I'll be very annoyed if I find I'm wasting mine and it has anything to do with you. How did you find out that Jane Boulter intended to be here today?'

'Come off it, inspector,' Brady said. 'You know I can't tell you that. My sources are sacred.'

'That sounds unlikely,' Thackeray said. 'But sacred or profane, you can be sure I'll find out when I get back to Bradfield, and if I find that you've been bribing my officers for your information I'll jump on you from a very great height, Mr Brady. I want a word with you anyway about the photographs in the *Globe* this morning. Call me when you get back to Bradfield, please.' It was an order, not a request, and Brady nodded with ill grace.

'Here's the RAC,' Val Ridley said, glancing towards the blue and white van which was inching its way round the bend in the narrow lane behind them.

'Thank Christ for that,' Brady said, flinging his screwdriver towards the cottage door in disgust. 'You can thank those buggers for their help from me,' he said, with an obscene gesture towards the front door.

'I shouldn't think they're amongst your most avid readers,' Thackeray said sourly. 'Did you see anyone in this green VW, by the way?'

'No, it was just parked,' Brady said. 'You don't think they could have taken my keys, do you? Who the hell would do that anyway? Some sort of nutter?'

'Perhaps the locals don't like your newspaper, Mr Brady,' Thackeray said. 'Or the way you park. Who knows?'

The chief inspector turned on his heel and walked up to the front door of the Everetts' cottage which was opened for him even before he knocked. The fact that Laura had evidently been to the cottage and was no longer there filled him with deep misgivings and, once inside, with Val Ridley close behind him, dripping water on to the flagstone floor, he listened with little patience to Caroline Everett's breathless explanation for why she was now alone at Honeysuckle Cottage.

'Did Laura Ackroyd say where she was taking your sister exactly?' he asked at length.

'Back to Bradfield to see you there,' Caroline said. 'Jane really didn't have much choice, you know, with that weasel banging on the door out there. It really is too bad the press found out about the meeting here. The leak must have come from your end, you know. My father and I certainly never told anyone, anyone at all.'

'But you told your father?' Thackeray asked. 'That was not part of the arrangement I made with you, Mrs Everett, and that might have panicked your sister just as much as Brady's arrival did.'

'Oh, don't be silly, inspector,'' Caroline said loftily. 'A father's entitled to see his own daughter, surely? Jane is being hysterical about my father.'

'As I understand it, what your sister is alleging is criminal conduct on your father's part,' Thackeray said circumspectly.

'That's monstrous,' Caroline Everett exclaimed. 'You couldn't possibly be taking that seriously . . .'

'Your sister has made no formal complaint to the police, as far as I'm aware,' Thackeray said, making no effort to hide his distaste. 'There's no action I can take about a crime which doesn't officially exist. But if Jane's problems impinge on a murder investigation then I'll certainly take them seriously.'

'Jane's problems can't have anything to do with your murder investigation,' Caroline said fiercely. 'She's talking about things which were supposed to have happened years ago, when we were children. It's got nothing to do with anything which has happened in Bradfield. Nothing at all.'

'Well, when I catch up with her I'm sure that will all become very clear, Mrs Everett. Until then I'm keeping an open mind,' Thackeray said mildly. 'But so far she and, I suspect, you have been doing your best to avoid that and I have to warn you that obstructing the police is a serious offence, especially when murder is involved. I hope your sister realises that too.'

Caroline Everett had paled perceptibly and swallowed hard before replying.

'She's gone to Bradfield,' she said, her confidence evidently seeping away. 'She's gone with Laura Ackroyd to talk to the police.'

'You're absolutely sure about that?' Thackeray pressed.

'Of course I'm sure,' Caroline said. 'Laura said she'd take her straight to police headquarters.'

Thackeray hoped very much that Caroline Everett was right. He had avoided Val Ridley's eye as they left the cottage but he knew that she knew as well as he did that there would be trouble of untold dimensions if Jane Boulter disappeared again. And if Laura were to be involved in that disappearance, he did not dare think what the future would hold. This was a case which was already threatening his sometimes precarious hold on his career. One impulsive miscalculation on Laura's part now could wreck it.

19

Laura dropped Jane Boulter at the central police station later that evening still unsure whether she had driven back to Bradfield with a murderer, a key witness or simply a deeply disturbed girl whose fantasies were running out of control. Jane had sat in silence for the first part of the journey until at last Laura had become aware in the fitful light of oncoming headlights that there were tears pouring down her cheeks.

'Why don't you tell me about it?' she said quietly.

'So you can write about it in your bloody newspaper?' Jane said, her voice an uncanny echo of Cassy Davis's.

'Not unless you want me to,' Laura said a shade wearily.

'Well, I expect it will all come out in the end, whatever my father says,' Jane said. 'Not even he can get away with murder, can he?'

'Your father?' Laura exclaimed, astonished at this turn of argument.

'Indirectly, yes,' Jane said vehemently. 'Except his hit man got the wrong person, didn't he? I would have expected my father to be more efficient, actually.'

'I don't really understand a word you're saying,' Laura confessed as she eased into the fast lane to pass two lorries travelling abreast, the little car shuddering up to eighty miles an hour. 'You're talking like something out of a James Bond movie.'

'He hired someone to find me, didn't he?' Jane said, almost overcome by sobs again. 'He admits that much. I think he wanted them to shut me up. You've seen him. He can't handle what I'm saying about him. He won't admit anything and he's desperate for me not to let anything out publicly. He'd be much better off with me dead.'

'But it isn't you who's dead,' Laura objected. 'It's Louise. Even if what you say is true, why on earth should it be Louise who was killed as a result?'

'Perhaps he thought she was me,' Jane said wildly. 'I don't

know, do I? He could just have made a mistake, turned up looking for me and got the wrong person.'

'But you were there that night . . .'

'Yes, but I never heard anyone arrive, did I? I was in the bathroom with the music turned up. If Lou answered the door to someone while I was out of earshot anything could have happened. If she thought it was someone looking for me she would have lied, she might have said anything. She knew I didn't want to see anyone from home. She knew what was going on. We didn't have any secrets between us, the three of us. Roz always insisted on that.'

'So you ran away because you were afraid for your own safety?'

'I thought he might come back for me,' Jane said tightly. 'I thought he might have another go. You don't know my father as well as I do. You don't understand what he's like. If he doesn't get what he wants first time he just keeps on going until he does. It was like that when I was small. I used to cry and tell him to leave me alone but he wouldn't, he took no notice, said I liked it really, kept on coming . . .'

From her own experience of the bulldozing Lord Boulter Laura found that easy enough to believe. She had only needed to prevaricate when he made demands, and pass him on to Ted Grant, who of all people was probably his match for pigheaded obstinacy, but she had still felt the full force of his displeasure. This frail girl at her side, twisting a handkerchief in her hands and gazing at the oncoming headlights as if mesmerised, was claiming that she had had to fend him off physically as a small child. There would be, Laura thought, no contest and the thought made her feel physically sick. If Jane had found some way of killing her father, she thought, it would be understandable if what she was claiming about her childhood were true. But the reverse still seemed a bizarre proposition in a bizarre case.

'But you didn't remember this until recently?' Laura asked, trying to keep the incredulity out of her voice. The idea that trauma on that scale could be repressed and forgotten for years had always struck her as unbelievable given a childhood of idyllic highs and tempestuous lows etched vividly on her own memory.

191

'I forgot why I was so unhappy,' the girl said firmly. 'My therapist says it's very common.'

'But it makes what you're saying almost impossible to prove after so long,' Laura objected.

'I'm sure Caroline knows,' Jane said, a note of petulance in her voice now. 'But all she's really concerned about is protecting her precious husband from embarrassment. I was a fool to trust her to meet me at the cottage. I should have known she'd tell my father, but I was getting very cold because I couldn't light the Aga and the food was beginning to run out. She said on the phone the police were determined to find me, so I thought I'd better get in touch with someone in Bradfield.'

'Why didn't you contact Roz?' Laura asked.

'My therapist says Roz is bad for me,' Jane said. 'She says she's smothering me and that's not what I need right now. Roz likes to have everything under control and all of a sudden everything at Number 17 was out of control. It was beginning to frighten me. That's another reason I decided to leave. Roz wanted everything under wraps about Lou, about the men, about Miles. I think she was trying to protect her, really, even after she was dead. She sees that as her role in life, protecting people. But I think Lou and I were both beginning to get a bit tired of being protected. I wanted to expose my father, and Roz kept telling me that wasn't a good idea.'

'And what did Lou want to do?'

'I think Lou just wanted to get away. I think Miles and Roz were making too many demands. She wanted to be off on her own somewhere. There always seemed to be a lot of rows for the last couple of weeks. I didn't take much notice. I'd enough problems of my own to think about. But I just got the feeling that Roz's little family was about to blow away and she didn't like that. She didn't like it at all.'

'Did you know Louise was pregnant?' Laura asked.

'No, I didn't. I was surprised about that. I didn't think it had gone that far with Miles.'

'It had to be Miles? Not one of her clients?'

'Oh, she didn't sleep with her clients. That's why she went in for the kinky stuff. I remember her talking about it to Roz and ˻z saying it was much less messy that way.'

'˻oz was advising her?' Laura asked, appalled.

'Roz advised us about everything,' Jane said slowly. 'Roz was our sort of mum. Real mothers were in short supply.'

'I can see the problem but you have to deal with the more serious case first,' said David Mendelson. On an infrequent visit to police headquarters he was closeted with Superintendent Longley and DCI Thackeray in Longley's office.

'Aye, that was my reading of the situation,' Longley said. 'The assault complaint will have to wait, Michael. If you want to talk to her again about the murder of Jason Beardsley then you must get on with it. If she chooses to complain some more then that's just a risk we'll have to take.'

'I was just concerned about leaving Mower in limbo any longer than we need to,' Thackeray said mildly.

'If I know owt about that young man, a spell in limbo won't do him any harm,' Longley said unsympathetically. 'He's too cocky by half.'

'I thought the evidence against him was pretty watertight,' Mendelson said, sounding slightly surprised. 'You won't be getting him back, will you?'

He took in Thackeray's tightening lips and needed no more indication that his friend was still deeply unhappy at the prospect of serious charges being laid against the sergeant.

'Come on, Michael,' the prosecutor said. 'You've never altogether trusted him. You've said as much.'

'I thought he might bend the rules to get a conviction,' Thackeray said. 'He's as ambitious as they come and ruthless with it. But this?' He shrugged. 'I know there are coppers who regard prostitutes as fair game. But I wouldn't have put Mower in that category. I thought he had too much pride for that.'

'I heard he had a reputation as a bit of a lad with women,' Mendelson said.

'Not a reputation for attempted rape, which is effectively what this girl is alleging,' Thackeray said sharply. 'If I'd ever thought that . . .' He shrugged again, 'I'd never have been easy with him around.'

'What does Val Ridley think?' Longley asked. 'She's a sensible lass.'

'Like every other woman in the station, I think Val Ridley's half in love with Kevin Mower,' Thackeray said. 'Half of her wants to believe he must be guilty because he's a man and we're all guilty of something. The other half is heart-broken at the prospect of seeing him go down.'

'You won't find a reliable character witness there, then,' Mendelson said.

'He'll have to rely on me for that,' Thackeray said and the other two men looked at him in surprise.

'Aye, well, happen it won't come to that,' Longley said. He glanced interrogatively at Mendelson. 'So we're agreed then. Michael can have another go at Cassy Davis without being accused of harassing a victim of crime, can he?'

'Undoubtedly,' Mendelson said.

'Right,' Thackeray said. 'I'll have another chat with her this afternoon. In the meantime I've Lord Boulter's private detective waiting for me in an interview room downstairs with some explaining to do.'

Rod Ferris was not what Thackeray had expected. Bradfield's private investigators were few and low key, not quite the unassuming men in faded macs of popular fiction, but certainly unassertive in their pursuit of missing spouses, errant debtors and the other detritus of modern urban life. If they came to police notice at all it was obliquely, apologetically even, armed neither with guns nor with confidence that their efforts would be much more than tolerated by the law. Rod Ferris was from a different mould.

He stood up to his full six foot four as the DCI and Val Ridley came into the room, making even Thackeray feel small. He was broad-shouldered, well dressed in a dark suit significantly more stylish than Thackeray's own, fair-haired and good-looking in a clean-cut, square-jawed, rather old-fashioned way, as if he had just stepped from the pages of *Roy of the Rovers*.

'I'm very willing to help the police with their inquiries,' he said, meeting Thackeray's sceptical gaze with eyes as blue and as guarded. 'But I have been waiting rather a long time.'

The accent was many miles from local. Thackeray already knew that Boulter had hired Ferris in London but there was more to the closed vowels and self-confident drawl than that.

'I was under the impression that I was the one who'd been kept waiting,' Thackeray said coldly. 'For more than a week in fact, Mr Ferris.'

'Yes, I'm sorry about that,' Ferris said easily. 'I went straight back to London after I'd been to Whitley Street and then I had to go abroad the next day. I don't do missing persons normally. Industrial espionage and security are my specialities and I had a couple of appointments in Amsterdam.'

'You don't read the papers, then?'

'Not that morning,' Ferris said. 'I was on the seven thirty flight to Schiphol having a quick kip. And I can't say for sure but I don't think I saw an English paper while I was away. I was pretty busy for three days.'

'So how did you come to be looking for Lord Boulter's daughter, if you don't "do" missing persons?' Thackeray asked sceptically. Ferris had Lord Boulter's arrogance without his employer's substance and Thackeray knew that he must not let his dislike of both men cloud his judgement.

Ferris shrugged.

'I met Lord Boulter when I did some work for one of his companies. When he asked me to trace his daughter it seemed worth the effort to do him a favour, you know?'

'And you had no idea there'd been a murder in Whitley Street the night you were there? I find that hard to believe, Mr Ferris.' Thackeray said coldly.

'I hadn't a clue, inspector. Not until Lord Boulter contacted me yesterday to tell me that his little lost sheep had been found and there was rejoicing in heaven ... or in Hampshire, anyway. Boulter filled me in on what had been happening up here.'

'So perhaps we'd better hear just exactly what part you played in what happened up here, Mr Ferris,' Thackeray said flatly.

'Captain, actually,' Ferris said. Apparently unabashed by his frosty reception, he unfolded his limbs elegantly back into the interview room chair, which appeared far too small for him.

'Army or navy?' Thackeray asked, knowing the answer. But Ferris was not to be put down.

'Left the Paras a year ago,' Ferris said. 'Felt there was no future in it now the Irish thing is calming down. Couldn't see myself in a daffy blue beret in some tinpot observation post at the back of beyond with orders not to shoot back. Not my style.'

195

'Not enough action for you?' Thackeray asked.

'Well, something like that,' Ferris said dismissively.

'So you set up as a private investigator? Is that more exciting?'

'Oh, it can be,' Ferris said although his enthusiasm failed to reach his chilly blue eyes.

'And how long did it take you to trace Jane Boulter to Bradfield?' Thackeray asked.

'Oh, a couple of weeks, not full time of course, I've other cases on the go, as I said. She'd chatted to friends about universities and mentioned Bradfield as a possibility. They remembered it because they thought it was such an odd place to come. Most of them were aiming for Oxbridge, of course.'

'Of course,' Thackeray said drily. 'And you discovered where she lived? How did you do that, Mr Ferris?'

'I'd found out from her friends what course she was likely to be on. After that it was just a process of elimination, really,' Ferris said vaguely. 'I asked around her department. I thought I'd run into her, but in the event I showed her photograph to someone in the union and they recognised her and said she lived with Roz Jenkins in Whitley Street, but they didn't think her name was Boulter. Watson or Watkins, they said. Anyway it was a firm enough ID to merit a recce.'

'I don't suppose you know who you spoke to in the students' union, do you?'

Ferris shrugged eloquently.

'One student looks much like another,' he said. 'Scruffy and unkempt. A couple of years' National Service wouldn't do any of them any harm, would it?'

'So you went to Whitley Street? What time would that have been?' Thackeray asked, ignoring the question.

'Nine, nine thirty, something like that,' Ferris said. 'Latish I suppose, for a social call, but I stopped off at the Clarendon in the town centre for a drink and a sandwich. I didn't fancy Euro-plonk and stale biscuits in some student dump, quite honestly.'

'And then?' Thackeray prompted.

'Then I drove to Whitley Street, parked, told some little tart who propositioned me as I got out of the car to sod off, and walked down to Number 17. It needed a couple of rings actually before anyone came. And then it was opened by this vision in a red kimono, blonde girl, well built . . .' Ferris's eyes flickered for a second towards an impassive Val Ridley who was watching him with daggers in her eyes. 'You know what I mean,' he mumbled.

'And she let you in to see Jane?'

'She let me in. Quite welcoming she was, in an odd sort of way. Took me into the front sitting-room and sat there not bothering to hide her charms much. But she said Jane Watson wasn't there and she didn't know when she'd be back. Denied knowing anything about her being Jane Boulter, or anything about her background. It was obvious she was lying her little socks off but I was getting a bit anxious by then because of the time and the Amsterdam trip the next day. There was a lot hanging on that. So in the end I made some excuse and left and shot straight off down the M1. I was home in Chelsea by about two, I know because I was listening to *After Hours* on Radio Five and it ended just as I got home.'

'Jane Boulter claims that she was at home that evening, that she never went out,' Thackeray said. His discussions with Jane the previous evening had been prolonged when, much to his relief, he found her waiting for him, staring blankly at a cold cup of coffee in an interview room at police headquarters.

The faint anxiety which had gnawed at him during the drive back from Derbyshire that Laura might have been tempted to spirit her friend's sister away again was unfair, he knew. And the guilt his unjustified doubts provoked prevented him from calling Laura when he finally let Jane go just before midnight to take temporary refuge at a women's hostel where Val Ridley had arranged a bed for her when she refused point-blank to go back to Whitley Street. Laura was too sharp not to sense his disillusion and home in on the reason for it. Better, he thought, to talk to her in the fresh light of morning when there was less chance of misunderstanding and recrimination.

So he had gone home alone, tired and dissatisfied by the evening's developments, haunted by Jane Boulter's intense, hollow-eyed stare, but reluctant to believe her wilder accusations against her father. Now, face-to-face with Lord Boulter's private detective, he was not so sure. Ferris, he thought, had the capacity to do what Jane feared he had been sent to do.

'So you never saw Jane?'

'I never saw Jane. I reckoned I could catch up with her when I got back. I just chatted to this other girl, her house-mate, she said,' Ferris agreed.

'Louise Brownlow,' Thackeray said flatly. 'You must have been the last person to see the murdered girl alive.'

'The girl in red was the one who was murdered?' Ferris stiffened, his powerful body unnaturally still, and if the surprise was feigned, Thackeray thought, he was a good actor.

'Slim, fair-haired, a pretty girl in a red kimono with a gold dragon on the back? Is that an accurate description, would you say?'

'Oh, yes,' Ferris said, subdued now. 'That's an accurate description.'

'And you left her at what time?'

'After ten, I think. I couldn't be sure. She made me some coffee. As I say, she was quite chatty. The other one I only got a glimpse of.'

'The other one?' Thackeray said very quietly.

'The fat one. She popped her head out of somewhere, the kitchen I thought, when I arrived, but she never appeared again. I heard her talking to Louise, though, when she went to make the coffee. A big dark-haired girl. Overweight and a bit punky-looking. Not my style.'

Val Ridley was very aware of the deep slow breath that Thackeray drew at that.

'Let me put another version of events to you, Mr Ferris,' Thackeray said. 'It goes something like this. Lord Boulter was finding his younger daughter an increasing embarrassment, a threat even?'

'Well, he certainly wasn't happy about her more esoteric accusations, that's true,' Ferris admitted.

'So perhaps he didn't just ask you to find his daughter, but to find a way of silencing her,' Thackeray suggested slowly.

'You can't be serious. To rub her out, you mean?' Ferris said, raising a laconic eyebrow.

'If that's the way you want to put it, yes. He was so worried by her threats that he wanted to get rid of her completely. That's why she believes you were looking for her in Bradfield, incidentally.'

'The girl's paranoid,' Ferris said, for the first time displaying some slight dismay at the way the interrogation was going.

'She's been in and out of psychiatric hospitals ever since she was a kid. She's off her trolley.'

'Mad enough to have persuaded her friends to protect her, even to the extent of pretending to *be* her if you turned up? Did you think Louise Brownlow was Jane Boulter and kill her by mistake, Mr Ferris? Is that what happened?'

Ferris leaned forward in his chair, faint beads of perspiration on his brow.

'Bollocks,' he said fiercely. 'I can tell you something, inspector. If I'd gone to that house to kill someone, firstly I wouldn't have been seen, either inside or outside the house, and secondly I'd not have made the messy job of it that your murderer seems to have made. If I kill someone it's quick, and it's clean and it's silent. That was the way I was trained.'

'At Hereford?' Thackeray asked quickly.

Ferris shook his head at the mention of SAS headquarters.

'Maybe,' he said. 'But this is all ridiculous. I've told you exactly what happened that night. I knew what Jane Boulter looked like. I had a photograph of her, for Christ's sake. Can I go now, or is this farce going to go on all day?'

'Yes, you can go, Mr Ferris,' Thackeray said cheerfully. 'But don't leave Bradfield, will you? I will almost certainly want to talk to you again very soon when I've checked up on a few things.'

'And who the hell's paying my expenses if I stay in this God-forsaken hole?' Ferris snarled.

'Oh, I should think Lord Boulter will oblige, don't you?' Thackeray said kindly. 'If you and he are as innocent as you say you are in this affair, I'm sure he'll be only too willing to do what he can to help us catch the killer of his daughter's best friend, won't he?'

'I'll book into the Clarendon,' Ferris said reluctantly. 'It looks like the only half decent place to stay.'

When Ferris had put on his jacket and departed in a palpable state of high tension, Val Ridley looked at Chief Inspector Thackeray with a speculative gleam in her eye.

'You don't think he did it, do you?' she surmised quietly.

'Oh, I think he could be persuaded to commit murder if the price was right,' Thackeray said. 'And Boulter could undoubt-edly pay the price and you could argue that he'd only employ an ex-SAS man, and that's obviously what he is, if that's what he had in mind. But I'm not convinced that was the way Boulter intended to silence his daughter. He said himself he wanted her committed to hospital, and I'd guess that was what he planned to do once he had tracked her down. Once she'd been compulsorily admitted to a psychiatric unit he could always claim that her allegations were just part of her illness. He didn't need her dead, just discounted.'

20

Cassy Davis burrowed under the thin blankets on the camp bed in the box room at 17 Whitley Street shivering uncontrollably and wracked by waves of nausea. By the time the police car which had come to pick her up earlier in the afternoon and had dropped her back home again had left, she had been barely aware of who she was, let alone where. Whitley Street was not where she wanted to be but with Jason dead she did not have ready access to what she craved. Until night fell she did not know where to turn for help in the pubs and clubs frequented by the dealers she knew. She had let herself into an apparently empty house, crawled upstairs on hands and knees and fallen into her bed.

She had slept fitfully, dreaming, as she often did, of her father, nightmares which inevitably woke her in a cold sweat of sick remembrance. She lay now staring at the tiny skylight in the water-stained ceiling above her head. Tomorrow – or was it the day after – was her birthday, her sixteenth birthday, the day, she thought, she finally became legal after all this time.

There had been, she recalled, some attempts at good times on her birthdays: times when she had been indulged with ice-cream and visits to a fun-fair somewhere, candy floss and huge heart-shaped silver balloons, even a party for school-friends once, though that had been spoiled by her mother's watchful eyes following her father's every move as he romped with a clutch of giggling nine-year-olds in skimpy dresses and tights and gold studs in their ears and no awareness of the adult signals their children's bodies were sending out. But the end was always the same, the breathless groping, the frantic grunts, the sweaty beer belly squeezing into her bed and a mother suddenly deaf and blind and wilfully uncomprehending.

She had told the reporter woman some of this, although she did not have the words for all of it. She could not analyse her own motives but knew that there had been some slight relief to be found in letting the images of years of hell out into the light of day.

And now, she thought, the police thought she had done what she wished she had had the determination and the strength to do years ago to someone else in another place. They thought she had killed Jase, killed her latest tormentor, the man she feared as she had feared her father and had found herself as helpless to resist.

It was me who was murdered, she had wanted to scream at the tall, grave policeman who had questioned her relentlessly all morning. I was murdered when I was eight years old, half my life ago I was left for dead. But she had bottled up the emotion which churned her guts and hammered in her head and answered him mechanically, monosyllabically: yes, she had approached the man she'd seen going into Number 17 the night of the murder; yes, he'd turned her down; yes, she'd seen a flash of fair hair as he'd shrugged her off; no, she wouldn't recognise him again but, yes, he was tall, very tall, a tall, strong man, the sort of man who should protect you but wouldn't . . .

And on the night Jason died, yes, she'd been there, but no, she hadn't seen him, Sherry had warned her he was about and she'd gone indoors to avoid him. No, she hadn't stabbed Jason Beardsley, she hadn't stabbed anyone, she had neither the strength nor the stomach for it, but Jesus Christ, yes, she wished she had.

She had scuttled back into the house from the police car, avoiding the eyes of the handful of dark young men who were hanging around outside but unable to avoid the murmured words of abuse as she fumbled to fit her key into the front door lock. 'Hoo-er,' they had said in that unique mixture of broad Yorkshire and Pakistani. 'Fookin' hoo-er.'

Cassy needed a fix. She knew that and also knew that if she lay in her bed for much longer she would hardly have the strength to go out on the street to begin the desperate search for what she needed. She sat up and pulled the blankets around her shoulders in an attempt to still her shaking limbs, when she heard the door bell ring below and, to her surprise, someone in what she had thought was an empty house answer it.

Kevin Mower could not sleep. That morning he had lain tossing restlessly in bed until noon and got up feeling dazed. As the days passed since his abrupt suspension from duty he found it harder and harder to keep in touch with any sort of reality. His life lay in ruins around him and like a caged animal he paced and paced up and down and around his small flat looking for a way out which he knew did not exist.

Today was the worst so far. It was a grey morning and, bleary-eyed and with more than a day's growth of dark stubble shadowing increasingly hollow cheeks, he opened the curtains reluctantly. Without interest he scanned the usual view of the downstairs tenant's washing hanging limply across the muddy garden where her small son and large Alsatian customarily played together in boisterous contentment.

But the almost grassless patch was empty this morning and Mower recalled vaguely that the child's mother had made some comment about him starting at a nursery soon. 'Shades of the prison house begin to close . . .' Mower recalled from some dim memory of his schooldays. He had always had a retentive memory, able to please teachers in spite of their mistrust of his cheeky good looks and his dubious provenance. Then he shuddered as the words brought vividly to mind the echoing desolation of prisons he had visited to talk to inmates turned grey and sullen by years of stodgy food and insufficient air and exercise.

He had no illusions about his fate if he went to gaol. Sex criminals were regarded as the lowest of the low by most inmates, convicted policemen lower still. He would do his time in isolation, his only companions rapists and child molesters, the very people he himself despised most.

He recalled Thackeray's frigid refusal to meet his eye at their last meeting in Longley's office, and the chilly correctness of his voice on the phone when he had called him, memories which merely served to fuel his bitter despair. He knew it was naïve to expect Thackeray to rush to his defence, naïve and stupidly optimistic in the light of the evidence against him, but he had expected some hint of humanity from the man he had worked with for long enough, he thought, to have earned him the benefit of even the slightest doubt. Speaking to Laura had been a desperate attempt to break that barrier down and had brought him nothing but a curt response to his telephoned offering of information followed by more silence.

From the rest of his colleagues he had expected less than nothing and had not been disappointed. To most he was still an outsider, arriving with an ambiguous history and unconcealed ambition from the London force, which was itself regarded with deep ambivalence by its provincial cousins. They tolerated his womanising, drank his rounds in the pub, but still he knew they kept their cautious northern counsel and had never granted him whole-hearted comradeship.

Thackeray, too, he thought, was an outsider, a loner, but when it came to it there had been no fellow-feeling there, just suspicion, a chilly refusal to get involved, which, Mower thought, was worse than the angry bollocking which is what he himself might have been tempted to hand out to a subordinate in his position. They all think I did it, Mower thought. They've written me off. If I'm going to get out of this I'm going to have to get out of it on my own.

It was not a thought which daunted him particularly. He had been going his own way, against the grain, since a boyhood spent on a rough, tough South London estate which should have delivered him, neatly labelled as the doomed spawn of a one-parent family, into the criminal sub-culture which surrounded him at school and in the neighbourhood. With no more than the offhand encouragement of a form teacher who recognised a spark of talent in the fatherless boy's dark eyes, he had stubbornly scrambled over every hurdle the system set him on his way to a down-town polytechnic and a hard-won degree.

Even then he had surprised and disappointed his weary mother, whose fantasies had hurled him higher into the stratosphere to one of those obscenely well-paid jobs in the City which, from their thirteenth-floor windows, gleamed glassily on the horizon through the London haze. Instead he had opted to return to the neighbourhood which had tried so hard to drag him down, this time wearing a copper's uniform. She had never forgiven him.

Mower drank two mugs of strong black coffee, and flung on jeans and a black designer polo shirt, before driving slowly through the drizzle to Whitley Street. What he planned, he knew, could finish his career even if it went as he hoped, but after days with nothing but his own thoughts for company, he had ceased to care. He parked at the end of the road and walked the hundred yards or so to Number 17. He ignored the two bedraggled women sheltering under a tree whose eyes had lit up with a spark of anticipation as he approached but who had turned quickly away as they realised who he was.

Outside Roz Jenkins' house, he could see that the vigilantes had been working overtime. The front door had been liberally splattered with red paint, and on the low wall which separated the scrubby garden from the street the word 'hores', without a 'w', had been sprayed repeatedly along the blackened stonework. As he reached out to open the gate he was startled by two young Asian men who leapt out of the bushes into his path.

'Fook off, you're not wanted here,' one of them said menacingly.

'I'm a police officer,' Mower said automatically, although he had no warrant card to prove it if either of them had been so well informed as to ask to see it, nor any right to the authority he claimed.

'Fook off any road,' the more assertive of the young men said.

'Nah, it's right, he's a copper,' the other broke in, tugging at the sleeve of his companion's jacket. 'I know him. He were here t' night t' church steeple come down. I saw him come out o' t' house here when there were that bloody great crash.'

Reluctantly his companion stood aside to let Mower pass and they watched as he rang the bell and waited until the door was opened by Roz Jenkins.

'What do you want?' she asked suspiciously, taking in Mower's hollow-eyed, unshaven state and scowling at the watchers by the gate.

'A chat,' Mower said.

'Can't your colleagues do anything about that lot?' she asked. 'We're in a state of siege here.'

'I dare say they'll move them on if you ask nicely,' Mower said. 'If they can be bothered.'

'Why shouldn't they be bothered?' Roz asked sharply.

'Oh, come on,' Mower sneered. 'You can't make serious complaints about coppers one day and expect them to come running to your assistance with undiminished zeal the next.'

'You'd better come in,' Roz snapped, running a hand through her dark, spiky hair. She bundled rather than ushered Mower across the threshold and crashed the door shut heavily behind him. He followed her into the front sitting-room, where the curtains were half drawn and the air even frowstier than the last time he had been there. Roz threw herself heavily into one of the sagging sofas, her loose black shirt billowing around her and wafting towards him a faintly sickly odour, half musky perfume, half, Mower suspected, unwashed flesh. She lit a cigarette with trembling fingers and for a moment the flare of the match threw the dark circles under her eyes into sharp relief. She was, Mower realised with a faint stirring of hope, a woman at the end of her tether.

'I came to talk to Cassy,' he said carefully.

'She's not here. I haven't seen her today,' Roz said, drawing deeply on her cigarette. 'Are you supposed to be talking to her?'

'A lot of people are going to want to talk to Cassy,' Mower said evasively. 'One more's not going to make a lot of difference. But if she's not in, you'll do instead.'

Roz looked at him for a long moment. The smoke wreathed around her eyes but could not hide the dilated pupils which, Mower realised suddenly with a sense of shock, were filled with hatred and contempt.

'What do you want to talk to me for?' Roz asked, calmly enough, although Mower found himself increasingly uneasy in the hot and stuffy room. He could feel a trickle of sweat running down his back beneath his shirt.

'To ask you the same question I want to ask Cassy,' Mower said sharply, deciding he might as well be hung for a sheep as a lamb. 'I want to know why you are telling a pack of lies about me. Why you and that girl set me up.'

Roz laughed, and Mower thought he caught an edge of hysteria in the brittle sound.

'What are you hoping to do?' she asked. 'Get us to back down? Pretend it never happened?'

'You know it never happened,' Mower said angrily. 'Why the fuck are you doing this to me?'

205

'Let's just say men enter this house at their own risk,' Roz said, with a giggle. 'There's a few of you got more than you bargained for, I can tell you.'

'For instance?' Mower asked.

'Oh, no one you'd know,' Roz said.

'You mean Miles Bateman?' Mower hazarded.

'Miles?' Roz said vaguely, and Mower began to wonder seriously just what she had taken to cause her confused and volatile state. 'Poor Miles,' Roz said. 'Those photographs must have been delayed in the post, you know.'

'Photographs? The ones the *Globe* published?'

'We took lots of photographs of all her clients. We were going to be seriously rich, Lou and I. Jane too, if she'd wanted to be in on it.'

'In on what, Roz?' Mower asked urgently, with the feeling that at last he was about to get a grip on this dark and, he realised with a flash of intuition, sexually indeterminate household.

But he never got an answer because at that moment there was a crash at the window behind them and a brick skidded across the carpet followed by a shower of glass. Roz screamed and cowered back in her chair as Mower jumped up and flung back the now flapping curtains to catch a glimpse of leather jackets and black hair dodging out of the garden into the street.

Almost without thinking he flung up the window and vaulted out to give chase. For a few frantic seconds he pelted down the street behind the boys, but they were younger than him and their start was too great and he bitterly regretted the lack of his mobile phone to call up the back-up he needed as he watched them disappear round the corner of the street by the cordoned-off remnants of St Jude's.

Slowly and slightly breathlessly, resenting his reinforced sense of powerlessness, he walked back to the house across the patch of garden to stand looking in at the open window. To his surprise he could see no sign of Roz Jenkins. Quietly he swung his legs back over the sill and, picking his way carefully between the shards of glass so as to make no noise, he scanned the room for anything that might help him discredit her as a witness against him. He had almost had her, he told himself bitterly, and photographs were undoubtedly the key.

The old oak bureau stood in one corner of the room. He

remembered that collection of informal framed snapshots arranged on its slightly dusty top shelf which had been the source of the pictures of Louise Brownlow and Jane Watson which the police had acquired early in the case. It had not occurred either to him or to Thackeray that there was anything unusual in the number of photographs around the room, nor had they wondered who the photographer might be.

There were some snapshots there still, most of them of young women Mower did not recognise, others of Louise and Jane. The bureau had been searched along with everything else in the house more than a week before and nothing of any interest had been found. It concealed, as he recalled, Roz's household documents, and piles of notes for her research. But that, he thought, was then.

There was no sound from the rest of the house as he circumspectly approached the bureau and lowered the desk lid. The contents looked much as he remembered, the jumble of books and papers untidy and disorganised. Very carefully he pulled open a shallow drawer in the centre of the desk and lifted up the pile of papers inside so gently that they did not even rustle.

The first thing he spotted was a screw of silver paper which he unwrapped with a satisfied smile, quite sure of what it would reveal. He sniffed the cannabis resin appreciatively, before wrapping it up again carefully and putting it in his pocket. Absorbed, he began to riffle through the papers which had concealed Roz's stash, so that the jarring blow from behind, just below the ribs, took him completely by surprise. It came with such ferocious force that it threw him across the flimsy bureau lid which cracked and gave way at one hinge beneath his weight and slid him helplessly to the floor as a second blow juddered into his shoulder and he felt the pain for the first time like a tidal wave in his chest.

'Jesus, help me,' Mower said into the dust-laden carpet as his hands scrabbled helplessly for a purchase and he began to gasp for air. But there was no help to be had and he was only half conscious, the pain coming in red-flecked waves now and drowning out both sight and sound, as he felt himself being dragged along the ground for what seemed like eternity and then dumped on to a cold hard surface before he fell for some distance down what he was only dimly aware must be a flight of steps. Somewhere very far away in another world a bell rang. After that, darkness.

21

A quick drink at the Devonshire, Thackeray had said briskly in an unprecedented call to the office, leaving Laura no time to protest. She took an early break and uneasily threaded her way through the bustling lunch-obsessed crowds, past the cavernous Victorian market building, with its tiled slabs of ice-packed fish open to the pavement, into a shaded back street where an elderly, unreconstructed pub cowered in the shadow of the town's glitzy glass and steel shopping centre.

It was not a haunt of Thackeray's CID colleagues or her own and she guessed he had picked it for that reason as she scanned the mainly male, raucously preoccupied press of drinkers who packed the stuffy bar. She eventually spotted Michael at a corner table in his shirt-sleeves, an orange juice and what looked like a vodka and tonic marshalled untouched in front of him.

He looked tired, she thought, insinuating her way between sharp elbows and expertly dodging pint glasses as she made her way towards him. The touch of grey in the dark, never totally tidy hair looked more pronounced than usual and she was suddenly conscious of an age gap which did not normally trouble her. This case, with its sleazy accusations and sour innuendoes, was getting to him, she thought, and felt a surge of inchoate resentment against a job which demanded so much and gave so little in return.

'This is a nice surprise,' she said, sliding on to a stool opposite him and touching his hand lightly. The welcome in his eyes was warm but his smile was strained.

'I haven't got long,' he said. 'But I needed to see you.'

'I always need to see you,' Laura said, turning her attention to the vodka and tonic to hide her disappointment. His present need, she realised, was a professional one, not the nagging longing which consumed her whenever she was not with him, which these days seemed to be most of the time.

'Is it about Jane Boulter?' she asked, and was suddenly assailed by an unwelcome thought. 'She didn't take off again after I dropped her off, did she?'

'No, no, she was waiting for me when we got back. Could you really not have waited at the cottage for me? It doesn't look good driving all that way and coming back empty-handed.' Thackeray's evident irritation, if not worse, with what had happened the previous night was measured but still apparent. He did not expect Val Ridley to underplay his humiliation in the canteen at having gone so far to find the bird had flown.

'Bill Brady is a persistent bastard,' Laura said defensively. 'It seemed like the right thing to do at the time. Have you discovered how Brady found out about the meeting?'

'No, I haven't,' Thackeray said grimly. 'I put off my chat with Brady when I bumped into him at the cottage for fear I was losing track of Jane Boulter again. But that's one of the questions still bugging Jack Longley.' And if it's bugging Jack Longley then it will be bugging you too, Laura thought, having gained more than a hint of the superintendent's expectations before now.

'And Kevin?' she asked, cautiously.

Thackeray shook his head impatiently.

'There's nothing new there,' he said. 'Nor likely to be until we've cleared up these deaths.'

'Have you seen him?' Laura persisted.

'No, I haven't. My seeing him would do no one any good. He hasn't been round pestering you again, has he?'

'No,' Laura said. 'I've not heard from him again.'

'There's nothing we can do, Laura,' Thackeray said wearily. 'It'll have to take its course. It will be the CPS which decides in the end whether there's a prosecution.'

'But you think there will be?'

'I think it's likely. Talk to David Mendelson if you want to, but I honestly don't think you'll like what he tells you.'

Laura looked determinedly away around the crowded bar to disguise her discontent but Thackeray was not that easily fooled.

'I don't think he did it, Laura, if that's what you want to hear me say,' he said. 'But I've neither the time nor the authority to interfere. And you'd be the first to complain if any woman making an allegation like that wasn't taken seriously.'

There was plenty of truth in that, she knew, but she was not in the mood to concede anything where Mower was concerned.

'What a bloody awful mess,' she said angrily.

'I'm sorry, Laura,' Thackeray said, deliberately distancing himself from her emotion. 'I haven't much time. I'm seeing Jack Longley at two, and then I have to go back to Whitley Street. Can we get back to Jane Boulter? Please?'

'So did she help your inquiries?' Laura asked, not averse to changing the subject, well aware that she too was probably on the list of Longley's current gripes.

'Yes, she did,' Thackeray said slowly. 'But I just wanted to check out whether what she told you tied up with what she told me. I assume she said something on the drive back?'

'It was difficult to know what was fact and what was fantasy,' Laura said slowly. She told Thackeray all she could recall, word for word, of what Jane Boulter had told her.

'Well, she seems to be consistent, anyway,' Thackeray said when she had finished.

'Do you really think her father wanted her dead?' Laura asked incredulously.

Thackeray shrugged and drained his glass.

'He doesn't look like a man who would be overcome by grief if she dropped out of circulation one way or another,' he said with a note of contempt in his voice which Laura understood only too well. 'But the notion that Louise Brownlow was killed by mistake is a bit far-fetched. I think the answer to that mystery is much closer to home.'

'Jane herself, you mean?' Laura asked.

'Louise was stabbed with great ferocity,' he said carefully, recalling the blood-spattered room he would never describe to Laura in anything but the most sketchy detail. There were so many memories that he consigned to a black hole in the recesses of his mind that in his dreams they merged into a baroque cavalcade of disconnected horrors which regularly woke him sweating. If Laura was beside him there was some comfort and he wondered for the hundredth time that week why he could not bring himself to make that comfort permanent.

'A crime of passion?' Laura said.

'Perhaps.' He pulled on his jacket. 'I have to go,' he said.

'Are you close to an arrest?' she asked.

'Off the record, Ms Ackroyd?' he asked, with a hint of a smile.
'I haven't a bloody clue.'

Laura sat for several minutes after Thackeray left, gazing into
the remnants of her drink. She was overwhelmed by a sense of
impotence, feeling more sharply than ever before the limitations
of her role as mere observer of events which she desperately
wanted to influence. Years ago her grandmother had warned her
passionately that she would regret not getting involved, as she
had always been involved, in the long struggle to make change
happen. This morning, Laura understood what Joyce had meant
and wished her youthful and dismissive contempt unsaid.

There was, though, one thing which she might alter. Ever since
Cassy Davis had spent a night at her flat, an act of kindness she
had still not told Thackeray about, she had been haunted by the
girl's desperate eyes sunk in that ashen, bruised face. She had
taken some time in the office to discover the names of drug
treatment clinics. Now was the time, she determined, to make a
difference, however small. Safe in the knowledge of her grandmother's approval, she swallowed the last of her vodka and, to
admiring glances from the crowd of drinkers, set off on a mission
of mercy.

Only as she got to the door did she notice two men she knew
deep in conversation, half hidden by a screen at the far end of
the bar. She looked again, hard, and caught Bill Brady's eye. He
gave her a nod of recognition, but it was not Brady who
interested Laura nearly as much as his companion.

'Gotcha, you bastard,' she said to herself as she turned away,
leaving the *Globe* reporter to resume his conversation with a
disconcerted PC John Franks.

Laura did not realise that the front door to 17 Whitley Street was
unlatched when she rang the bell and stood waiting on the
doorstep. The rain had begun in earnest now and the street was
deserted, the trees dripping relentlessly on to bedraggled gardens full of weeds and newly washed paving, the water forming
puddles where the old York stone had cracked and shifted with
the years.

To her right she noticed the shattered glass in the main pane
of the stone-silled bay window, where the curtains were flapping

gently in the wind, getting wet as the rain gusted through the jagged hole. The house, she thought, had taken on an abandoned air and there was no sound at all from inside.

She pressed the bell again and it was only then that she realised that the door was very slightly ajar. She pushed it experimentally and it swung back, to reveal the dark, narrow hallway with its worn carpet and chipped paintwork, a pile of letters and free newspapers in a higgledy pile at the foot of the steep stairs.

'Cassy,' Laura called, stepping cautiously over the cracked mosaic of Victorian tiles beyond the scuffed maroon paint of the doorstep, inhibited by her sense of invading a private territory where she was by no means sure of a welcome. 'Cassy, are you there?'

The hallway was airless and dimly lit only by the filtered daylight from behind her and from what she took to be the kitchen door, also ajar, at the far end of the passageway. The silence grew oppressive as she stepped further into the house, ignoring the two doors to the left which were firmly shut and making her way quietly to the end of the hall.

'Cassy?' she said again, pushing the door open and glancing into a small kitchen where an electric kettle sent a wisp of steam wafting in the sudden draught of air. If there was no one in the house, she thought, there had been someone here very recently. She glanced around the cluttered work-tops and the sink full of washing up soaking in soapy water, transported back suddenly to student houses she had shared. Nothing much changes, she thought wryly. Rotas for the washing up, drawn up in optimism to grow yellow on cluttered notice-boards, never ever worked.

Yet this was not like any house she and her friends had lived in. There was an air of desolation here, a sense of life abandoned, of the *Marie Celeste* floating aimlessly on a grey uncaring sea. Through the kitchen window she could see the narrow yard which was all houses like this usually boasted at the back. On a washing line strung from a hook on the stone wall to the gate post some bedraggled underwear flapped, like a remnant of a defeated army made sodden by the rain. A green plastic tub of spring bulbs and a couple of black plastic dustbins huddled by the high wooden gate which swung in the wind at the other end

212

of the narrow stretch of cracked flagstones. She was uneasily aware that she was standing uninvited in Roz Jenkins' kitchen where normal life seemed to have been interrupted without explanation or apology.

Laura gripped the edge of the kitchen sink tightly, overcome with a sense of deep depression and doubt. What was she doing here, she asked herself, interfering in lives which were well beyond her control and far beyond her understanding. Cassy had touched a raw nerve the night she had invited her home, moved to an impulsive gesture of kindness which had evidently done no good. She touched the piece of paper in her pocket on which she had written the addresses and telephone numbers of the clinics she wanted to recommend to the girl. It was a sort of arrogance, she thought, a self-indulgence for which she certainly would not be thanked. Far better to sort out her own emotional entanglements than waste time and energy where she would almost certainly not be welcome.

She turned back into the hallway, resisting the temptation to open either of the other doors, and she would have left the house, embarrassed by her intrusion, had she not heard a sound from upstairs, a sound so faint that she was not even sure that she had not imagined it.

'Cassy?' she called, hesitating with one hand on the knob of the bannister, looking upwards into the gloom of the upper floor. There was no reply, but another noise, half-way between a groan and a sob, which filled her with anxiety. Without thought, she ran up the steep stairs to find herself on an ill-lit landing where all the doors were firmly closed.

'Cassy!' she shouted this time, afraid now. She flung open the first door and glanced into a bedroom, exceptional only in its orderliness, the bed neatly made, books ranged precisely at a work table and on shelves, chair at a ninety degree angle to the desk, a bathrobe folded exactly and laid across the foot of the bed. There was no one there.

The next door still had a loop of blue and white police tape tacked across it and wound around the handle. No one, she thought, could have gone in there without snapping the tape, and she was relieved she did not need to gaze at the bed-sit where Louise Brownlow had died.

On the other side of the landing were three more doors. The

213

first opened on to a bathroom. The air was heavy and damp and scented as if the room had been recently used, the bathmat marked with wet footprints, the mirror steamed up.

The next gave on to a tiny box room, lit by a small skylight in the ceiling. It was furnished only with a rickety-looking camp bed on which a couple of blankets and a pillow lay in disarray, and a single wooden chair bearing an ashtray overflowing with cigarette ends and a discarded, empty box of matches. This, she thought, must be where Cassy Davis had found a temporary refuge, though of Cassy there was no sign.

The last door, Laura thought, must give on to the main bedroom at the back of the house. For a moment she hesitated, her hand on the handle. Then she heard the same noise again, a subdued sound, a faint moan which was not quite a sob, and she opened the door gently and looked inside.

At first Laura thought that this room was empty too. Heavy curtains were drawn across the window but she could make out an unmade bed, the patterned quilt half on and half off, a wardrobe door left open, a bedside table piled high with books and papers. The room smelt even more strongly of the same musky perfume as the bathroom and eventually Laura located the figure of Roz Jenkins, sitting hunched on the floor close to the window, wrapped in a blue bath-towel and rocking gently with something clutched in her arms.

'Can I come in?' Laura asked and, getting no reply, she felt the wall beside the door to locate the light switch and turned it on. The shade was draped with some sort of flimsy blue material to shield the bulb so that even now the illumination remained dim and ethereal. As Roz continued to rock and moan faintly, Laura crossed the room and stood at the foot of the bed gazing down at the enormous bulk of the woman.

She had wrapped the towel around herself and tied it, like a thick sarong, under her armpits. Her upper arms and shoulders were still beaded with water and her short hair clung tightly to her head like seal-skin. Her face was blotched with streaks of damp mascara and in her arms she nursed what could have been a baby but Laura realised with horror was a doll wrapped up in an enveloping white shawl.

Almost lazily, without rancour or apparent threat, Roz looked up with huge dark eyes, and from where it had been hidden by the folds of the towel pulled out a large kitchen knife which Laura could see was smeared with blood.

Laura felt her mouth go dry. She found it suddenly almost impossible to breathe as her heart began to pound.

Imperceptibly she began to edge backwards towards the door.

'I was looking for Cassy,' she said in a voice which sounded to her like little more than a whisper.

'I haven't seen her since this morning,' Roz said in tones of complete normality. 'Annie was a little sod in the night so I slept late.' She looked down at the bundle in her arms with a smile of great sweetness and Laura realised with horror that in some part of her mind she believed the baby doll was real.

'Then some man came trying to...' For a moment Roz hesitated and looked puzzled. 'Trying to sell me something? Maybe? I'm not sure why he came.' Her voice had imperceptibly taken on the uncertainty of a young girl. She looked down at the bundle in her arms again and gave that same little half-sob which had first attracted Laura's attention. 'I haven't seen Cassy,' she said again. 'I think Cassy's gone away.' She sounded utterly lost.

Laura had reached the doorway by now and glanced behind her to see how far she had to run back to the top of the narrow steep staircase. It looked like a marathon in itself. Before she tried it, though, there was something she had to know.

'Is Cassy hurt?' she asked, trying to put as much insouciance as she could into the question but still hearing her voice shake. She had to drag her eyes away from the knife as she waited for an answer. But Roz looked at her uncomprehendingly.

'Cassy?' she said. 'I don't think Cassy's hurt. Who's hurt Cassy? It was Lou who got hurt. All that blood. Such a mess. Silly girl. Silly, silly girl, wasn't she, Annie? You could have had a baby sister if it hadn't been for Lou.'

'You wanted Louise to have the baby?' Laura whispered.

'Of course we did, didn't we, Annie?' Roz said. 'We wanted that baby and Lou said we couldn't have it. We all wanted the baby except Lou. Jane did. I did. Miles did. But not Lou.'

'And Lou got hurt when you told her that?' Laura prompted.

'She was going to kill the baby,' Roz said. With a sudden movement she flung away the doll and undid the towel exposing her naked body with its heavy breasts and rolls of flabby fat and

215

aimed with the point of the knife low down on her stomach an inch or so above her bush of dark pubic hair.

'There,' she said. 'They killed my baby and told me I could never have another. Like that!' She made a sudden stabbing motion with the knife and Laura screamed in horror as the tip drew a pinpoint of blood and then stopped.

'Like that,' Roz said dully. 'Dead.'

'Oh God,' Laura said softly, feeling behind her for the door handle and wondering whether, if she turned and ran, she could slam the door shut and prevent Roz from following for long enough to make it out to the street. But there was one question to which she still urgently needed an answer.

'Did someone else get hurt, Roz?' she asked, her eyes on the blood with which the knife was already smeared – not, evidently, Roz's own blood, but if not hers or Cassy's, then whose?

Roz glanced at the knife for a moment. Laura waited, her breath coming in short gasps as she teetered on the edge of panic. Suddenly Roz flung the knife across the floor into the corner of the room where it lay spinning for a moment, the blood glinting redly in the dim light. She clutched the towel back around her massive bulk and stood up.

'I had to have a shower again,' she said. 'There was so much blood. Such a horrid mess. I'll show you where he is. Downstairs.'

Feeling sick, Laura went ahead, not wanting to let Roz come between her and the still open front door. At the bottom of the stairs she waited for Roz to come down the last few steps and turn along the narrow hallway to a wooden door beneath the staircase which Laura had not noticed when she had passed by on her way to the kitchen. As Roz unlatched the door and reached inside to turn on a light to illuminate the cellar steps Laura noticed with horror that the threshold was smeared with thick gouts of still sticky blood.

Feeling sick, she followed Roz cautiously down the stone steps to where Kevin Mower lay unmoving in a pool of blood. Above them she heard the door slam shut and a bolt slide home.

Chief Inspector Michael Thackeray stood in the draughty sitting-room of Number 17 Whitley Street, the curtains drawn across

216

the shattered window pane, with his arms tightly clasped around Laura. Her hands were still smeared with blood which had transferred itself, along with damp patches of tears, to his shirt. Outside he had left Val Ridley to supervise the phalanx of police officers who had arrived at the house to assist, and had then closed the door firmly in her face.

'You came quickly,' Laura said faintly.

'Cassy Davis called us,' Thackeray said. 'Told us where you and Roz were. How she'd locked the door on you. She was here when Mower was stabbed. She saw it all.'

'She's safe?'

'She's gone,' Thackeray said grimly. 'We asked her to wait but when we got to the call box she'd gone.'

'And Kevin? Are you sure he's not dead?' Laura asked for the sixth or seventh time, and for the six or seventh time Thackeray reassured her that the blood-soaked Kevin Mower she had stumbled over at the foot of the cellar steps had still been breathing when the ambulance carried him away at speed to Bradfield Infirmary. He spared her his conviction that Mower would be lucky to survive.

'We tried to stop the bleeding, she said. 'We used the towel to try and stop the bleeding.'

'I know, I know,' Thackeray said. 'It wasn't your fault, Laura my love. You did your best.'

Laura pulled herself away and looked at her bloodstained hands.

'I don't think,' she said very quietly, 'I'm cut out for this.'

Thackeray put down the colour magazine and gazed for a moment at Laura, who was sitting on the edge of the hospital chair opposite him, her hair pulled severely back from her pale face, tension in every inch of her body. Between them Kevin Mower dozed fitfully. He was swathed in bandages but after a week of intensive care some semblance of colour and animation had begun to return to his dark eyes and thin, sardonic face, barely recognisable under the piratical growth of black beard that the nurses had not yet helped him shave off.

'Will it do?' Laura asked nervously.

'It's very good,' Thackeray said. 'You can write with passion

217

as well as intelligence. You're far too good for the *Gazette.*' If the compliment came reluctantly it was because it carried the implicit expectation, tinged with fear, that eventually her talent would take her elsewhere.

Laura took the magazine and smoothed out the glossy pages. She had told two stories about two young women who shared a similar childhood experience of exploitation and betrayal, the stories of Cassy and Jane, pieced together from what they had each told her and what she had been able to glean from friends and relatives.

Only the resolution diverged. Jane was now in an exclusive private clinic, where the best psychiatrists were trying to untangle fantasy from her fractured past. Cassy had been found dead and emaciated in a sodden squat, the victim of a fix of unusually pure heroin she had bought in desperation from a stranger on the street, the day after Roz Jenkins' arrest.

'Will it make any difference?' Laura asked sadly, touching the full-page photograph of the beautiful child Cassy Davis had been. 'I couldn't use their real names. Their fathers are still out there . . .' She shrugged.

'You can't ever tell whether it will make a difference,' Thackeray said. 'You just have to believe it.'

'That's what keeps you going, is it? Faith?' she asked doubtfully. She knew he had hated the interrogation and the subsequent committal on remand to a prison hospital of Roz Jenkins. She had not felt able to be in court herself that morning. The memory of those desperate moments when she had crouched beside Roz, cradling Mower's head in her lap as they tried to staunch his stab wounds with the towel Roz had been wearing, was still too fresh.

When the police and an ambulance had arrived, Roz had walked, majestically naked and smeared with bood, back up the cellar steps, head held high, and graciously accepted the blanket an ambulance man had held out to her to cover herself before she acknowledged the presence of two startled police constables. It had been left to Laura to explain that Chief Inspector Thackeray would undoubtedly wish to talk to Ms Jenkins, and to Thackeray himself, when he arrived soon afterwards, to ask Roz with gentle courtesy to go to her room with Val Ridley to dress for the journey to police HQ.

'Faith, hope and bloody charity, isn't it, guv?' Kevin Mower said with the first hint they had yet seen of a crooked smile as they realised that he was awake again. 'I thought I'd missed out on all three, for a while.'

Thackeray looked at him consideringly for a moment, keeping him waiting, although there was a hint of affection in his eyes.

'What you had was the luck of the devil,' he said. 'By rights you should be dead.'

'Wishful thinking, guv,' Mower said. 'Did you find Roz's photo collection in the end, by the way?'

'Yes, we did. She told us where they were hidden in the cellar. She told us everything in fact. It all came pouring out,' Thackeray said. 'She'd lost a child when she was about twenty. They told her she'd never have another so she set about building a surrogate family for herself, except that it never really worked. Her lodgers generally got tired of her manipulation and left. But with Lou and Jane she found herself two vulnerable young women who went along with her mothering and tolerated her increasingly bizarre fantasies. The photographs were to blackmail Louise's clients with, and Miles Bateman, if he became a nuisance.'

'And Beardsley?'

'Cassy was Roz's last and most desperate recruit to the family. Beardsley was on Cassy's back so when the opportunity offered Roz simply got rid of him,' Thackeray said.

'And me?' Mower said hoarsely.

'You?' Thackeray said. 'By the time you attracted her attention she was running out of control. She'd sent pictures to the *Globe*, she'd precipitated national headlines, it must have seemed as if anything was possible. Getting Cassy to accuse you must have just seemed like another line of defence. Distract the police, set you up, discredit Bateman, it all had a sort of logic from her point of view. Cause the maximum confusion. And John Franks feeding information to the *Globe* just added to the mayhem. He's been suspended, incidentally. When Bateman brought the church down around his head Roz must have thought the Almighty Himself was on her side. He's regained consciousness, by the way. And decided that perhaps we didn't treat him so badly after all. I think he's quite grateful we saved his life in the end.'

'So I'm in the clear,' Mower asked. 'Roz Jenkins has admitted it was all lies.'

219

'Oh, yes,' Thackeray said. 'I'm not sure Val Ridley's totally convinced, but you're cleared.' So far as any of us will be able to wash off the mud flung with such vigour in a peculiarly messy case, he thought.

'Val's never forgiven me for standing her up one night,' Mower said thoughtfully. 'Pity she's got such gross legs. She'd be quite presentable otherwise.'

'You're incorrigible,' Laura said, standing up to go, and giving him a kiss on the cheek.

'Now, if you're really not going to make an honest woman of this one . . .' Mower said to Thackeray, with another brave attempt at a grin, as he sank back on to his pillows.

'We might still be able to find some reason to put you back on traffic duty if we try hard,' Thackeray said, turning to follow Laura to the door. He put his arm around her as they left the ward.

'Your place?' he said and she nodded.

'Do I have time to go and get my suitcase?' he asked.

Epilogue

The dream was fading now, the city street was empty, and Roz knew, although she could not remember anyone ever telling her, that the child she was searching for was dead. The passers-by still went on their way, although one or two now reached out a tentative hand, though whether in appeal or to offer sympathy she was not quite sure. But they were wasting their time. She knew that. Just once, at last, the child had turned and met her eyes and she had recognised herself. Now she knew that she would walk the streets for ever searching for what had been lost and would never be found. When she woke she was aware of screaming, of thrashing the clothes off the narrow institutional bed, and then of hands and a needle and the advancing mist of a blessed oblivion. As she coiled herself tightly again for sleep she knew it would be the same tomorrow and the next day and for ever. But she felt safe now and was comforted.